Praise for Roger Elwood's

Angelwalk NOVELS:

"The Angelwalk trilogy is easily one of the most moving books (or rather, series) I've ever read. Elwood clearly and passionately portrays the greatness that can come out of tragedy, the pervading evil that can hide behind even the most seemingly harmless facets of modern life.... The trilogy is nothing short of a work of genius. Both engaging and breathtaking as a novel and peppered with enough spiritual truths to be used as a devotional, Roger Elwood's Angelwalk trilogy is essential reading for the literary Christian."

—Elias Emmanuel on Amazon.com

Coming soon from

ROGER ELWOOD

Three brand-new Angelwalk novels

Survival in the Wilderness
on sale in March 2000

Chances of the Heart
on sale in June 2000

Wings of Angels
on sale in October 2000

AN *Angelwalk* NOVEL

ROGER ELWOOD

WENDY'S PHOENIX

Published by Steeple Hill Books™

STEEPLE HILL BOOKS

Steeple
Hill™

ISBN 0-373-87089-2

WENDY'S PHOENIX

Copyright © 1999 by Roger Elwood

Visit us at www.steeplehill.com

Printed in U.S.A.

A Note from the Author...

Angels have changed this writer's life, at least my professional life, in addition to the lives of readers.

Nineteen eighty-eight.

The first *Angelwalk* novel was published that year, but only after being rejected by six other publishers throughout 1987. I had moments of temptation to throw in the towel, as the expression goes. Finally one publisher expressed interest, read my detailed concept and put me under contract.

Ten years later...

As I write this, that much time has passed. *Angelwalk* and the sequels have been read by millions of people in half a dozen or more countries, and my publishers and I have received countless letters about how deeply these books have reached into people's lives and provided help of one sort or another.

That is where the rubber hits the road, as far as I am concerned!

For words on paper to be translated into emotions and for those emotions to be really meaningful to a vast throng of people worldwide is about as gratifying as it can get for any writer.

And now there will be a fresh direction to the continuing *Angelwalk* series, a new spirit, if you will, and a manifold expansion of what always has been the international outreach of these books.

Whereas all but one of the five previous novels were vignette-oriented, the new ones are going to be more traditional in narrative style, with a single plotline, or two at most, throughout. This will allow for even greater depth to every aspect of the story, especially the characterizations.

We all are aware of how interest in the subject of angels has mushroomed since 1988—coincidentally the first year for *Angelwalk*—begetting a hugely successful television series. Such films as *Michael, City of Angels, The Preacher's Wife* and others capitalized on the trend. But the truth is that not one of them was theologically correct. All tampered with the concept of angels as delineated in the Old and New Testaments, assuming that it did not matter, that angels were fantasy figures anyway.

To the credit of *Touched by an Angel,* the producers of that series have seldom violated any scriptural insights into angels. It can be watched without injury to one's personal faith. In fact, more often than not, the series reinforces faith.

The new *Angelwalk* books will do no less than that. And our goal is to have no inconsistencies between what we publish and what the Bible presents.

Above all, we want to be sure that these books are more accessible, both in terms of their availability in a wider range of stores and in terms of the subject matter being dramatized. To help and enlighten readers everywhere—what a blessing that would be!

Roger Elwood

Rick Pritikin—
For being truly a friend

Part One

Angels.

They exist.

Call them creatures or beings of light, call them ethereal phantoms, call them what you will, or have no description at all beyond some vague expectations based upon sketchy portions of the Bible. Regardless of the words used or not, they are here, and they are real, and they can change our lives.

Despite the contentions of skeptics, angels are not and never have been creations of the wishful thinking of desperate men, women and children.

Angels have been with us since the beginning of time, whether we see them or not, and angels will continue to be with us, since they cannot be doubted into oblivion or discouraged by our resistance to them.

Patience. They have that, you know, literally a vast eternity of patience.

In a sense angels have existed since before God called them into being, they were in His eternal mind, nourished among His thoughts, and being readied for their own majestic birth.

Companionship. That was why God created a whole new species of creatures called angels, to be His companions as well as His helpers. From the beginning of their existence, they were invested with remarkable abilities that came from their heavenly Father. They could traverse time and space, could appear and disappear in an instant, could go back and forth between heaven and earth, could do so much more than humans, making them second only to God Himself.

Angels have existed since before the human race began, their involvement in history beginning from the moment of the first man and the first woman in Eden, and continuing on from there.

Yes, skeptics say that there are no such creatures but then skeptics are not to be believed. Those who are nonbelievers of angels often do not believe in God either, and those who have no time or thought for Him will one day need Him, but since in their sad, wretched world, He is dead if He ever existed, how can they call on Him, how can they turn to One Who, for them, is not there?

Angels have been influencing history since time and space began, perhaps more than kings and queens and prime ministers and presidents, perhaps more than heroes, scoundrels, whatever else.

Angels have been the power behind many thrones and yet flesh-and-blood rulers were seldom, perhaps never, truly aware of them. How many have stood and listened, vaguely aware, but not more than that, and then giving up, fallen prey to the rational instead of accepting the supernatural?

Angels aid the progression of history but they do not rewrite what God has ordained, do not contest His declarations and admonitions, act only in obedience, act only to please the One Who gave them life. They are the trusted messengers of the heavenly Father, sent by His command to do His bidding.

And if that were the sum total of the essential story of the existence of angels, the human race could rejoice.

Sadly, though, that is not the entire drama about angels. A darker side exists, a darker side mired in pain and suffering and sin and corruption.

There is more about angels to be told, tragically so, and it has been thus long before human beings witnessed their first sunrise, sat in awe at their first sunset, looked up during the night at the wonders of heaven spread out in a tapestry of twinkling shapes to the very limits of vision and beyond.

In the greatest tragedy of time, space and eternity, ten thousand or more angels rebelled, perhaps considerably more, causing a cataclysm in heaven, a kind of warfare that shattered the harmony of that place and brought forth something that had been unknown to the whole of creation until then.

Evil.

Unholy, rank, chilling, overwhelming.

As a result, evil was born aeons ago.

And it came in the form of dissident angels, egomaniacal creatures bent on the destruction of everything God Himself had created.

These angels—no longer content to live under the encompassing benevolence of their Creator, no longer satisfied with life as He had given it to them, a life of glory and majesty—these angels resisted the pleas of their obedient comrades, yes, resisted even the entreaties of God Himself, for He knew what their departure would mean, knew the ages of suffering and calamity that would ensnare all of creation.

None of this mattered. None of what God said changed what the rebel angels wanted, enslaved as they were to unleashed ego.

And they were led, countless aeons ago, by the most beautiful of angels, Lucifer, the archangel, the one second only to God, Lucifer, who succumbed to ego and thought himself higher in authority than his Creator.

Only that once. It would never happen again.

But that singular act of thoughtless rebellion would change everything, would change the course of all of history to follow.

The angels who chose to remain with God rather than follow that path carved out by Lucifer have been witnessing through the passage of time since then exactly what their former comrades are doing with their so-called freedom.

Anguish. Centuries of it.

Angels-become-demons seem delighted to inflict all kinds of suffering upon a world that was once literally an idyllic Eden but has now become little more than a jungle of relentless crime, pain, any manner of sin and degradation, conditions that were never intended by God but which represent Satan's revenge.

Revenge.

Satan's singular obsession drives him, propelling him and the loathsome entities chained to his will to one horrendous act after another, multiplied blasphemy on top of multiplied blasphemy. In fact, Satan would not exist without revenge at the center of his being; it and he, one and the same.

Revenge is the oil that fuels every thought, every action, every word of this monstrosity, this devil, this incarnation and origin and cause of evil, and those who acknowledge him as their master.

And he uses his influence accordingly.

All angels—fallen and unfallen alike—influence, yes, they influence individuals while at the same time influencing history as a whole, since history is the compilation of the acts of men and women since the dawn of time.

The unfallen ones bring about that which is good, decent, honest, true, that which uplifts and edifies and sanctifies, encourage our better instincts, assure us of the continued Fathership of Almighty God.

But not the others.

Not the dark, unholy ones who spend the length and breadth of their existence attempting to thwart holiness, attempting to turn altruism into perversity, decency into immorality, nobility into savagery.

The fallen angels, the corrupted ones are behind all of this, taking the responsibility for infamous acts from those of Cain through to those of Hitler, Stalin, Amin, Gacy, Bundt and others, destroying unending numbers of innocent and usually defenseless human beings rather than uplifting them.

All unfallen angels leave an imprint on the lives they touch, an imprint that says, "We love God and this is how we show our love."

While the others, the ones that once inhabited heaven but now have only hell as their domain, will leave behind that which shouts, "We have brought evil this way, and we leave despair in our wake."

Unfallen angels often assume human form, perhaps that kind stranger who saves someone from being hit by a car.

Or someone who puts her arm around a lost, confused child.

Or the new friend who seems to enter our life at just the right moment with advice that changes the way we live.

On occasion, yes, they do assume human form, and they walk among us who are from the same Creator. They may appear like us outwardly, when it is necessary, but they are quite unlike us otherwise. For when they look human, they are simply engaging in a kind of masterful masquerade, not to mock us, not to toy with us, but to be guardians, our guardians, to do what God has commanded in our regard, whatever and whenever and wherever that might be.

But, mostly, angels *are* invisible, sometimes whispering to us, not through our ears, of course, but into our minds, perhaps our very souls as well, not impeded by the confines of flesh and blood with which humankind has been saddled for all of history.

The majority of angels are remarkable unfallen ones, mysterious and beautiful extensions of God Himself, for they were His first children, children brought to life, as it were, by the mere thought of divinity. And they are never to die—as do human children from time to time—never to get sick, never to watch their parents die, for they have Almighty God as their father.

And they stand with us, here in this life that we lead, sometimes seen, sometimes not, but here just the same, an enduring link between us and God, ministering to us, and preparing us for whatever the present and the future hold.

Do angels prevent tragedy? Frequently. But not always.

It seems that they fail more than they succeed.

How could that be? How could it be that tragedy is allowed, seemingly slipping past the vigilance of Almighty God?

If good angels are sent continually, dispatched by a merciful God, why would they ever fail?

Because something may seem tragic at the moment, until it turns into a triumph, a course of events that only God Himself can see from beginning to end.

And thus it was with Wendy MacPherson.

Chapter One

May 10, 8:30 a.m.

In something resembling a cattle drive, hundreds of teenagers had begun converging on the same spot—the local high school.

And, inside, scores of teachers were preparing to do battle, as some would characterize the day's activities. In an era of guns being smuggled into a great many schools, that description might not have been entirely bizarre.

So many of them, Wendy MacPherson thought as she watched the stream of students crossing the street while she was stopped for a red light, surprised by the numbers because the high school she had attended was considerably smaller. *There was a time when I was one of them, hurrying to attend my first class of the day, and looking forward to summer when I would be on my own.*

She sighed with a bit of wistfulness, the baggage she brought with her from those years feeling a little heavier just then.

We didn't have computers in those days, she recalled, feeling a bit "ancient," *and there was no Internet. We didn't have to worry about weapons being carried inside, or wonder if our school would be the site for some unbalanced young man blasting away at anyone and everyone he happened to see.*

Wendy brushed that thought aside, shaking her long, red hair as though to clear her head, but this did not work.

Her thoughts refused to be controlled. They were like rebellious chess pieces refusing to pay any attention to their master's wishes.

And then another insight seized her.

It was unplanned, not a thought to which Wendy had been devoting any attention previously, yet it was stunning enough to make her tremble, to tighten her insides into a collection of knots.

Only boys.

Girls were never involved, girls just did not—

Holy—! she started to say to herself. *Why hasn't anybody said that yet? All the reams of copy and cassette after cassette of videotape, and yet that fact has not been spotlighted by anyone anywhere.*

The cases in Oregon and Virginia and elsewhere involved disturbed boys. No instances were on record as yet of girls going on a rampage.

Girls have as many frustrations, likely more. She wondered, *why aren't they reacting in the same manner? It's a good thing they're not, but what, really, is the explanation? Are we actually more civilized after all?*

Wendy pondered briefly the significance of that fact, but her anxiety in getting to the office where she worked shoved the thought aside and made her concentrate on the human and vehicular traffic directly ahead.

It was otherwise a fine Southern California day, the temperature mild, the air clean and sweet with scents carried on a vagrant breeze that teased her nostrils and then left, leaving behind a fleeting reminder of their pleasantness.

Nice, Wendy thought, *really nice... like some kind of perfume.*

She relaxed a bit, having to admit to herself that, apart from the traffic-induced pressure of that moment, she actually felt pretty good.

In fact, she'd felt good since the early morning. *I got up, lurched my way to the mirror in my bathroom, looked at myself, and didn't pass out,* Wendy reminded herself.

Feeling that way about her looks was a bit of a victory since, for a long while, she had not especially liked what age had done to her, wrenching her from a "cute" teendom to what she was now. Although quite attractive, she couldn't ignore what time had done to her.

Age brought more wrinkles, skin that was more pale than ever, hair that while still resplendently red and beautiful, nevertheless required constant attention since it tended to be dry and rather brittle.

Yet that morning, that one morning, Wendy saw her reflection, saw that age had not been as unkind as she once thought, saw that, to a degree, she looked perhaps better, more mature. She knew she painted her face with greater expertise than she'd applied the heavy layers of makeup she used as a teenager, causing some other girls to snicker behind her back.

Until she wised up.

That was when Wendy started off in the other direction, applying as little makeup as she could.

And this morning I decided that, though I was no longer a hot babe, I still had some of that old look left, which seems amazing, what with all that has happened since I left high school and entered married life.

Nowadays Wendy's life had fallen into something of a routine, which displeased her, but there was little she could do to alter that routine, since it was mandated by her profession, her relationship with each client following a specific approach, always beginning the same way, the words from some well-worn motivational script. It was like being the star of a long-running Broadway play—she had to figure out some way of keeping the lines feeling fresh day after day.

Seeing those high school students made her smile a bit.

The relief of summer vacation was just ahead for them, but to get there for many would mean wading through piles of final exams, and sweating out their averages and often trying to con teachers and counselors alike into helping them squeak through...somehow.

So many, she thought, compared to the rural school she had attended just over a decade earlier, *and a much broader range of ethnic types.*

She saw a number of Asian students, black students, Latino students, along with the average WASP students, and others. Most were walking, at least two were using crutches, three were in wheelchairs.

And then she noticed one tall, dark-haired, quite good-looking young man who was blind. He used a walking stick and right beside him, helping with single-minded loyalty, was a German shepherd rigorously trained as a Seeing Eye companion.

How close those two must be, Wendy thought. *What a bond. But what will happen when the dog dies? To be that close and lose him!*

A wave of humbleness hit Wendy as she studied that student, studied the friendliness with which he greeted people who approached him, studied the smile on his face, and the casual manner he seemed to have quite naturally.

It comes from inside, she told herself, *and it is incredibly genuine. He's not play-acting, not at all.*

Wendy had had to form opinions of people in a very short span of time, and she already had one of that blind student.

Grateful.

He seemed grateful to be alive.

Though surrounded by other young people who were blessed with the gift of sight, this teenager seemed to have gotten beyond feelings of bitterness, though it could hardly have been easy for him.

Of course, she could not discern how long he had been blind, from birth or much later, perhaps as a result of an accident.

To have never known sight...

She shivered at the thought.

To never know what his loved ones really, truly looked like, she went on in her mind. *Not to have seen a sunrise or sunset, not to know the beauty of a monarch butterfly, never to have even the vaguest idea of—*

How many of his young classmates truly *appreciated* the gift of sight or ever considered it at all? They fussed and fumed over broken relationships, outbursts of acne, being grounded by their parents or whatever else.

"But you can see!" Wendy screamed, though no one could hear her, the car windows closed, the air-conditioning on full blast. "Don't you realize how important that is? Don't you *understand* what you have when you open your eyes each morning *and see?*"

Wendy was good at putting herself in the place of others. That was one reason she had become a successful public defender. She projected a great deal of empathy for her clients, enabling her to understand them better.

The blind student was entering the high school, and she whispered goodbye to him.

Wendy sighed, wondering briefly how blindness would have changed her life, how she would have adjusted.

I might not have, she confessed to herself. I might have been a nightmare patient, moaning and wailing all the time.

She turned her attention, while waiting for the red light to change, back to the swarms of students.

All of them were destined to endure the same pressures or, at least, similar ones, and react with varying degrees of intensity.

The loners would have it the roughest, Wendy decided. For them, turning to someone else would not be an option.

For students, the already overriding importance of social ties was heightened, for they could share their worries about the present, their fears for the future with others, who undoubtedly would understand, with an empathy that came from going through similar emotional turbulence.

The same peer group that could be so destructive on one level could also get each member over the rough times.

"Belonging..." Wendy said out loud, an almost palpable wistfulness in her voice. "How could they get through without that?"

She could not have done so, could not have endured the nightmare into which she once had been thrust, could not have—

Thank you, she thought, remembering the students and the adults who rallied around her then.

Wendy was lost for a moment back in her own times as a teenager, times when she was so burdened with concern about her grades, about her acne, about her weight and whatever else that she thought the accumulated fears would tip her over into paranoia, and force her into a breakdown.

I always wanted to succeed, to be accepted, she recalled, at whatever I attempted. That made me fierce in sports and in anything else, for that matter. And I always wanted to look my best.

Ah, the memories there!

She was popular, respected, at least during her first year or two of high school.

And she was determined to stay that way.

Her weight tended to be up and down, and she fought quite a battle to keep it within limits, dieting, then gaining a few pounds, dieting again, and all the while, concerned about anorexia nervosa.

A difference.

The difference that set Wendy apart from other girls who fell prey to that condition was her determination and her awareness.

Looking good meant being thin, she thought ruefully.

She drove herself to lose pounds, desperately switching from one diet to another if any did not work as quickly as she wished.

And none did.

She knew her behavior was strictly compulsive. She never lied to herself about that.

But, still, despite this self-awareness, it took Wendy many months to break the cycle, to make herself realize that she had never been overweight in the first place, and that she had nothing to prove to anybody.

So Wendy found herself caught up in a cycle that was wholly debilitating, as well as dangerous.

How I worried and worried and worried, she thought. *And yet I survived without any lingering problems.*

Friends. They were the answer for Wendy.

Her friends were understanding, patient with her periodic nervous outbursts. Though no wiser than she was, since they had some of the same hang-ups and few answers, what they did succeed in doing was reassuring Wendy that she was not alone, that they would survive together.

I could never understand how they managed to put up with me, Wendy thought. *I wonder how often they felt like giving up.*

But they stuck by her.

And she did the same with them as she saw her moods reflected like mirror images in their own.

We laughed together, Wendy remembered, *and we cried together, my friends and I. We talked into the night, and shared the pain we felt, the pain of being young, of wanting to be noticed by the best-looking boys in school, shared all the rest of what we agonized over during those years.*

She did not know where most of them went after high school was over. And she felt quite sad about that, sharing so much pain and so many tears with other teenagers, thinking that they were bonded forever.

And then the friends she had treasured were gone.

The bulk of them were off to universities across the United States, and one or two in another country altogether. Letters were exchanged early on and then everyone, including Wendy, was caught in other relationships, other obligations.

Wendy MacPherson was among a very small minority of students whose high school years ended in a unique way.

Marriage.

Not what used to be called the shotgun wedding but a marriage filled with mutual need, mutual passion, mutual hope, or so she had thought.

Marriage for Wendy.

A whole new world.

Chapter Two

The thought, the hope, the dream of marriage had been with her since her early teens and accelerated as each year passed. Most of her school-mates were interested in the intimacy of marriage but were repelled by the idea of a certificate of paper that bound them to their husband for the rest of their life.

Wendy felt differently.

Sex outside of marriage was verboten for her, as much from her sense of self-respect as any religious upbringing her parents had given her.

Ironically, regarding marriage, she did not have to wait nearly as long as most other girls for that to enter her life, for she met the apparently remarkable young man she was to love passionately during her sopho-more year.

Seth Darfield.

Despite the baggage she carried with her from that relationship, she still got sweaty palms when she thought of him periodically, remembering the warmth of his firm body against her own, the touch of his lips pressed against hers.

Oh, Seth, she asked of the air and the sun, *I wonder, if you came back to me, and pleaded with me to forgive you, what would I do?*

She was biting her lower lip.

I just might get you alone, and unbutton your shirt and…and…

Her hand. It was slippery on the leather-wrapped steering wheel.

Even now, even today, even after all that you did to me, I—I would still let you make love to me.

He was a young man in his late teens who came from English ancestry, including not a few dukes and princes.

And less than fourteen months after they first met, Wendy MacPherson and Seth Darfield were married.

My husband became my best friend, replacing just about everybody else, Wendy recalled, *until, one morning, I discovered the truth about him.*

That nightmare morning.

They had not made love during the night but she knew in advance that this was going to be the case since he told her just before they got into bed that he was bone tired, that there were some matters at work which were causing him stress.

"Forgive me..." he asked plaintively, his thick lips teasing her as they always did. "It's not you, believe that, okay?"

She had no reason to dispute him, so they kissed, and fell asleep, Wendy completely at peace.

Until 7:10 a.m.

Wendy awoke slowly, her sleep during the night a deep one, and filled with dreams as usual.

"Morning..." she spoke in her softest, sweetest tone, with a special edge to it that she knew he found quite sexy.

No answer.

Wendy assumed that Seth was still asleep so she raised her voice just a bit, sure that he would respond this time.

Still no reply, muttered or otherwise.

She generally detected the odor of the men's cologne that he used, Lush Meadow. That was the odd name but she also liked it, liked it as much as he did, perhaps even more because just smelling it reminded her of him, made her anxious for him to get home so that she could stand at the door, and reach out and hold him in her arms.

Wendy instinctively sniffed, searching for it.

Once, twice, again—then a final time.

Nothing...

She smelled nothing but the scent of roses drifting in through an open bedroom window.

Berating herself for overreacting, and yawning a bit, she stretched, waiting a few more seconds.

And then she turned over, expecting to see him sitting in a chair and looking out that open window, a pensive expression showing that he had not answered her because he was in the midst of a brief, personal reverie.

But—

"Good morning, dearest," she started to say, then sucked in her breath, her eyelids shooting wide open.

His side of the bed was...empty.

Empty!

Instead of seeing that familiar body, his well-defined chest with just a hint of hair, his strong legs sticking out from under the covers, his—

He was gone.

She tilted her head toward the bathroom, listening.

A shower. *Yes, of course!* Surely he was taking a shower and could not hear her. But he generally sang while he was doing so.

Not this time. No sound was coming from that direction.

Her heart was beating faster.

No! she thought. *I'm overreacting. I'm—*

She sat up in bed, sat there quietly, sat there and waited, and hoped and...

...listened.

For the sound of water in the shower enclosure. Or the car being started. Or Seth on the telephone.

Nothing. Absolute silence.

Wendy got out of bed, threw on some clothes, went out into the hallway, and looked in both directions.

"*Seth!*" she cried out, her level of anxiety mushrooming.

She waited for him to reply. He did not.

"You're scaring me," she said. "I don't know why you're doing this, but it's awful. It's really—"

Still no response.

Cold perspiration begin to cover her, sticking her nightgown to her body.

A thought.

What about a—?

Yes! Of course, that was it.

Seth had gone out, that much was obvious but, knowing that she would be concerned, had left her—

A note!

Surely Seth had done just that so that she would not be reacting as she, in fact, was.

Wendy searched the apartment, looking on the door of the refrigerator, on the kitchen countertop, on a little table near the front door where they put the mail each day until they could deal with it.

No note.

She got down on her hands and knees and looked on the floor, from one end of the apartment to the other, lifting up the throw rugs to see if somehow a note had been accidentally kicked underneath.

Seth apparently had left no note.

Not even that.

Trembling, hugging herself, Wendy stood finally, hurried over to the telephone on the wall in the kitchen, and started making phone calls, to mutual friends, to where Seth had been working.

No one knew anything special about him or his plans for that day but they all asked her to call back if she needed help.

Wait.

That was all Wendy could do.

So, she sat back and waited, checking the clock in the kitchen every few minutes, as though she could persuade time to move just a bit more quickly, and bring her closer to Seth's return, and his explanation for what was going on, an explanation she was telling herself would be honest and true, and they could go on as before. And that morning, that initially disturbing morning, would be forgotten.

Tick-tick-tick.

She could hear the clock, hear its ticking louder than normal, the sound taunting her with the passing seconds, seconds with Seth gone.

An hour.

No phone calls from Seth.

Her gaze darted to the front door, fixing on it for a moment or two.

She tried to *will* the knob to turn, tried to will the door to open, prayed quite desperately that, on the other side, standing in the hallway, would be the man to whom she had pledged the rest of her life. Looking sheepish, but with a full and responsible explanation for his disappearance.

The knob did not turn. The door remained shut.

More seconds turned into a ever expanding pool of minutes, and the minutes kept piling up until—

Two hours.

Her nerves were rubbed raw by the waiting.

She started crying.

"What's happened?" Wendy asked out loud, her entire body shaking, a headache beginning, and intensifying as the minutes passed, the back of her neck tight, like a piece of wood, hurting whenever she turned her head.

The relationship that existed between her and Seth was the sum total of her existence.

And now—!

At first she gave no thought to the possibility that Seth had run out on her, which seemed so remote. Their married life was so satisfying in every respect. And she would have sensed any problem, at least that was what she tried to tell herself.

Noon.

By then Wendy was nearly hysterical, the walls of that apartment feeling like some kind of mausoleum in which she found herself inextricably trapped, trapped inside a place of death.

Another hour.

Sobbing, nearly passing out from the strain, she waited another hour.

After that, Wendy called the police, her hand shaking as she dialed the number, hysteria underlining her voice.

The officer who answered was respectful but also a bit cavalier, accustomed to calls from overwrought women.

"We can't do anything for 48 hours," he told her.

"But if he's been injured and can't get back to me, or to a hospital," she said, "he might be dead by then."

"Regulations, ma'am."

"But—"

"Ma'am?" the officer interrupted, with no particular embarrassment. "Were you and your husband—?"

"Yes?" she interrupted, impatient.

She could hear him clearing his throat before speaking again.

"Were you and your husband having marital difficulties?" he asked, a cynicism in his voice that was unnerving.

Wendy MacPherson slammed the telephone receiver down on its cradle, and started sobbing.

Darien and Stedfast were in the car with Wendy, though she never knew this, never suspected.

"She is so fine, this one," Darien remarked. "She has been through such a great deal. If only she could give herself a rest."

"Yes, she needs that," Stedfast agreed. "She has never really confronted the past and banished its demons. I use that word figuratively."

"Of course. We have been by her side for...how long now?"

"A day or two."

"No, I mean finite time," Darien corrected the other angel.

"I see—perhaps ten years."

"I suspect you are right. It is awkward keeping track, would you not agree? After all, we have to be traveling from heaven to earth and back again."

"Most awkward, my comrade."

"A day to God and others like us is a thousand years to humankind," said Darien.

"Then I was wrong, was I not?"

"About being with her a day or two?"

"Yes. It seems like much longer, but it has been only a few minutes."

"A few minutes for us...a decade for Wendy."

"I have felt her pain," Stedfast confessed.

"As I have," Darien assured him.

"I will be very glad when there is no longer any more pain, any more tears, any more suffering throughout the whole of creation."

Thoughts of that eventuality occupied them for some while. Then the two left the car and went where they could be alone and ponder the fate of a young woman of whom they had grown very fond.

Chapter Three

So long ago...

Or had it ever happened?

She toyed with that absurdity, toyed with it because it had the advantage of being delusional, a delusion that she could deal with better than the reality.

Had there ever really been a Seth Darfield?

Did he even exist?

A couple of years after she became a public defender, and had already gathered together an impressive list of contacts, she decided to see if she could trace Seth's whereabouts, no longer with any intention of revenge but as a matter of curiosity.

A friend of hers lived in Washington D.C., and Wendy called, gave her Seth's name, and then waited to see what would turn up.

The friend called the next day.

"Wendy?" she spoke.

"What did you find out?" Wendy asked.

"Very little, I must say. There are a couple of Seth Darfields listed in the public record."

"You're kidding—"

"I thought it was a mistake myself. It's hardly a common last name, and to have Seth attached to it seemed more than coincidental. But there it was. He's forty-five years old, fat, kind of ugly. I figured *your* Seth was ruled out from the get-go."

"The other one, the second Seth Darfield," Wendy probed. "Anything there?"

"I couldn't find out. All records relating to *that* Seth are sealed."

"Sealed? Why in the world would they be sealed?"

"Can't tell, Wendy."

"Why not?"

"They were sealed by express order of the director of the Federal Bureau of Investigation."

Wendy did not return often through memories to that time when she went from the mountain to a dark and miserable valley, did not return because she did not want to relive the anguish of what ultimately occurred.

It seemed that a lifetime had passed since then, however clichéd it was for her to look at her past in that manner. Sometimes she was so tired that she could not think any more originally than that.

So long...

It was true, shopworn description or not. A decade could change the course of history, and it had certainly changed her life.

For the better.

Certainly for the better.

And now that Wendy had achieved what she convinced herself was necessary, she need never again risk being deserted by any man, because she could get along without men if she had to do so.

At last! she muttered in exasperation, as the light finally changed. *If nothing else holds me up, I'll be okay.*

Wendy breathed a sigh of relief, as everyone must have who was waiting to go on about their business for the day.

She turned and glanced at the man who was sitting behind the steering wheel of the car in the next lane.

He sensed that she was looking at him, and smiled pleasantly.

Any other time, she sighed wistfully, *any other place.*

Wendy returned her attention to the street ahead.

The light's green now! she thought, her stress level rising, *so what's stopping everybody from moving ahead?*

She saw the answer a moment or two later.

Teenage pedestrians.

An ever constant flow of line after line of them, crossing the street, reluctantly heading back to school.

As a result, vehicular traffic was jammed bumper to bumper, congestion inexorably set in directly in front of the attractive brick-red-and-ivory-white Spanish-style school building where most of them would spend four years. Although not a prison, for many, it would come to feel like that.

Pleasant enough on the outside, she remarked to herself, though her experience had been that, inside, such schools were often drab by contrast, smelling of disinfectant and unwashed sneakers.

Wendy was impressed by the entrance, which was bordered by scarlet-colored bougainvillea at their most beautiful. And the grass in front was exceptionally well kept, as though the building was a very large residence or a hotel, and not part of the often maligned public school system.

Hundreds of teenagers.

They were coming in from as far away as twenty miles in different directions, brought either by buses or driving in their own sometimes rusty, battered cars or simply walking if they lived but a few blocks away.

The school itself was situated in a predominantly upscale vicinity, one of a series throughout the affluent San Fernando Valley area just north and slightly west of Los Angeles, California.

Most of the students were dressed fashionably even if that meant wearing what appeared to be threadbare jeans and other current examples of teenage attire, clothes expensively manufactured to look weather-beaten.

Amused, Wendy chuckled at the various displays of what was currently fashionable, reminding her of her own teenage attempts to stay current, a frustrating, wasteful and expensive business.

Earrings.

More boys wore these than girls did!

A few went so far as to have pierced noses as well. Some would have gone even further down that road, with purple or pink or green hair but the school administration had stepped in a year or so earlier with a flat-out ban, while allowing students some flexibility otherwise.

Chattering. Massive waves of it! The sheer volume gave the illusion of an even larger crowd than the one she was seeing all around her.

But that chattering would have to end soon after they entered the school building for the next several hours, so they got in all they could beforehand.

Undoubtedly, its total absence inside the thick walls bordered on being rather eerie, but was due merely to a set of definitive behavioral rules that were applied with surprising military school-like exactitude. Years of laxity regarding the conduct of students had ended, and the new generation paying the price for the unruliness of the previous one.

Chapter Four

Standing on a street corner, ready to cross...
Wendy noticed that one couple immediately—out of the many either passing by or simply standing—noticed them as though they were outlined by a glow of some sort, making them impossible to ignore.

Which was in itself unusual since she had seen endless numbers of young people over the past decade, either passing them by on the street as at that moment or, especially, in the course of her longtime work.

As a public defender, she'd crossed paths with many teenagers.

Wendy's career direction was unusual for a young woman such as herself. If her parents had been alive, they would have protested any such choice, but eventually bowed to her wishes.

"You can't be serious!" her mother would have said. "It's not what you should be doing, dear."

And her father would have spoken almost those words as he tried to dissuade her from any such career direction.

"And what should I be doing?" was undoubtedly the question Wendy would ask the two of them in return.

The only question possible, given the way she felt.

In addition, her father would have pointed to the types of people she would have to defend.

"Scum, Wendy. Don't you realize that? Kids on drugs. Mothers who have been sleeping around with any man they please. They're not your kind."

"Mom, Dad? What about the poor people, the innocent poor people who can't afford a lawyer? What happens to them?"

Both would have remained silent, and both would have reconciled themselves to accepting what their daughter wanted to do.

There was nothing but love between us, Wendy thought, *even in the midst of our disagreements.*

But, in retrospect, she had to admit that being a public defender was not what most high school girls dreamed of doing.

Originally, she had no intention of going in that direction.

She was tinkering with the idea of psychoanalysis. The appeal of being an airline stewardess was fleeting, since she never had much regard for her appearance.

Yet how much that sort of life beckoned, she acknowledged to herself, *especially traveling overseas.*

Wendy had never been out of the United States nor visited many states. Her parents and she had spent part of one summer vacation on Maui, Hawaii, which whetted her appetite for other exotic places.

More than one friend thought that she would have been an ideal stewardess, tall, attractive, a good personality. Her parents agreed with those friends and urged her to aim toward such a career.

Yet Wendy turned away, deciding that she was not appealing enough, with virtually no charisma, and that being rejected by all the airlines would have been more devastating to her than making the attempt in the first place.

But being a lawyer was something else altogether.

I don't have to be glamorous, she convinced herself. *What is necessary is that I have a good mind. I could handle any of the pressures, and I probably could do a very good job winning cases.*

Her parents wondered what in the world she could be thinking of, worried about the unsavory character of some of those individuals she would be required to represent, and the possible danger involved.

"Wendy..." her mother pleaded, "you might have to defend rapists, pornographers, prostitutes, awful people like that."

Wendy's view was that somebody had to do it because, whatever their crimes, the U.S. Constitution guaranteed them representation under the law.

"Besides, Mother, some of them, though accused, are actually innocent," she said, "and *should* be protected."

From that point, her parents said nothing more in protest.

And then, when she did decide, she went through the rigors of law school with top honors, and a few years later, had been so successful that she became a respected and exceptionally busy public defender.

But not long after Wendy had begun building a track record, she nearly threw everything away.

And all because of a wrong turn.

A wrong turn supposedly by sheer accident.

Which brought her face-to-face with pure evil.

Chapter Five

Wendy was in her early twenties at the time, a vigorous young woman who was, on the surface, shaking the trauma of having her marriage annulled.

She was an exceptional student, had graduated from law school at the very top of her class, and, during the years to follow, would compile a burgeoning list of awards and commendations that would continue through the years to follow.

Every reason to be content. And relax.

But that was not what Wendy did.

She kept pushing harder, campaigning for an even heavier workload, confident that she could handle anything the district attorney gave her, no matter how demanding.

Until that one day, a day without a remarkable start to it, in fact, rather ordinary, she got out of bed and readied herself for the next few hours, although there was nothing to prepare Wendy for what was to happen....

She felt a bit tense, though she could not imagine why.

I need to relax, she told herself.

Wendy went on a drive to clear her mind of the pressures of an over-burdened schedule, and got lost, her mind on the future, not on the road ahead of her.

The barrio area of Los Angeles.

As soon as Wendy realized where she was, she panicked, having seen the media coverage of such neighborhoods, a large percentage of the cases she tackled coming from barrio related situations.

Fortunately, at least she would not have to face any of those forbidding and unfamiliar streets after dark since the analog clock on her car's dashboard indicated that the time was two-thirty in the afternoon, and as much as she admitted that she would not make a good navigator, even she could never remain lost for three or four hours.

She glanced from side to side, appalled at the conditions: the piles of trash; the men lying in gutters and leaning against old buildings, some holding liquor bottles to their mouths and pouring the poison down their throats; the rest room-type odors that permeated the entire area, it seemed.

Lord, she thought prayerfully, *no wonder there is crime in these places. What else in life do they have?*

Not much better than a slum. That was Wendy's first impression as she searched for a sign pointing to the nearest freeway entrance.

So many, all tortured in one respect or another, a majority of them not much interested in going on living if the life ahead of them was going to be little better than what was already driving them to despair....

Most of her cases concerned men and women well out of their teen years but the percentage was changing, the age of those in trouble slipping dramatically.

She had been involved with clients who were as young as ten years old.

One *looked* younger than that. Johnny Perez.

He could not be tried as an adult, and yet putting him in with hardened teenagers was not acceptable as far as Wendy was concerned. Even the bureaucrats in the creaking system of government with which she had to deal daily recognized this, and she was asked what solution she proposed.

At first Wendy had no answer.

What *could* she say?

Though rehabilitation was being trumpeted as a goal, the emphasis was still on punishment. And, admittedly, Johnny *deserved* to be punished.

Arson. Months before, he set ablaze a nursing home, ironically one of the better-run establishments.

Wendy heard about this during a television news program the evening it happened. She was alone, which was how she spent most of her after-hours time. There were occasional office parties, a rare date, dinner with friends, that sort of thing but, usually, she went from the office straight home, and cooked for herself, watched videos.

When the report was broadcast, she stopped eating, and was transfixed by the images on screen.

"Those poor souls!" she exclaimed out loud, watching the terrified expressions on deeply lined faces and hearing the fear in their voices as they looked at the news camera and expressed their bewilderment, "Why us? Why here? We just want to be left in peace."

Fortunately, no one died in the flames but there were many injuries, and trauma-related deaths occurred within the next few weeks, frail hearts and veins and arteries unable to endure the stress for very long afterward. In most of the cases, the heart attacks or strokes or other conditions were caused by the awful fear, accelerated by age, of being burned alive. Yet not all of these occurred hours or days later, a delayed reaction syndrome taking over and erupting as much as two months afterward.

Why?

That was the question Wendy had for Johnny Perez as she confronted him in his solitary confinement cell in the local jail where she was fighting to keep him so that he would not be transferred elsewhere.

A boy like Johnny, toughened by the life he had been leading, would be an attraction for prisoners with pedophile tendencies or those who would be interested in a one-time fling with someone as young as he was.

"Why?" she asked, knowing that she had to do whatever she could to probe past the tough exterior he projected, the get-out-of-my-face attitude that so many barrio youngsters had to adopt to survive in the jungle around them.

"It felt good," he told her.

So cold, so—

"To torment people?" she probed, confident that she could break through and uncover the truth.

"Whatever...."

"Have you done this before?" Wendy continued, her pulse quickening as she tried to prepare herself for the answer.

"You're my lawyer, right?"

"I am."

"Anything I tell you can't be repeated unless I let you, right?"

"That's correct," Wendy acknowledged as a sudden chill began at the base of her spine and fanned outward.

"Three times."

He was smiling as he spoke, his eyes reflecting the excitement that he felt, the flow of adrenaline through his body.

Suddenly Wendy's throat was dry.

"You're happy?" she asked with effort.

"Sure," Johnny told her matter-of-factly. "It's cool, real cool. I mean, what else could I want?"

Trapped people screaming...confused by the encroachments of age...terrified by the flames and the smoke.

"Did you stay around and watch?" Wendy spoke.

"Man, did I! That's part of the fun, you know."

That's part of the fun...part of the fun...part of the fun...part of—

Wendy wanted to shake the ten-year-old, wanted to shake him until he dropped that stone-cold facade and sobbed out to her some kind of repentance.

But she restrained herself and asked as calmly as she could manage, "What did you see, Johnny?"

A look of unrelenting terror...skin splotched with liver marks...vari-

cose veins...eyes bloodshot...not knowing what to do...where to go...

"This old guy came running outside," Johnny Perez continued. "His arm was on fire. And he was screaming. That was great."

It was not an act from this ten-year-old, the act of a callow child trying in some perverse way to act like an adult.

I wanted to watch him die.

Wendy heard those next words but they seemed to be coming from somewhere else, or perhaps it was a trick of her mind, a defense against overload.

I wanted to see the expression on his face. But I had to run. I had to run so that the pigs wouldn't find me, and I could go on and do it again.

Wendy was feeling nauseous by then, and had to strain to keep from grabbing his neck and...and...

"Anything else?" she asked, keeping her voice at a monotone, for if she did not, she would say things that her job did not permit.

"Yeah."

"What?"

"Not old people this time."

Wendy's heart began to beat faster, straining against her chest, as she asked, "Who then, Johnny?"

He was licking his lips, looking a little like one of those movie vampires who had just claimed a victim or was anticipating the next one.

"Babies!" he exclaimed. "Lots of them!"

Wendy's hands were clenched into fists, her palms sweaty.

"What did you do to babies?" she probed. "And how many, Johnny, how many were there?"

"Four, I think."

"You think?"

"I don't remember sometimes. It might have been more."

Wendy's next question was not one that she *wanted* answered, because she dreaded what Johnny Perez's answer would be.

Lord, she prayed to herself. *I need to know this. I need to know it so that we can try to understand, so that—*

She *had* to find out, had to have the question and his response in her report, had to do what her job demanded.

"What was it that you did to those babies, Johnny?" she spoke, the words nearly burning her mouth.

"Stole them," he replied, his fingers tapping some obscure rhythm on the tabletop between them.

"From where?"

"Carriages."

Murder. Kidnapping. He must have started earlier, a year, two perhaps, when he was only eight or nine.

"Where were the mothers?" Wendy asked. "What were they doing?"

"Talking to somebody...in person...or on their cell phones."

"They didn't know what was going on?"

"I was good at that. It was too late. I ran fast. The babies were asleep. They didn't start crying until later."

...until later.

Wendy found it difficult to swallow.

What caused the babies to cry later? What had Johnny Perez done to them to make them cry...later?

"And then—"

"I broke their fingers one by one...like toothpicks, you know...it didn't take long. That was when they started to cry."

"What did you do then...Johnny?"

"I put them on the ground and threw things at them."

"Threw—!" Wendy gasped, starting to lose her self-control, fighting hard to keep it but not succeeding.

"Anything I could find, you know. Bricks, stones, bottles, cans. They didn't know what hit them."

Wendy's face was pale, her lips trembling.

Johnny saw that he was having an impact on her, and chuckled, "You should have seen the last one. His head caved in like a rotten melon!"

Wendy jumped to her feet, and called frantically for a guard, who came running, a pistol in one hand.

"He's—" she started to say as she nearly ran out of that room.

"A monster?" Johnny Perez yelled behind her. "You bet I am, bitch. What else is there for me? I never had a dad. My mother was a twenty-dollar hooker on Santa Monica Boulevard. I started on drugs when I was six years old."

Wendy hesitated, turned and looked at Johnny.

For an instant, just that one fleeting instant, he seemed vulnerable and then it seemed that a dark mask settled over his face, and a malevolent look transformed him as he rushed toward her.

Wendy was at the door when he reached out, his hands closing around her wrist. The guard stepped forward but Wendy held up her hand, needing to hear what he had to say, desperate to understand him.

"Go ahead!" he yelled. "Write me off. That's what you're gonna do, isn't it? Like all the rest!"

He spat at her and launched into a stream of obscenities.

She had heard bad language before, had heard it throughout her career. This was different.

Darker, unholy, so severe that she noticed the veteran guard's reaction, his cheeks beet-red, barely able to contain his own anger.

The guard grabbed Johnny and broke his hold on her wrist.

Wendy was shaking by the time she was out of the building and had reached her car in the parking lot adjacent to the jailhouse. She wanted to get away from that place as soon as she could, start her car, and floor the accelerator.

Chapter Six

Her throat muscles had tightened.

And she felt dizzy.

"My God...!" Wendy said out loud, though not profanely, more as an impromptu prayer. "I...I saw real evil back there. I—"

Though a relatively new public defender at that point, Wendy had done so well that she was being handed more cases than was usual.

And yet, as severe as some had been, not the worst of them were even remotely like Johnny's.

"My God...!" she repeated, taking slow, deep breaths to keep from passing out. "It was—it was like getting a glimpse of—"

She brought her hand to her mouth as she leaned weakly back against the hood of her car, a much dented aquamarine coupe that had preceded her black Swedish wagon by a number of years.

A hand on her shoulder. The gentle touch of an unexpected hand.

"—hell," a voice spoke. "It was like getting a glimpse of hell, is that what you intended to say?"

Gulping, Wendy was startled, and swung around, confronting a thin-faced elderly man, slightly stooped, who was leaning on a cane with a rather elaborate, old-fashioned handle.

He winced as he saw her reaction.

"I am *very* sorry," he spoke. "I thought you were in distress. But I see that *I* have caused you some myself," he added.

Relieved that she was not facing an assailant, Wendy dismissed his concern with a wave of her hand.

"You don't know the half of it, sir," Wendy replied. "I was tense already, as you observed."

She looked back toward the old brick jailhouse, nervous about doing that, but unable to resist, because along with her fear was something resembling fascination.

I broke their fingers one by one—like toothpicks, you know.

She shivered visibly, and she thought that she might be on the verge of losing whatever food she had eaten earlier that day.

"*All* the color is drained from your face," the old man spoke sympathetically, examining her closely.

"Not surprising," she said, "because of what's back there."

"What or who?"

Wendy was surprised by that insight.

"Both, I suppose."

"The who, yes, that *is* the worst part, *knowing* who, I mean," this elderly stranger added cryptically.

"A ten-year-old boy."

He raised one finger. "Not that," he told her. "He's flesh and blood. It goes ever so much deeper than that, young lady."

As someone who believed in God and angels, she likewise accepted the reality of Satan and demons though she never fell into the trap of thinking that evil was behind every unfortunate event, every tragedy throughout history.

But, now, after spending time with Johnny Perez, she had that creepy sensation of sheer darkness, of a chilling presence that she could not as yet shake. It had gotten through to the center of her soul.

So she could agree, at least in part, with the old man.

If all evil was mental illness of some sort, then the demonic reigns of Hitler, Stalin and other madmen could not be explained, for these went beyond dementia or a related condition. And what about Dahmer, Gacy and others of their ilk? Were psychotic aberrations enough of an explanation?

"Of course, sir," Wendy replied politely. "Psychiatry does not have all the answers. And I have never thought that Freud was as profound as he was purported to be."

As part of her law school curriculum, she had had to study Freud, Jung, Menninger, others, and became convinced that they arrived at incomplete conclusions in many instances, with the exception of Menninger who allowed for a spiritual dimension in many of the cases of schizophrenia with which he was involved.

"There's more to it," the old man said.

"I don't understand."

"There's the 'who' you can *see*—and the one you cannot."

Wendy was beginning to wonder if he suffered from the early signs of senility.

"Thank you, sir," she said, hoping that he would take the hint. "I really do have to be going now."

"Can't I be of some help?" he asked.

"I am afraid not. I have to be heading back to my office."

"May I say something?"

"Go ahead," she said impatiently.

"To be honest, you look very queasy."

The way Wendy felt, she knew that she could not protest his appraisal.

"Won't you join me for a cup of coffee?" the old stranger urged sincerely. "Across the street is a very nice little shop. They have some wonderful Danish pastries there."

Wendy knew that she had waiting for her a heavy workload at the office but she was shaking inside and needed to calm down, or else she would cease to be of value to anyone for the rest of that day.

"Who are you?" she asked. "I am not accustomed to strangers being so nice, not in this day and age."

"I have lived long enough to understand that you and I are here, this very moment, for a reason."

"Predestined?"

"You could call it that."

The old man seemed so kindly that Wendy decided it would not be unwise to accept his offer.

"I *will* join you for coffee," she replied, "and I will share one of those pastries with you, sir."

"How fine!" he exclaimed with such good cheer and a burst of youthful energy that he seemed to be the grateful one instead of her.

Chapter Seven

After they had sat down in a booth next to the large window at the front of the coffee shop, and she tried to get her nerves back under control, Wendy told the stranger essentially what she had encountered just a short while earlier, leaving out enough detail that she would not be breaching her client's confidence.

When she had finished, he did not react for a minute or two.

"You seem surprised by the extent of the evil you witnessed," the elderly stranger finally spoke, raising his voice a bit because of the noisy crowd. The coffee shop had been a success for some years, its neon sign outside and garish decor inside part of a calculated attempt to evoke another era, an attempt that evidently was paying off since the place was seldom less than filled to capacity.

He leaned forward intently, grimacing a bit from what Wendy assumed was the onslaught of rheumatoid arthritis.

"Or have I misunderstood?" he asked.

Wendy assured him that he had not.

"Unrelenting evil," she agreed. "I sometimes see flashes of it in my work but not like this time."

The old man sighed with a weariness akin to that which Wendy herself felt from time to time.

"I have seen such evil also," he remarked.

He was not humoring her, his expression serious enough to make her believe everything he said up to that point.

"When?" she asked.

He sat back and closed his eyes, the images not ones that he enjoyed recalling, and said, "Over the course of many years...not just once but innumerable times."

"Any examples?"

Wendy had no idea why this stranger fascinated her to the extent that he did, or why she should be interested in any of his experiences.

He nodded with a kind of solemnity that seemed almost regal. "More than I could ever recite in their entirety," he replied.

"But a little boy?" Wendy asked incredulously. "Were any as young as the *boy* I met there in that jail?"

"He is an exception, yes...an exception, for the moment."

...*for the moment.*

"You expect more, don't you?"

"Especially in this day and age."

"What is so different about now?"

"Defiance..." he told her, spitting the word out as though it tasted quite bitter on his tongue.

"Is that it? Simple defiance. We both know that young people have been defiant for generations."

"Not like at present..." he emphasized. "It's more severe now, darker, an unholy edge to it."

As he spoke those few words, Wendy felt a wave of cold touch her body, worse than she had ever before experienced.

"But what's causing it—?" she started to ask, then realizing she did not know his name, added, "May I address you by name?"

"I am called Darien," he told her.

"Is that your first or last name?"

"It is my *only* name. Now tell me, what is yours?"

"Wendy MacPherson."

The two of them shook hands with a warmth that seemed uncommon under the circumstances.

"Darien, what's causing this outbreak of such total—?" Wendy asked.

"Evil..." he stated. "Use that word again, Wendy. That's what you were about to do, right?"

"I was, yes," she confessed.

"Then you would be quite correct...but not in the way I suspect you typically would mean it."

"Evil is evil."

"No, evil is not always just some psychological aberration," he said. "And we must never fall into the trap of thinking that it is."

"What else is there?"

"From the soul, Wendy, from the human soul. It often has nothing to do with psychological impulses, though such evil may start out that way."

"I believe in the soul."

"You should. In that jail cell, you just witnessed a soul completely given over to forces of evil."

"Schizophrenic, you mean?"

Darien was showing some frustration. "Forget the Freudian language."

"You're losing me."

"I see that I am. I'll try to be more direct but you may have difficulty handling what I am about to say."

"Go ahead."

"More than that, Wendy, more than schizophrenia, manic depression or any of those other conditions or illnesses. The *symptoms* are those of schizophrenia."

"You honestly see something else?"

"I do, because, young lady, the real source is control, control by the most awful evil imaginable."

Wendy was fascinated.

"Can you tell me more?" she asked.

"I can *tell* you a great deal more. But can you absorb more? I worry about overwhelming you."

A flash of anger. "I am close to being offended by that, Darien," she said.

"Sorry to hear that," he added. "I hope that you will believe I was speaking purely out of concern."

Wendy was at the point of getting up and leaving this pedantic stranger, not wanting to waste any more times with riddles.

"Don't leave just yet," he requested. "I've not told you what I think is allowing evil to spread among young people more completely, more rapidly than ever before."

"You seem to have the ability to read minds, so you must know why I am getting out of here."

"I don't have that ability, as you wrongly suspect," Darien corrected her, "but Someone else does."

Wendy allowed a smirk to cross her face as she said, "I believe only God can truly read minds."

"Precisely!"

He reached over and placed both of his hand on top of hers.

So soft, she thought. *So soft—like feathers.*

"God told me what you were thinking of doing," Darien spoke.

Now she *knew* she had to leave that coffee shop.

"Sure, sure," Wendy said, mocking him with an edge of sarcasm, and asked a passing waitress for the check so she could pay for the coffees and pastry each had ordered.

"Wendy?" he said.

"Yes?" she replied, anxious to be gone from his presence, and betraying this by tapping several fingers on the tabletop.

Darien held on to her.

"Wendy, listen," he asked.

She tried to pull away but could not, surprised by the strength of someone as old as he appeared to be.

"I've *been* listening until now, but you are beginning to sound major league weird, Darien," she said. "Now let go of my hands or, I promise you, I will start screaming so loud that everyone in this coffee shop will be on top of you in seconds."

"It isn't the first time, you know."

"The first time for what?"

"Remember the man in that park so many years ago? At first you were uncomfortable with him as well, remember?"

The waitress had come to give them their bill but as far as Wendy was concerned, she might as well not have existed. She left it and walked away, unacknowledged.

...like the man in that park so many years ago.

Wendy was certain that she had been alone with that man. She didn't remember Darien being there.

Now every detail of that encounter came back vividly. It was a day not long after Seth had left her. She was alone with the man, a man who later turned out to be an angel incarnated in human form.

"How—?" Wendy started to ask. "How could you know? How could you tell me anything when you weren't there?"

"I *was* with him," Darien said.

"You could *not* have been!" she protested. "I saw the two of us, nobody else. There was only that man and me."

"I was sitting next to him on that park bench. I heard every word of what you and he talked about."

"Nonsense! I'm warning you—let go—*now!*"

"Wendy, look at me! You say 'that man.' You *know* he was more than that, you know in the center of your being."

"I *saw* only—" she repeated, clinging to those words as though they were some kind of life preserver.

"That's right. You emphasize saw, Wendy. You saw only the two of you. That's the operative word...*saw.*"

"That man was the *only*—"

"Say what he was, Wendy. Say it."

She hated revisiting that moment in her mind because of the awful disappointment of knowing that she realized what the stranger was only after she'd left.

"An angel!" she blurted out. "I know *now* that he was an angel. I heard his wings. I *felt* him as he really was, but too late."

"And closing yourself off from the truth has cost you, has it not, Wendy?"

She had to admit that he was getting very close to the center of a truth that she had not confronted for a long time.

"I...I hated myself for being so blind," she told him. "I hated myself for not letting myself be close to one of God's miracles. I let that time pass, and look at what I could have learned from him. Look at—''

Darien smiled benevolently.

"Learn from me," he said. "Learn from me."

"I have to ask why, Darien. Why you, Darien? That stranger was an angel. How could I ever learn from—?''

She gasped even before he spoke next.

"As I am, Wendy, my dear woman...as I am.''

She fell back against her seat.

"I've got...got to get out of here!'' she exclaimed. "I can't stand any more of this. I must not allow this to continue!''

"As you did then, and regretted it. You turned away, understanding the truth only a short while later, and wishing for all the years since then that you had not been so rash, that you had paid more attention, that you had believed what God was trying to tell you.''

By then some of the other customers in the coffee shop had turned around and were glancing at the two of them.

Wendy was sweaty, sensing that unwelcome attention, embarrassed that she and this stranger were the center of it.

She looked at him and tried to decide what to do.

"Just listen, my dear,'' Darien spoke, knowing her confusion. "What harm could come from listening?''

"My caseload,'' Wendy answered lamely, grabbing for any excuse to run, to turn her back again as she had done before.

"Is that the best you can do?'' he added. "Besides, is it going to hurt your clients if you come to them a little wiser than before?''

Since their voices had lowered quite a bit, the other customers lost interest and returned to their own conversations.

"Go ahead then,'' she said.

"You have to be prepared for evil. You have to understand that some of those for whom you gain freedom are going back on the streets with only one intent...to spread the evil that grips them to others.''

"So I should refuse to represent them? I should break down my clients into two categories—possessed and not possessed. How am I to do that? And how could I explain it to the district attorney if I did?''

"Discernment,'' Darien stated simply.

"But I have no choice. I have to take whatever cases the DA gives to me. I can't refuse without an impeccably good reason.''

"That is not what I am suggesting.''

"Then I have no idea what you *are* talking about, mister.''

"Be prepared, really prepared to deal with your cases, as you call them.''

"I am prepared from the first moment,'' she protested.

"Prepared *spiritually* as well as psychologically. The one is pointless without the other. Don't always bring in simply a psychoanalyst, and no one else. As there are angels, there are also..."

"Are you suggesting that a clergyman be added?"

"That is exactly what I am urging you to consider. Or at least someone with *spiritual* training."

"I don't think I could—"

"Get away with it? That was what you were about to say, isn't it, Wendy? Be honest, please."

"Yes, Darien, I would not be allowed to introduce any kind of religion into something that was being paid for by public funds."

"How sad. People go to an early grave or end up in a padded cell because bureaucrats disavow the spiritual altogether. Those public funds you speak of were paid into the system by the very people who clamor for help but are often denied use of the funds that *they* contributed in the first place."

"I...I *would* like to do it differently," Wendy acknowledged. "But my hands *are* tied, as much as I hate to acknowledge that this is the case."

"Someday you *will* do it differently."

Darien made that declaration in a manner that suggested he knew something Wendy did not.

"How can you honestly say that?" she demanded.

"You are going to be a pioneer, who places the greatest emphasis on rehabilitation. The results will be amazing."

"I'm not all that special," Wendy protested. "I'm not the sort of person who is able to change anything."

Darien pooh-poohed that notion. "The mayor might be receptive," he suggested. "After all, you and he are going to be increasingly friendly."

"I can't count on that. I hardly know the man and—"

She was stunned once again.

"You really are an angel, aren't you? You must be to make a prediction as wild as that."

"Yes, Wendy, I am, and you can believe what I have just told you. This mayor will be re-elected and—" He tapped the back of her hand. "There is much in store for you."

"God has told you this."

"He has, Wendy, that He has," Darien said, firmly showing his disapproval of her tone of condescension.

"Can you tell me anything else?" she asked.

"A peek into the future? No, I am not allowed."

"But I am to believe you, anyway."

"If you believe in angels, yes, Wendy, you are to believe what I am telling you in this little coffee shop across the street from the dark and terrible evil that you witnessed only a short while ago."

He paused, his head tilted slightly to one side.

Wendy studied this old man who claimed to be an angel, and it appeared that he was listening.

"Is God—?" she asked.

He held up his left hand, and she fell into silence, wondering why she was obeying him.

Seconds passed.

His eyes were closed. And he was not moving.

He seems frozen, like a videotape that has been paused, Wendy observed, as she glanced over her shoulder to see if anybody else in the coffee shop was paying attention to his strange behavior.

No one was.

Then his eyelids shot open, startling her a bit.

"I want to show you something," Darien said.

"Is that what God told you?" she asked.

"It is what the Creator told *us.*"

"I didn't hear Him."

"You weren't listening, were you, Wendy MacPherson. It is fine to have angels around when you think that they are needed. It is fine to pray to God with supplications dealing with what you want Him to do for you." Darien paused, then told her, "But when you think you can handle everything by yourself, you tend to forget Him, us."

She nodded toward the ancient jailhouse. "I couldn't handle what I saw in Johnny Perez," she acknowledged, still feeling chilly at the very recollection.

"Precisely, young lady. I must say that I wonder if you can handle what I am about to show you."

He was trying to provoke her, and succeeded.

"Just try me!" she declared.

He stood, said, "Follow me," and started to walk out of the coffee shop.

Wendy did what he asked as soon as she paid the bill. The waitress looked at her and asked, "Is everything all right? Do you want me to get someone to help you?"

"When is anything all right?" Wendy said cryptically, then assured the other lady that there was no problem.

She left the coffee shop and approached Darien, who was standing outside. "Where are we going?" she asked.

"The answer will be obvious to you in a few minutes."

Wendy had no idea why she suddenly felt so tense. But she soon found out.

Chapter Eight

A teenage boy, dressed in a tank top and faded jeans, was standing on a street corner.

"Look at him," Darien told her. "He has just reached the age of sixteen years, and already his life is being wasted. He has no income except from the drugs he sells," Darien continued. "He is not being educated. There is certainly no church influence. He makes it big again and again and thinks he has the system beat."

"I am familiar with kids like him," Wendy said, nodding sadly.

"He just bought his mother expensive central air-conditioning for her home. And new furniture. He wants to take her to a store in one of the shopping centers so that she can buy a new wardrobe."

"I have represented many, many others who have a story to tell identical to his own," Wendy replied. "How do you convince boys like that not to do what seems to solve their economic problems, gets them whatever material things they could want and yet involves so little work?"

"Not until they are thrown into jail," Darien pointed out.

She remembered one boy who told her that he was much better off than a friend of his who had taken to hustling along Santa Monica Boulevard in order to scrape together sufficient funds to live in places better than condemned buildings.

"After a couple of stints like that, they are hardened more than ever," Wendy recalled. "It is no longer enough to make money. They now want revenge. Revenge drives them day after day."

Darien put a finger to his lips, then pointed across the street.

"Look harder than ever before," he told her.

Wendy was not certain what it was that she should be searching out.

"It would help if I knew what you had in mind," she said.

"You will know when you see it," he replied. "You will see something for the first time right there across the street, something you shall remember for the rest of your life.''

Her car was parked close to the opposite corner. At first she could not begin to imagine what Darien was getting at, the scene apparently the same as when they arrived less than five minutes earlier: a teenage pusher, with an acne-scarred face, trying to convince another young man to sample some white powder in a two-inch-by-two-inch plastic bag.

''What's new?'' she asked.

''Reinforcements,'' Darien remarked. ''What you are about to see is reinforcements, Wendy.''

It took her only a short while to—to see *something!*

''Something'' was the best description, perhaps the only one. Not a shape so much as a presence.

''Dark—'' Wendy muttered, clenching her teeth. ''Darker than any bottomless pit.''

''They always are,'' Darien spoke, his own tone sombre, reflecting long awareness of and experience with the evil being discussed.

''They?'' Wendy asked, noticing the personification of evil, rather than simply referring to it as a cosmic force of some sort.

Darien betrayed some exasperation as he replied, ''Creatures, my dear Wendy, the most loathsome creatures.''

''What I'm seeing is *alive?*''

The thought that she was witnessing living things collided with the rational side of her nature.

''Very much so, alive and deadly,'' Darien assured, his patience returning, ''and ready to swallow up another victim.''

Movement.

The darkness seemed to be moving, some vague sort of shape to it.

''Is that—?''

She guessed what Darien's answer was going to be, guessed it in the very center of her soul.

''Evil?'' Wendy asked. ''*Real* evil? Not some Hollywood producer's hokey special effects fabrication?''

''Yes, *that* is living evil,'' Darien spoke knowingly, ''not some theological doctrine or some philosophical abstraction.''

He pointed for emphasis.

''That, my new friend, that is undiluted *real* evil. It is with us every minute of every day. It never leaves.''

''It? Evil is not personal? Is that what you are saying? Evil is a force, not beings like Satan, demons? I thought you were going in the other direction.''

He shook his head. ''Just a manner of speaking,'' he remarked. ''Evil is their brainchild. Evil is their constant progeny, Wendy. Demons and devils create it and let it loose, to go on a rampage.''

"But where is the good? Where—?"

"Wendy?"

She waited for him to continue.

"Do not become fixated on the evil. That is the mistake the movie people make. Look now and you will see something else, something altogether the opposite."

And Wendy did see them.

Creatures of light so intense, so multicolored, each completely different and so overwhelmingly beautiful as they came together that she could do nothing, say nothing, because what she was witnessing transcended language itself.

"My G—!" she started to say.

"No," Darien interrupted, "no, not God at all. But like Him, Wendy. After all, they were created directly from His mind. He spoke and they came into being, *we* came into being, my comrades and I, Wendy.

"We have existed for aeons, you know. We were before evil was. Evil came later, wrenched from us, angels corrupted by Lucifer. And now look at them, Wendy. Look at the good and the evil side by side."

"It looks like a fight," Wendy observed.

"And a fight it is," Darien confirmed. "A fight in a long series of these, battle after battle, as part of a monumental war, a war not for land, not for money or power or politics but for something quite different...the human soul."

He touched her arm. "It is time to leave," he said. "You have seen enough for the moment. The rest is not for someone unaccustomed to the *results* of evil."

"But I haven't seen what will happen," Wendy protested. "Should I do that, to be prepared, Darien?"

"You should see no more."

Darien's authoritarian manner was becoming quite galling to her, and she now reacted against it.

"Why not?" Wendy persisted, showing him clearly that she was irked.

He was not fazed. "It would destroy you," he said simply.

"It hasn't thus far."

"But, my dear, this is only the prelude. You could have no conception of what surely will follow."

He threw his shoulders back. "What is going to happen next is..." he began, then stopped.

"Are you ill?" she asked.

"Not this temporary body, Wendy, but ill of spirit, ill at the knowledge that such evil could be rampant in this world."

He cleared his throat. "The damning of a soul, Wendy. No human being could ever, ever, ever witness that and hope to remain sane. It takes all the strength of an experienced angel to avoid being overwhelmed."

Under other circumstances, Wendy might have protested all the more but this stranger named Darien had won her trust completely, and she determined that she could not disregard his advice.

"Where do we go now?" she asked.

"Kindly take me to a certain place of worship," Darien told her. "It is just three blocks away." He smiled serenely. "I need to be alone for some while," he added.

She turned in that direction. "I will miss you...." Wendy acknowledged, genuinely sorry to have to say goodbye to Darien.

"You never know when I or another of my kind will show up," he told her a bit mischievously.

"I have believed in angels for a long time."

"But belief is often a matter of simple faith, a kind of hope in what is or will be. In a way now, my dear, you no longer need faith as such because you have seen the *reality* of what you believed."

"Back there..." she muttered, hardly able to refer to what she had seen, hoping the effects would not hang on so that she spent one sleepless night after another, thinking and wondering.

"Yes?"

"Was that...the devil himself...all that terrible darkness?"

"It was not. He is not able to be everywhere, as God is. Satan has severe limitations, Wendy."

"What was going to happen back there?"

"Demons were ready to enter that boy's soul. I did not want you to stay because you would have seen something so ugly that it might well have been the cause of a nervous breakdown or worse."

"But you see it again and again, don't you?"

The old man seemed gripped by a special despair, despair that made him appear older than he was. "Through the centuries, Wendy, through the *many* centuries, whether it be demonic influence or oppression, or actual possession...yes, I have seen it."

They were at the church where Darien had wanted to go.

"Wendy," he faced her, "I have seen people corrupted who once could have helped this world but instead just deepened the crime, the violence, the disintegration."

Darien seemed to know that what he was ready to say next would test the credulity of any normal person, and so he went on to speak with a deliberateness that emphasized his astonishing contention.

"I saw Adolf Hitler *before* he was taken over. He did not hate Jews. One of his closest relationships was with a Jewish college professor."

According to Darien, Hitler was searching for direction in those days. He was fascinated by that professor, saw in him levels of wisdom as well as a certain weariness that made him feel oddly protective for a young man who'd begun to have preliminary flashes of anti-Semitism.

"What happened?" Wendy asked.

"I cannot say. I was given another assignment. I know only the result. We all do...the millions of victims, the piles of corpses, the crematoriums and—"

Even he could not continue but needed to pause briefly, the sights, sounds and odours of Dachau, Auschwitz, Treblinka, Bergen-Belsen and other concentration camps returning in a rush that he would have hoped he could have stemmed but was unable to do so, the memories with him like leeches, hanging on, hanging on, hanging on.

"I was with so many souls as they left those wasted bodies," Darien continued. "The relief on their faces, but also their concern for loved ones left behind, to suffer whatever madmen prescribed to do to them!"

He saw Wendy's expression and kissed her on the forehead. "Be of good courage, dear one," he said. "Think of the One Who sent me when you feel as though there is no hope. Do not think of me. I am but the messenger. God overcometh, dear one, God overcometh."

"You call me 'dear one'?" Wendy spoke. "Why? I'm just one person. I feel so inadequate. There are others far more worthy of your attention, your time."

"Angels do not know time. Angels look at a clock ticking and hardly know what it is there for, because they are beyond time and space. They can go from one universe to another, from one so-called time period to the next. When I leave you, I can be in an instant in ancient Rome or mediaeval England."

"I am Wendy MacPherson. I am not Joan of Arc or Madame Curie or anyone else even remotely as great."

"That is correct. You are not."

Wendy threw up her hands in bewilderment. "Then why bother as you have been doing? How do I warrant you and the other angel in that park years ago and other angels on yet more occasions? Can you explain that to me? I always have believed in angels but I never assumed they were with me constantly. Please help me out here."

Darien was learning to be patient with her. "Because you, too, were created by God," he replied.

"Is that all?" Wendy asked, sensing from the old man's manner that there was something else.

"Someday, countless numbers of men, women and children in this country and elsewhere will look to you, my dear Wendy, for you will have made an impact on their lives beyond what you could possibly guess right now."

Wendy laughed rather heartily, appreciating his feel-good comment but scoffing at the same time. "Thousands? Surely you are joking. I know who I am, what my capabilities are. But thank you anyway."

"Angels are not creatures of jest, believe that. Nor do they harbor deceit. Surely you understand that."

"Why would thousands care anything about me?"

"Because of what you will come to mean to them."

"I help a few needy, hurting people every week. That doesn't add up to the thousands you suggest."

"In time," he said, "in time you will know and understand."

Darien got slowly out of the car, and walked to the steps of the church before turning around. The now familiar body, bent with age, was being replaced even as she watched, replaced by—

Creatures...countless numbers of them...creatures of light so intense, so multicolored, each completely different and so overwhelmingly beautiful.

And Darien had become one of them.

Wendy could hear those words of his once again, spoken as though from ten thousand tongues.

Be strong and have courage...countless numbers will look to you.

Then they all were gone, and she found herself staring at the empty steps of an inner-city church.

Wendy did not go to work but called in sick from a nearby pay phone, and found her way through the unfamiliar barrio streets back to her apartment where she stayed alone for the next several hours, alone and in prayer.

Until evening.

She halfheartedly threw together a hodgepodge of a dinner, ate the mess slowly, reluctantly, her stomach not entirely settled, her head throbbing from all that she had seen and experienced.

Chapter Nine

As a result of her experiences that day, Wendy MacPherson made taking on cases involving teenagers a top priority. She had had a number of such cases already but she soon began *looking* for these, asking her staff to pass any new ones to her as soon as they became aware of the details.

I was fanatical, she recalled, *as though I could correct the ills of a portion of the younger generation all by myself.*

And most of the ones she learned about came from the barrios of the inner city, which used to be many miles away but the infestation of the drug-and-gang culture had eventually spread well beyond its traditional boundaries. The onslaught had forced a redrafting of rehabilitation methods based upon a new brutality and recklessness that was showing up in boys as young as seven or eight years old. By the age of ten, many had been on the streets at least a third of their lives.

Wendy was very much at the center of the revamping of efforts to reach young people throughout Southern California. She introduced a motivational approach that showed results over a period of time, though she faced critics who were interested in results quicker than what Wendy's could offer.

At one speaking engagement, Wendy nearly had a physical confrontation with someone in the audience.

"You act as though we have all the time in the world with these kids," said the short, round-faced woman in her midforties, her tone not much short of a shout. "We have to do better than that."

"Better?" Wendy repeated. "Better in what way?"

"Quicker! If we don't make progress right away, we will lose them back to the lives they had been leading before we were given a chance with them."

"Quicker?" Wendy went on, toying with the woman. "I see what you mean." Then she slammed her fist down on the program. "You've been watching too much television," she retorted.

"What does that have to do with it?"

"Everything neatly resolved in an hour, all loose ends tied up until the next episode. Life isn't a trite TV drama or a quick pop-in-the-oven TV dinner. These young people got into their behavior patterns over a period of years. You want a magic wand that you wave through the air and everything is fine afterwards."

"Nonsense!"

"Yes, I agree, what you expect *is* nonsense."

"I didn't mean it that way."

"Of course, you didn't. But I *do* mean what I say. You want instant gratification. But that is part of the disastrous mind-set that gets teenagers into trouble day in and day out. They take drugs because they want to escape. Sniff something up their noses and, in an instant, their troubles go away. But they have to buy more drugs, and indulge themselves until they are hooked. Quick fixes are seldom the answer."

Wendy knew she was on solid ground from years of success as well as failure, knew that quick fixes were an illusion, creating the image of having accomplished something, only to have that victory slip away.

Wendy was also familiar with the attraction of a regimen that meant reduced costs, always a political favorite.

"Is it saving young people from themselves that motivates you?" she asked severely. "Or the cost? Quick fixes mean less dollars spent. My approach requires a greater budget in each case. Is looking good before the politicians at the heart of what you are trying to shove down the throats of anyone blind enough to give you their time?"

The woman in the audience was incensed. "We don't have the time!" she protested. "It's not the money, never has been. How dare you say otherwise?"

"What happens when your so-called solution turns into the same problem, because your so-called help isn't anything more than a little disinfectant and a bandage over what is *really* wrong? You are forced then to fight disillusionment, a growing sense of inevitability. Where are the savings then? And what of the toll on those young lives you claim you are reaching to help? Answer me that!"

Wendy's critic was abruptly quiet.

"I don't feed the kids I work with anything other than the truth. They will need patience. They will have to have courage. And they must expect reversals. But taking that first step is important, moment by moment. Gradually I pull them out."

Wendy's tone softened. "The Gallup Organization did a poll," she added, "and this one consisted of information about young people one year after they went through what my approach mandates. The recidivism rate was less than ten percent.''

Wendy smiled the kind of smile that Bobby Fischer must have had after winning an important chess game. ''Are you going to call *their* facts fallacious?'' Wendy persisted. ''Everyone is wrong but you, is that it?''

The other woman mumbled, ''If only that were true with my kids,'' and sat down without protesting any longer.

Chapter Ten

Wendy had been praised by Nancy Reagan, Barbara Bush and others. The Bushes invited her for a private dinner at the White House, and she accepted the invitation. Only hours before her evening with the President and the First Lady, Wendy succumbed to a bout of extreme nervousness and insecurity. She felt as though she could not leave her hotel room when the time came.

"What am I going to say?" she asked out loud. "I'll make a fool of myself for sure. How can I advise someone as knowledgeable as the President of the United States?"

It had been a long time since Wendy needed to deal with such pervasive feelings of inadequacy.

"I have to leave," she said. "I have to find some excuse. This was a dumb thing for me to do."

For the first time in years, she felt something in the hotel room with her, a voice that seemed to whisper not into her ear but directly into her mind.

Be not afraid....

Words sensed but not spoken.

Be not...

"But I am not able," Wendy complained, interrupting. "I know my limitations. I cannot change with the snap of a finger."

She heard a rustling sound like the one in that park so long ago. And the voice in her mind continued, ever so gentle, sweet, kind.

The peace that passes all understanding...

"What about it?" she demanded.

Let it surround you. Do not hinder.

"No!" Wendy said, nearly shouting defiantly. "I am not smart enough or glamorous enough or—"

Be still....

"Yes, I know all about that!" she declared. "Please tell me something different."

Be still and of good courage.

"But—" she spoke.

And it was gone. Wendy knew because immediately the room seemed to be unspeakably empty.

"I've sent you away!" she exclaimed, panic filling her. "Please come back."

No use. The visitor was gone, and no amount of pleading would change that.

Wendy got down on a chair, and put her head in her hands, and started sobbing, but then she stopped quite abruptly.

Have I run out of tears at last? she thought. *After all this time, all the pain. There are none left!*

Finally, Wendy put on some makeup, got dressed, placed her hand on the doorknob, ready to open it and walk into the corridor outside, and froze.

"I will bring shame to my work, to the people depending on me," she said out loud. "There must be a better way, a better person to do this instead."

A hand. Wendy jumped, startled. The vivid sensation of a hand actually resting on top of her own, resting with infinite tenderness.

Go....

A pause.

The words will be given to you. Let them flow out from you to the President and the First Lady. You will bless them, and they will be a blessing to you.

So she went.

The President and First Lady were charmed by her, moved by the stories she had for them of the young people and others who had been helped over the years.

In a matter of weeks afterward, Wendy was able to get the amount of federal funds budgeted for treatment increased in an era of accelerating cutbacks.

I've seen the young ones who were tragically wasting away every bit of potential they ever had, she thought, *as well as those who never got into drug and similar problems, were thankful about this, and stepped forward to offer their services as volunteers so that funds could be stretched for housing, supplies and the necessary paid personnel: doctors, nurses, psychiatrists and others.*

How proud she was of the unaffected teenagers who gave up summer vacations to help out, as well as those who were the objects of that help, the ones who broke away from the hopelessness that had trapped them almost since birth, through to their teenager years, and would have continued until they ended up in jail or a city morgue.

The teenagers who had been abused as children were the most pathetic of a heart-wrenching panorama.

Annabeth... Wendy recalled one whose only defense against her father's and brother's sexual abuse was to develop multiple personalities. When one of these felt threatened, another surfaced quickly, and another after that, always an escape route available to her, until she herself was lost in a neurotic maze.

Escape was the only way for Annabeth to survive. At least it was some form of survival, survival that in itself was destructive.

You eventually managed to get away by marrying the first man who truly seemed interested in you, Wendy recalled about Annabeth. *But that marriage ended in divorce because he wasn't able to cope with your illness.*

Annabeth came very close more than once to taking her own life, but always resisted the urge. And yet, for a very long time, she never did much with that life, either. "I don't know," she would say. "No guy will look twice at me. And I'm not into women. Where should I go, Wendy? Maybe death is the best answer." A warning sign. It did not take much insight for Wendy to detect the possibility of regression, regression to Annabeth's devastating previous state of slipping from one personality into another and another one after that.

"Never," Wendy assured her. "It is not an option."

"But what else do I have? I live alone. Nobody calls me and I have no social calendar to look after. I make good money as a secretary but money isn't everything."

Her weight. She was not like a fat lady in a circus but she had enough extra pounds to make her unattractive to any possible suitor.

"I think I'm getting past the psychological damage," she said. "It's the way I look that I've not been able to conquer."

And her physical condition could cause her to slip back into the multiple personality syndrome that had haunted her. So Wendy helped her to start the right diet and put together an exercise regimen that she hoped Annabeth would follow zealously. For a while, it was a struggle. For a while, she needed to fight the return of her multiple personality disorder.

"That's not unusual," Wendy told her. "I don't think it ever goes away, at least completely."

"Then that means I will have to be on guard for the rest of my life?" Annabeth asked wearily.

"I'm afraid that that's the case."

"You know..."

"What, Annabeth?" Wendy asked.

"You know what my main problem is?"

"Tell me, okay? I want to hear."

"You *want* to hear?"

"I do."

"Why?"

"Because once I know what it is, I can try to help you break free of it. You can understand that, can't you?"

"I can."

"Okay..."

"You'll tell me then?"

"I will, Wendy."

And it poured out of Annabeth in a seemingly unstoppable surge.

"I want to go up to my father and my brother *and beat them!*" she cried out. "I want to *punish* them for what they did to me. But I can never do that. They have denied me that kind of satisfaction."

Both Annabeth's father and brother were dead, killed one night as they were driving home after several hours in a bar.

"All I can do is go and spit on their graves!" she added. "That's not enough. I want to choke them, kick them, do some terrible things and...and..."

She stopped, her cheeks bright red, perspiration on her forehead and trickling down the back of her neck.

"It's happening," she said, her eyes half open, her breathing heavier.

"Another personality?" Wendy asked, but knowing the answer.

A gurgling sound in Annabeth's throat. "I can feel her trying to get in," she confirmed.

Wendy was not a licensed psychiatrist but she had had to get some training before being allowed to become a public defender, since being able to analyze personalities was helpful to her as she became familiar with each client.

And she knew that Annabeth was on the verge of an "episode."

"What is she like?" Wendy asked.

"She wants to take me over, to control me, to dominate everything that I do. She wants *me* gone forever."

Wendy knew what to expect, knew not to push too hard without a psychiatrist next to her.

"Annabeth?"

"Yes..."

"Will you allow that to happen?"

"I don't know if I can stop it, Wendy. I am not very strong yet. That will take a while if it *ever* happens."

"You are stronger than you allow yourself to think."

"No, no, I'm not, Wendy. Don't do that! You mustn't tell me something that's not true. Don't—"

"You're wrong," Wendy interrupted. "You can no longer let yourself think like that. It's one weapon she has, your insecurities, your feelings of inferiority, playing on them continually. She thinks you will allow her to take over because she is the dominant one, and you are too weak to resist.''

"I don't *want* that to happen," Annabeth cried. "Please help me! Will you please, please help me?''

"Yes, of course, I will. Annabeth?''

"Yes, what?''

"Tell me something?''

"I'll try, God knows I'll try.''

"All right, then, tell me this. What *would* happen if she did take over, Annabeth?''

"I would go and...and...''

"Tell me," Wendy urged patiently, her voice as calm as she could make it under the circumstances. "Go ahead, dear. Don't be ashamed. There's really no reason at all to be ashamed, you know.''

"She's awful" Annabeth continued. "She wants to sin over and over, with men, with women, with—''

Annabeth threw her arms up in the air and swayed them from side to side, arching her back, thrusting her breasts forward.

Her eyes were wide-open, and she was getting to her feet.

Suddenly Annabeth dropped her arms, relaxing her body from head to foot, and folded her hands together in a praying position.

"I'm not going to let her through!" she declared. "She has had victory too long now. This cannot continue.''

"I will stay with you for as long as you need me," Wendy promised, realizing that she was on dangerous ground as someone not licensed to conduct such a session.

Over the next several hours, the two of them in Wendy's office, the staff members knowing that they should not interrupt under any circumstances, a battle was fought, two young women against forces that seemed dark and unholy.

"I think we are not alone," Annabeth said toward the end.

"We are never alone!" Wendy declared.

"Are *they* our friends? Or are they—?''

"Friends, yes. They want to make sure there is victory here today. They want all presences to leave.''

Victory. It *was* a war of sorts, a war for the stability of a young woman named Annabeth, a war for her soul.

And there *was* victory.

Annabeth succeeded in remaining who she was and not letting any other personality come in and take over.

And, later, years later, she became the mother of two sons and a daughter.

The day the third child was born, Wendy arrived at the office and found an extraordinary floral arrangement on her desk.

Chapter Eleven

Dear Annabeth...

It was not uncommon for thoughts of that one young woman to come back vividly to Wendy.

"You suffered so much," she would say out loud, "for those years, sexually abused by a father and a brother who should have been protecting you."

But Annabeth pulled through, and Wendy was at the center of her recovery.

She kept in touch with her former client periodically, but because they now lived hundreds of miles apart, the contact between them was not as regular and as intimate as once was the case.

Knowing Annabeth had deeply affected Wendy. The one "case" that she promised herself she would *not* lose, could not lose! There had been a helplessness about the young woman, her emotions so fragile.

In some ways Annabeth was so pitiful, in others an example of pure courage and faith, faith that, in the end, God would not desert her.

But marriage changed her. Annabeth's husband was a tall, chunky, young man only slightly less handsome than a movie star. And those three children!

"I am so fortunate," Annabeth told Wendy. "He's a wonderful husband. But look at us! Beauty and the beast all over again. And I'm the beast!"

Wendy winced at that, though aware that the other woman was being entirely facetious. "Brad loves you," she remarked.

"Yes, I know. Sometimes, though, I wonder how long it can last. Will I wake up one morning and find him gone?"

Annabeth had not known about Wendy's own marriage. "I can understand your feelings," she said.

"You can?"

That was when Wendy told her the basic facts of what had happened with Seth. When she was finished, she added, "It will be different for you. You are going to be married for the rest of your life."

Wendy decided to let Annabeth know about something she had just learned a short while before. "One more thing," she ventured.

"What is it? Good news, I hope."

"Very good."

"Then go ahead."

"Brad took me aside at the end of last Sunday's worship service," Wendy revealed, "and we talked for quite a while."

Annabeth's eyes widened.

"What did he say?" she asked.

"That he loves you very much, that he saw from the beginning what your soul was really like."

"Are you...serious?" Annabeth asked, not quite letting herself accept what she had been told.

"I am. And he told me something else."

"What?"

"That angels were responsible for bringing the two of you together."

"Angels?"

"That's what he claimed."

"Do *you* believe in angels?" Annabeth asked. "I do. But I wasn't sure about Brad. I am so glad he does."

"Yes, and I have for many years," Wendy assured her.

"Have you had any experiences with them?"

Wendy told her about the encounter she had had in that park a decade earlier, and how much she regretted not realizing the truth until it was too late.

"It was something like that for me, too," Annabeth recalled. "I wish I had known so that I could ask him questions."

"I was like that," Wendy acknowledged. "I could have spoken to him about God, could have asked him what Heaven really is...and—"

Wendy bowed her head.

"Are you all right?" asked Annabeth.

"Yes...I was just thinking that I could have asked that angel in the park how my parents were doing. He might have taken a message to them. How wonderful it would have been to know that he was going to tell them that I loved them very much."

"Wendy?"

"Yes?"

"Did you ever think that God didn't want that to happen? Just then? That we may not know why but that He had the best reason?"

Wendy smiled, grateful for what this troubled, overweight young woman was telling her that day.

"You know what, Annabeth?" she asked.

"What?"

"I think He spoke through *you* just then."

"Me?"

"Yes, you...every bit as much as He spoke through the angel I met in the park."

"Praise God!" Annabelle exclaimed.

The two of them talked for another couple of hours, and then each had to take care of other obligations.

Annabeth went on to a happy life, her multiple personality disorder gradually dissipating until she was as close to being normal as she could expect.

Praise you, my dear, Wendy thought. *Bless you, sweet, sweet one.*

Other young women were not so fortunate. Just two weeks earlier, one of Wendy's clients attempted suicide for perhaps the twentieth time.

I think you will be successful one of these days, Wendy told herself at the time, *wasting all that could be accomplished if you just waited, if you just held on and saw what God had in mind for you.*

It did not turn out that way.

This client was more the average than Annabeth. Ransacked by personalities that took her over, she was eventually destroyed by them.

Often clients like these would go on existing for many years, would live what could be called a "normal" life span, but in fact the length of it was all that *was* normal.

Constant anguish. Physical anguish could be treated, could be alleviated and even cured. But the kind that ravaged the human mind, that caused each bright sunrise to be greeted with fear.

Fear of the very worst variety. For people riddled with this fear, life itself was a constant battle, a battle not to survive against cancer or AIDS or a crippling accident but a battle to survive the horrors that their minds inflicted on them.

"I get up in the morning sorry that I have to," one client of Wendy's confessed to her. "I get out of bed, a bed in which I have slept alone, as I have been alone for so much of my life, and I dread the next few hours. Then when I get through *those,* I dread the next few after that.

"There is no hint of joy in this plodding struggle of mine, this struggle that drags me from morning until evening. There is only dread. Who will betray me today? Who will reach into my life and cause not happiness, not fulfillment, not some sense of satisfaction, but, rather, more tears, more depression, more of an obsession to end it all, to pull the plug, to let it be known that I could not go on, that death seemed the only direction in which I could go."

Young people who grew up in abusive environments had no security or stability within their own homes. They were raised not to face life and live in triumph but to *endure* it and die in despair. And they *were* dying at an accelerating rate, whether through drugs or alcohol-related traffic accidents, or suicide.

Suicide.

So wrong, Wendy thought morosely. *It is a deceptive one-way street, ending six feet underground.*

For those who lived in the barrios, there seemed an answer that drew them like a magnet that was so strong, so compelling that it could not be resisted.

Gangs.

And so they turned to gangs which did offer a measure of what they had been missing for so long.

Lord, thank you for letting me be with them, she prayed silently. *Thank you for helping me to reach out and bring some hope to their lives.*

Chapter Twelve

To reach out and bring some hope to their lives...

That became the motto of Wendy's career and, to a great extent, her life since her career was such a large part of it. And the resulting benefits seemed to be both for her clients and Wendy herself.

For her, reaching out and bringing some hope into lives desperately needing it proved a blessing of no small proportion for her, a reason to look forward to each day, to the opportunities for instilling hope.

She had seen so much hopelessness, had been submerged in it herself when she was younger. She knew about the value of hope, the necessity of it from the most personal of experiences.

I know what so many young people are going through, she thought. *They seem to detect this in me, as though I was a soul mate of sorts or, at the very least, that they can trust me, trust me with the most intimate of revelations.*

And now, over a decade later, Wendy had come full cycle to this one couple just outside this one modern high school in this one largely affluent district, light-years away from the run-down barrios, the rat and cockroach havens in which vast numbers of families were forced to live.

She was quick to realize that her response to *these* two was not the same, not the same at all as her response to the kids in the barrios.

For one thing, this girl and boy looked as though they belonged in a slick television series since both were remarkably attractive and well groomed, not scruffy and acting more like punk rockers.

But then there was something else—she hesitated, on the basis of a fleeting glimpse to use the word *chemistry* to describe what was going on between them, for first impressions carried a high fallibility quotient— something that Wendy herself had not experienced since she was their age, hardly due to unattractiveness on her part but through a choice she had made, a choice that caused her to shy away from any relationship that had any potential of becoming intimate. She had lived by that choice for most of her adult life. Her past experience dispelled one of the most pervasive romantic truisms of her own youth, a truism that seemed so powerful that it was unassailable: *It is better to have loved and lost than never to have loved at all.*

Wendy no longer subscribed to that notion. She would rather have never known love than to have known it and lost it one cold, lonely morning.

"Was it love at all as far as Seth was concerned?" she asked out loud. "Or was it just lust? I represented a challenge to him. Once he had caught and conquered me, he lost interest very quickly."

Shivering, Wendy gripped the leather-wrapped steering wheel so tightly that her hands started to go to sleep.

A wave of dizziness grabbed hold of her for a second or two, and she worried about losing control of the car but it quickly faded.

Look at them! she exclaimed, returning her attention to the couple. *What a wondrous Creator You are, Father. You deserve the praise, honor and glory!*

They did stand out from the rest of the stream of students who were flowing into school for the day.

So pure and beautiful, Wendy thought. *They have everything to live for. How fortunate they are.*

It was impossible to know whether or not anyone else was noticing them as she was or if the two were just accepted into the fabric of that high school's social structure and not thought to be at all special. It was similar to how movie scouts often discovered young people that their own family and friends took for granted. Scouts, trained to decide who had the charisma for acting careers, could see their potential.

If I were scouting, Wendy told herself wistfully, *I would pick such a couple immediately, and pray that their screen tests turned out well enough to justify acting classes.*

The route she normally used to reach her office was closed off because the street was being repaired, potholes filled in and a new layer of asphalt spread over it, the odour as unpleasant as ever.

Wendy was in a bad mood by then.

She had overslept, her body protesting the degree of strain she placed upon it. Rushing a bit frantically to get ready while thinking about the day's work caused a headache that was momentarily so severe she had to stop altogether, sit down and close her eyes. Afterward, she got a bottle of pills from the third shelf of the medicine cabinet in her smallish bathroom, a bathroom that she had decorated herself, using floral print wallpaper and a felt tile floor covering that was medium beige and very thick. The pills were not aspirin but a Chinese herbal medicine that banished a headache in less than half an hour.

And then she was on her way to the office, which was her destination sometimes six days a week, glad as ever to leave the house behind her for a while, since when she returned to it in the evening, sometimes as late as just before midnight, she was surrounded by its encompassing emptiness. It was not empty of quality furniture or bright colors or rugs into which her feet sank comfortably, but of people. This was an attractive three-bedroom rancher in a neighborhood dominated by families that she shared with no one, and having no one to whom she was close seemed to mock every minute of every day she spent inside it.

No one. She felt a chill as those words echoed in her mind.

Fathers and mothers and children were all around her, up and down the street, unavoidably reminding Wendy of what she'd thought she would have with Seth Darfield.

After Seth left, I wanted to get out of an apartment, she recalled. *I wanted to get away from elevators and landlords. I wanted to have some hope for the future, with a home of my own, ready for a family of my own.*

And nothing that reminded her of Seth. Wendy bought new furniture, including a fifty-five-inch projection TV with a striking dark cabinet, enjoying the shopping experience which a friend from the office who helped out with suggestions about color schemes. And she had new kitchen appliances delivered: a refrigerator with a built-in ice maker for the first time in her life; an electric range with a ceramic top; deluxe dishwasher and garbage disposal.

I remade that house as I wanted it to look, she told herself. *I picked the curtains, the rugs, the wallpaper, the wood paneling—everything new.*

And she moved in and lived there alone.

Was that foolish, Lord? she thought prayerfully. *Or did You foresee a purpose in what I did, and I was following Your will without realizing it?*

It started out well, how very well it did.

When she first moved in, she was given a welcome the first couple of days by one neighbor after another.

"We want you to be happy here!" exclaimed a dark-haired middle-aged man and his attractive, younger wife.

"I'm sure I will be," Wendy replied, delighted at the open friendliness they showed to a stranger.

"It's just a great place to live," his near-model pretty wife added. "You and your husband will fit right in."

"I'm not married."

"Oh..."

She seldom saw them after that.

And other attempts at welcoming fell flat as well. Wendy was just not gregarious enough to socialize, as seemed very much the norm for everyone else up and down that particular street, a block that happened to be an exceptionally long one.

Free time was not abundant. She spent time with an endless line of clients, at the office, in court, in jail and, sometimes, at rehab centers as well as sanitariums.

Still, people kept in touch the first few weeks, for, Wendy suspected, she represented a challenge to them as they tried to win her over.

Somehow it seemed artificial, contrived. *I've become a sought-after trophy,* she would think from time to time, wondering if there was some sort of secretive betting going on about whose invitation she would ultimately accept. All of this was somewhat amusing to her, and she was quite sure that she caused a stir when she agreed at last to go to the church that, coincidentally, several of the families attended.

It felt good that Sunday, she recalled warmly, *felt good to praise God in prayer and song.*

Building a new life for herself, Wendy assumed that she was finally being accepted into the community, despite how she tended to isolate herself. And she had to admit that the attention felt good. Part of the reason was that she was with people who did not have the severe kinds of problems that she had to deal with daily.

Finally someone asked what she did for a living. And that was when budding relationships in the neighborhood started to deteriorate or disappear altogether.

They'd been smiling and friendly and accommodating at the start.... Until her neighbors found out the kind of people she represented, the kind she would be inviting to her home from time to time.

It was hardly an overnight change but, as far as Wendy was concerned, it was unmistakable.

The cheery phone calls dropped off. And so did the knocks at the front door, accompanied by fresh-baked pies or homemade soups or other friendly offerings designed to make her a part of that community.

In time, Wendy's social calendar was abysmally empty again, and other than casual and rather forced hellos as she passed by people on the street, no one invited her to anything. She was being ostracized just as surely as though she were a black woman in a Ku Klux Klan neighborhood. Only the burning crosses and the rocks thrown through her front window were missing. However, since most of her clients were Latinos and black people, she recognized that a racist mentality was at the core of what was happening or, rather, what was not happening. At least this was how she looked at it later. Initially she could not imagine why.

What have I done? she would ask herself, ignoring any suspicions as paranoia on her part.

Then someone on her staff and she were having a coffee break a few weeks later, and Wendy mentioned what was going on or, rather, what was *not* going on.

"I know I'm being ridiculous," she confessed with some weariness, "but it's become total rejection."

The staff member was a young man named Bret Atherton, over six feet tall, who looked like a soap opera hunk, with an easy manner that made him a target for any woman who came in close contact with him.

If she had allowed herself, she could have encouraged a dating relationship between them, but decided against doing so.

"Complete isolation?" he inquired.

"I believe so," Wendy replied. "I mean, when they can't avoid me in the local supermarket or at the post office, places like that, they are friendly enough. Even then, I can *feel* a difference, Bret, and it's unsettling to me. I had such high hopes."

"Scared," he said.

"Are you serious? What is there to be scared of?"

"I'm dead serious and, yes, from what you tell me, I would have to say that the good folks in this new neighborhood of yours are very scared," he repeated wisely, not that this surprised Wendy since she had hired him for his intelligence and rather striking perceptivity.

"That seems mindless, utterly mindless," she repeated. "They are thinking, reasoning adults. What's the problem?"

"They are scared, as I said, and you are a symbol of that fear because of your connection to the harsh realities of the world."

That was hardly a profound statement but it made Wendy even more attentive.

"Me?" Wendy asked, tapping her chest with a finger. "Bret, really, am I all that intimidating?"

Wendy could clearly read his reluctance to speak any more strongly, and tried to make him feel more secure about doing this. "Go ahead, speak. Your job is not on the line," she assured him.

"If you say so."

"Really."

"All right, as I said, they're scared, but not of you. They're scared, I imagine, of what you *do* for a living."

"Helping people?" It was the only way Wendy could envision herself making a living, the only way she could get a degree of personal satisfaction. "They're upset over *that?*"

Bret shook his head. "Not that exactly," he said.

"Then what's the problem?"

"It's the kind of people you usually help," Bret remarked, his voice trembling slightly as he forced himself to be frank.

Dangerous men and women...wallowing in crime and immorality...destroying their lives, and in some cases the lives of others.

"Oh..." she said, not altogether surprised.

"Are you following me then?"

"Precisely, Bret."

"It's a shame but understandable from their point of view, I suppose. After all, you do have drug addicts, hookers, accused murderers, robbers and others as clients. Your neighbors must feel threatened."

"And I wonder..." Wendy was biting her lower lip.

"Wonder what?" Bret asked.

"If they think I'm no better than the people I defend. Otherwise, why would I have anything to do with such low-life criminals?"

"Listen, are the lowlifes any worse than some of the clever millionaires who run savings and loans, and cheat elderly people out of whatever money they worked most of their lives to save?"

Wendy's temper was flaring. "That's the way I feel, too," she went on.

"But your neighbors may not. I would wager that most of them see you as somebody responsible for gaining freedom for dangerous criminals who go out again on the streets, and rape women, rob convenience stores, shoot up on drugs, and often getting AIDS in the process, which then spreads to the population by infected blood supplies."

"How narrow-minded!" Wendy exclaimed.

"I guess seeing innocent children die from the AIDS virus can corrupt anyone's outlook," Bret told her. "I won't argue the moral implications of what started AIDS in the first place. Whatever side you're on, you shouldn't turn away from the plight babies face as they experience the ravages of the virus."

She looked at him intently. "You speak as though from experience."

"Yes, I do."

"What happened?"

"My little sister..." His voice suddenly trailed off.

Wendy placed her hand on his shoulder, and whispered, "Don't talk now. We can do it later."

"It's okay. Just give me a minute."

Bret seldom spoke about his personal life, and she had once thought he might be gay. But he'd vehemently assured her that this was not why he was prone to keeping some facets of his past and present quite private.

"They're too emotional," he had said. "It's difficult to say anything without breaking down, Wendy."

She understood, understood better than most, and felt closer to Bret than the rest of the staff members.

He bowed his head briefly, then looked up at her.

"My little sister died because of AIDS just five years ago," he remarked sadly. "And I've been struggling with my feelings ever since. She had received an infected blood transfusion. Oh, it made me want to die as well. To see her go from being a healthy four-year-old to...to being a human skeleton, whimpering in pain, coughing up blood. The agony she experienced!''

''So that's what gives you such insight into what I've been talking about, Bret—now I understand. Sorry to be so obtuse.''

''You couldn't have known.''

He paused, his mind turbulent, not sure that he was doing the right thing but compelled to go ahead anyway. ''I could be like one of your neighbors,'' he said, ''if I allowed myself to slip into that kind of provincial thinking.''

''How can you say that? You seem so totally different.''

''I am now but I've changed.''

Wendy went back to work after that conversation—a conversation that helped in one respect, and hurt in another.

I have no one even on the street where I live, she thought. *I moved from a lonely apartment to a lonely house, with just more space to walk around in. I have no one who will say good morning to me, and no one to...*

And so it went for Wendy MacPherson, her life apparently what it would be for many years to come, no real change on the horizon.

Until that singular moment, that nearly incandescent moment, when she came upon a special teenage couple one morning, apparently quite by accident, a couple who were destined to have more of an impact on her world and the way she lived in it than she could have imagined was possible.

Chapter Thirteen

That morning, managing with some effort to force a patently phony smile as one of her neighbors cheerily called hello, Wendy had jumped into her station wagon, satisfied that she would arrive at the office early.

She had driven the same route for nearly ten years, and knew every building along the way by heart. Turning a corner here and there had become a Pavlovian example of conditioning, then stopping for a series of traffic lights, and waiting as a woman walked her dog across the street at the same hour daily.

And then that unexpected detour. Wendy did not doubt that it would cause her to lose valuable minutes. And there was the real possibility that she might carelessly make a wrong turn since she was accustomed to a singular route leading to her office and had never explored the surrounding area sufficiently enough to know where the various side streets would take her, giving new meaning to "one-track mind," a fact that she knew about herself.

The change in direction was especially irritating since she was someone for whom control was important, that and precision, and if the day was going to become steadily worse, her mood would get more sour as the time passed. The more she controlled the elements of her life professionally and personally, the more secure she felt, and feeling secure was all that mattered to Wendy MacPherson.

Schedules were invariably all-important for Wendy. Once she had one set for each day, she hated deviating from it. And she generally worked one out several weeks in advance, at least as often as she could.

But this time she had no choice.

It's ridiculous, Wendy muttered to herself. *I have so much to do, and now this delay hits me.*

She tended to personalize such matters, which betrayed a touch of paranoia over such a common incident as a street being reasphalted.

Chapter Fourteen

I have so much to do....

That was a bit of an exaggeration, at least to describe the next few hours, a bit of self-deception that was unconscious. The truth was that Wendy's morning calendar was actually quite empty but the schedule that listed her afternoon appointments was jammed.

One of the individuals she was supposed to be seeing that day happened to be that Southern California community's mayor, a man who viewed any current political office as just one step closer to the next one—Robert Friedl.

His supporters had subtly suggested to him that he consider a TV or movie acting career when politics lost its magic. But Wendy would not go along with that. She told him that he should set his sights much higher.

"I think you would try to be president someday," she told him during a budget lunch months back.

"You are right, Wendy," he admitted. "Could I do any worse than that buffoon we have now?"

"Buffoon? I had a different word for him."

"So did I. But for once I wanted to express myself with some modicum of pleasantness. And calling him merely a buffoon is about as polite as I can manage at the moment, given his present shenanigans."

They had met more than once. The fact that he was divorced and available probably would have given the gossip columnists a bonanza if anyone had found out about those occasions.

Actually he's rather good-looking, she told herself. *Tall, broad-shouldered, a nice head of slightly graying hair, and probably more ethics than most politicians.*

Wendy snickered knowingly, well aware that the man was susceptible to flattery, and if she slipped in a certain quota of praises through the

Grunting irritably, Wendy made the necessary left turn, drove two long blocks, and then turned right.

In addition to the detour, she now had to face traffic caused by a funeral possession, plus all the cars driven by other men and women on the way to *their* jobs as well.

A heavy dose of traffic bumper-to-bumper...

The pallbearers carrying the gold-trimmed mahogany coffin to the awaiting black hearse caught Wendy's attention. They were young, in their late teens or early twenties.

Who could it have been? she wondered. *Under ordinary circumstances, they avoid funerals like the plague. And, yet, those pallbearers were young men, all six of them.*

A police officer was standing at the intersection ahead, directing traffic. Wendy leaned her head out the window. He recognized her immediately. And Wendy remembered him as the scrupulous arresting officer in a number of cases that she had been given during the past few years, a man who was not a bully like many of his colleagues.

"How are you?" he asked, his tone friendly. "Sorry for all this confusion."

"What's behind it all?" she inquired genuinely curious. "Do you know who's being buried?"

"I sure do," he said sadly, stopping a moment to let a few cars pass in the opposite direction. His shoulders drooped as he went on, "Very sad. Another school shooting. No motive can be found yet."

Wendy had read about it in a late edition of the local newspaper.

"The one three days ago?" she asked.

"That's right. The victim was a special young man, this one."

She remembered some details. "At Pemberton College, wasn't it?"

"One dead and five wounded, including the dean of the college.

"He died on the way to the hospital. He died talking about angels gathering all around him, and...and...taking him to heaven."

"Did you know the victim?" Wendy asked intuitively.

The officer wiped his eyes with the back of his hand.

"My son's best friend," he told her. "This is a terrible world, you know. Not even high schools and colleges are safe these days."

She patted him on his arm, and then the traffic opened briefly, and she was able to drive ahead.

Noticing the pain on the faces of the pallbearers and most of the mourners, Wendy MacPherson turned away and concentrated on the few miles that remained before she reached her office.

meeting, he would do almost anything she wanted, including promise a bigger budget for the next fiscal year.

And then she felt guilty about mocking him. *You really have been so helpful,* she thought, chastising herself as she remembered his support of the entire public defender system, a system that had come under fire for being the pawn of elements within the city responsible for all conceivable types of crime, the critics forgetting about the genuinely needy cases.

Two years earlier, the mayor, fresh off a landslide win on election day, had become interested in her program for rehabilitation, and, in addition to what he had promised afterward, had recently signaled a willingness to secure additional funds in order for her to rent a bigger office, and hire a larger, more qualified staff.

"And I still have to prepare for that meeting," she snapped. "People seem to think that since I've been doing this so long that I can just jump into a case without—"

Her foul mood made her a bit careless with her driving. She had to swerve twice, once to avoid an obviously aging dog who was crossing the street as fast as it could, and the other time to avoid hitting an eight-year-old girl.

And now—a red light, directly in front of her!

Wendy's reflexes were quick, and she reacted immediately, slamming on the brakes to avoid running the light.

And that was when she saw the two teenagers for the first time. They were already about a third of the way across the street, but hesitated in an instant as her tires squealed.

Wendy gasped as the two of them turned and looked directly at her, her gaze making contact with theirs. No anger or irritation! No obscene gesture either, just a serenity that cut through to the center of Wendy's soul.

She could not help but give them a smile as she glanced at them. Which they returned!

For Wendy it was followed by a hint of tears momentarily affecting her vision, but she wiped these away quickly enough, and went on studying the couple as much as the fleeting few seconds permitted.

At peace. They seemed almost oblivious to the rest of the world around them, though not entirely detached from it.

So young, so fresh, she thought, with some wistfulness. *They have a lifetime together ahead of them, if they can remain in love long enough....*

She sucked in her breath.

And if—

Wendy continued hesitating to formulate the rest of what she had been about to say to herself, words implicit with forlorn recollection.

If love is there in the first place...

Tears, trickling in a tiny stream down her cheek. Again. Tears that resisted her efforts to hold them back. More this time, many more, tears like a river, as an old song's lyrics stated with such accuracy.

Tears were flowing so freely that Wendy wondered what was happening to her at that moment, wondered if there would be a traffic accident because she really was not in full control of herself, her attention instead riveted on two strangers whose abrupt appearance had turned her inside out.

Don't go, she thought. *I want to spend some time with you, get to know you. I want to learn from you.*

Impossible. Wendy was an adult. She counseled teenagers. How *could* she learn much of anything from those so young? She had lived far more of life and for far longer than they had. It was a patently silly idea to think that they had anything to offer her, and even sillier to hope that they would be willing to try.

Wendy swallowed hard once, twice, a third time.

Her palms became sweaty as she dealt with emotions that she had endeavored to keep buried for nearly a decade, emotions she had never wanted to confront again but now could not sidestep.

The light changed finally just as the couple reached the opposite corner.

After pausing for a moment, reluctant to leave them, Wendy cautiously accelerated her black Swedish-made station wagon.

A creaking noise.

There had been something wrong with the springs for some time but she kept putting off any repair work because getting to the dealer, and arranging for a rental car, was invariably inconvenient.

Loud. Disconcertingly. Like chalk across a blackboard.

The two teenagers slapped their hands over their ears and glanced at her with bemused expressions.

They must have one terrible impression of me by now, Wendy thought, *me and the way I take care of a car!*

She could see as the wagon passed them that the two blissfully involved teenagers were lingering at the opposite corner, now holding one another close, apparently not paying attention to anyone or anything around them.

Ignoring that she was in moderate traffic, Wendy braked the car just to look at them, just to look and remember what she herself had once had...and lost. Fragments still clung to her very soul, it seemed, refusing to be brushed away, though she wondered how different life would have been for her if she had looked as radiant as this girl, this beautiful girl with hair like a halo.

And then they were behind her.

No! Not yet! I can't let you go just like that!

Wendy panicked momentarily, not wanting to dismiss that image, not wanting to simply let them pass by so quickly, and become just a memory, a fragile, beautiful, endearing memory.

Her gaze drifted to the rearview mirror. *Do you really know?* Wendy thought, some jealousy surfacing. *Do you have any idea of what it is that you—?*

They could be like self-centered people everywhere, people who were being blessed and yet showed little or no thankfulness, walking without being aided, living and breathing without pain, having enough food to eat, eyes to see, ears to hear, yet giving no thought to the One from whom the blessings came.

"Do you really *know* how fortunate you are?" she continued, this time out loud. "How precious those moments are?"

Wendy wanted to reach out to every boy, every girl in that school and elsewhere who took for granted everything that was good and decent and loving about their lives, and inculcate into them the truth, truth that was harsh but necessary, truth that could prepare them for the pain surely to come.

Never treat what you have lightly! her mind shouted, while, she really wanted to stick her head through the open window and shout aloud. *It is precious and you should treasure such moments before these are taken from you.*

And Wendy knew what she was talking about, knew it as intimately as anyone could know anything.

She continued watching the couple for as long as safe driving would allow.

In a matter of seconds, however, Wendy was too far ahead to see them any longer, and sighed melancholically, as though she was once again saying goodbye to what had been and would never be again.

"If only we could reach out and give her what she needed," Stedfast said.

"We do not have that power," Darien reminded him but with no irritation. *"I was just wishing that—"*

"There will be plenty of opportunity to be at her side, I suppose."

"No supposing about it. She will need us desperately."

"Has God not changed His mind?"

"He was just speaking with me, my dear Stedfast. Today is the day. Everything is in place."

Stedfast was more than a little sorry to hear that, though he would never explicitly admit this to his comrade.

"Oh..."

But Darien knew him well, and hinting at what his friend could not acknowledge openly, he asked, "Are you wishing that there was another way?"

"Yes, I was wishing so hard I thought God might—"

"Rebuke you?"

"Yes, that was it."

"Your thoughts are out of love, out of sympathy. How could our Creator rebuke you for that, dear comrade?"

"I just want to please Him so much. I worry when I seem not to be doing that."

"As I do. For the moment, though, we have someone who will need us as much as the air she breathes."

"Yes, I see. You are quite right. We must not let her down."

"She will assume that we have deserted her altogether."

"At the beginning. Yes, I am sure about that as well."

"But, later, Stedfast. Think of what God has promised for later."

Chapter Fifteen

Just a dozen years ago. But to Wendy MacPherson, it seemed longer.

An eternity but not really that at all, Wendy reminded herself reluctantly. *Seth and I were beginning our relationship.*

Her insides quivered briefly.

Becoming lost in one another, the outside world no longer important to either of us just as long as we could be with one another.

He looked so good, so fine. Wendy sucked in her breath at the memory of Seth emerging from the surf, tanned and muscular, and full of energy. How charismatic he was! The best-looking boy in school, the most charming, the most athletic, and the most sought after by hundreds of girls, few of whom had any hope of spending any time with him away from school.

How she loved him!

How she later hated him!

Other memories of their relationship returned, memories of what it seemed at the time they had meant to one another, memories that came to the surface when stirred unexpectedly in such moments as that one, or when Wendy happened upon a few photos stuck on the pages of a forgotten dust-gathered album, quickly putting it away to avoid any more exposure to what the past had been.

Gone.

My one love, my only love, Wendy whispered, *once it was just the two of us like that young couple, like those two so much in love. Or so it had seemed with you and me, Seth, so it had seemed until a couple of years after we were married, and you decided to run off.*

She was trembling.

No one else...

There had been no one before Seth entered her life, and no one after him, no matter how much she ached for someone to take his place. Wendy had given this teenage boy her virginity on the night of their honeymoon and he seemed to begin taking her for granted not long thereafter, though she realized this in retrospect, and not at the time, her love for him covering a multitude of truths.

Wendy raised a finger first to her left eye, then to the right to wipe away the onslaught of some more tears.

For a very long time, she had fought showing how she felt. But all of a sudden she was failing. And she was failing quite desperately.

If this continues, Wendy knew, *I will have to pull over to a nearby curb and take time to calm myself down somehow. I can't have my staff at the office suspecting that anything is wrong with me!*

And yet surely they would *know*, anyway. Surely the redness in her eyes would betray everything, and the disciplined, rather reserved image she had worked so hard to build up would start to unravel, and how could she allow that, how could she?

Wendy caught her breath, her insides shaking.

But what am I to do? She begged of the emptiness around her. *How can I pretend that this hasn't happened?*

So many reminders were now abruptly fighting for Wendy's attention, a rush of happy, sad, angry memories, all clustered together, all demanding her attention as she tried to continue driving the car.

She remembered the dark circles, showing beneath the makeup that she carefully applied each morning.

Back then, the nightmare for me started to show there, she continued in her reverie, *dark circles which no amount of makeup could hide.*

Wendy sighed wearily, realizing that the changes wrought by the outcome of her relationship with Seth were even more apparent inside her.

She had had an active dating life before she met him. While not spectacularly beautiful, she was nevertheless very attractive, her long red hair crowning her features and looking almost like a fiery halo.

But she never dated one boy more than a few times, and that part of her life seemed more like a series of predictable rituals.

I wouldn't sleep with any of them, Wendy recalled. *I allowed my convictions about the Bible to guide me and no area was more important to me than the biblical standard for sexual conduct.*

So, she got into a syndrome that drove her from boy to boy, hoping to find one who was more sympathetic. But it seemed that there was no one who shared her moral and spiritual standards.

"I won't do it!" she would protest to each boy when she finally saw what each one had in mind.

"We're all the same," one or more would tell her. "It's part of life. Why deny yourself, Wendy? Don't you want to have any fun?"

Those were words with which Wendy would beat herself more than once, causing her to question the standards of morality which had been hers since she was old enough to understand life.

Sex was at the center.

"Not that way," she would retort, "not before marriage."

And so the routine went, date after date, week after week, and soon enough, the ridicule started, harsh, unrelenting.

She knew it was going on behind her back. Occasionally, she heard portions of comments made just before they realized she was passing by, comments that made her appear unapproachable. In a new era of greater sexual freedom, she seemed little more than an odd relic from the Victorian era.

In time Wendy found that she was not dating at all. She spent Friday nights either at home or going to a movie by herself. Her parents did the best they could to reassure her but she was on a downward spiral, and increasingly worrying them and the handful of teachers and student friends who really cared about her.

Then Seth came along.

Lord, Wendy would pray at night, *thank You for showing me that it is possible for my dreams to come true.*

Seth gave Wendy every reason to trust him, and that in truth made it all the more easy for her to love him. Step by step Seth gained a hold on her, took over her life layer by layer...by seeming to agree, by being ever so patient, by agreeing to wait until after they were married before the two of them had intercourse.

He made her think that she was the center of his universe, and it was no leap for her to feel the same way about Seth. They talked about a marriage that would last forever, that would take them both through to heaven itself.

Those nights, she whispered to herself.

Nights when she and Seth would sit by the shore of a lake some few miles away and look up at the stars, and be thankful that they were alive and together, that they had one another.

Wendy had no hint then of any hidden agenda on Seth's part.

And even when he walked out on her, she refused for a short while, out of lingering fragments of her devotion to Seth, to believe that he did so in any way willingly, and tried to convince herself that he would attempt somehow to contact her.

And she would wait by the telephone, not eating very much, if anything, sleeping fitfully, waiting for it to ring, while praying whenever it did that she would pick up the receiver and hear Seth's voice at the other end. But it never was that way, it never would be, her prayers unanswered, her future as she had assumed it would be shattered into hateful, melancholy little pieces.

"I hoped in the early days that I could hold you whenever I wanted," she spoke to the car and the air and the solitude, "that all I had to do was reach out, Seth, reach out, and you would be there."

Seth *was* with her at the single most traumatic moment in her life.

Oh, God, Wendy remembered, something that, of course, she could never truly forget or completely push back into some remote corner of her mind.

"Mom, Dad!" she exclaimed out loud.

She could see the position of their bodies in the midst of the wreckage, the two of them seemingly hugging each other for the last time. Their lips were actually pressed close together!

A kiss? Wendy wondered. *Could they have been kissing for a moment or two just before they died?*

No longer.

They were ripped from Wendy's world in an instant in an automobile accident.

They had died seconds after impact with the other car, which was driven by an elderly man whose poor eyesight had not been flagged by DMV. He did not notice a stop sign, and went past it at nearly fifty miles an hour.

Seth drove Wendy to the location where the accident had happened. The old man was still there. She ran up to him, intending to beat at him with her fists, her anger and loss exploding as though from some flesh-and-blood volcano.

But then he looked at her, his eyes bloodshot, tears streaming down his own cheeks, yet oddly disconnected from the scene, and he was mumbling, "What's happening to me? I killed them...God help me, I killed them!"

"Yes, you *killed* them!" she shouted. "You *murdered*—"

She could say nothing further, she could do nothing but collapse into Seth's strong arms and sob so much that she lost consciousness, awakening in a nearby hospital, the same one where her parents' bodies had been taken.

"What am I going to do?" she said after she came to, Seth standing by her bed, holding her hand. "How can I go on?"

Seth's tears joined her own; he seemed to have liked her mother and father. His own had been claimed by death as well just a couple of years after he was born, and he was raised by well-meaning but rapidly aging grandparents.

"You have *me*," he told her, "and someday there will be kids. We'll build a new life. They're in heaven now, Wendy, with the angels. They are beyond pain, tears. Be happy that they didn't suffer."

Seth literally seemed a Godsend, comforting her as she cried continuously well into the night, *many* nights, nights that stretched into weeks.

You were my emotional salvation! she cried out in the confines of her mind. *Without you, I might not have survived because they were everything to me.*

And then he was gone, by her side in bed one night and gone at dawn, leaving her to cope with a sense of such total isolation that it had grabbed hold of her sanity and threatened to drive her into institutionalized care.

How close I came! she exclaimed as fragments from that time floated to the surface of her mind like debris from a wrecked and sinking ship. *How close!*

But she survived. She survived because of friends she thought she never had. She survived because of the prayers of the entire congregation at the church she and Seth had been attending. Survived because of them. Yes, and something else, something that seemed to run thick through her veins, a special kind of adrenaline that provided the energy needed for her to get up each morning, to get up and somehow manage to face the next twenty-four hours....

Hatred. Very real, very powerful. Love corrupted into hate.

And it nearly destroyed her all over again.

Chapter Sixteen

In the rush of that kaleidoscope came bits and pieces—happiness, joy, melancholy, despair—spinning faster—engulfing her, unwelcome, once banished but now returning....

Wendy strained to keep her attention on the street ahead of her, strained to avoid hitting another car, strained to keep from losing control.

The old anger.

Returning.

The old anger was returning—a seething hot mass of it, like lava out of a once dormant volcano—anger repressed for years but now exploding.

Wendy hated herself for allowing that to happen. But she was not a programmable human computer and had no button marked Delete so that she could rid herself of memories or feelings.

What you did to me! she exclaimed to herself. *The pain I felt after you deserted me. There was no warning, no hint. I almost didn't survive. I didn't want to, Seth. I wanted to stop living because life meant not being able to reach out and touch you, and knowing why I couldn't, feeling the awful sting of it right in the center of my heart.*

Isolation. She constructed it for herself with such totality that it seemed she had disappeared altogether, abducted by an alien spacecraft's crew or retreating to a mountain cabin that had no phones, fax machines or any other means of communication.

And then it was over.

After a period of shutting herself off as completely as she could manage, she eventually emerged from isolation. But she had changed drastically, was far less outgoing than before, trying to shield herself from the slightest involvements, platonic or otherwise, deciding that she would be less vulnerable this way, that she would allow no one to catch the slightest glimpse of her inner self.

*Oh, Seth, my first love, my only love....*she thought. *How much harm you did to me. How much of life you trashed!*

Suddenly, horns were honking, each one sounding slightly different, all blending together into a cacophony of frustration and impatience.

Wendy shook her head slightly, saw that she had been driving so slowly that she was beginning to back up traffic behind her.

"Goodbye, sweet kids," she said to the couple now long out of sight. "Treasure what you have."

The honking was more strident, drivers protesting furiously, one of them reaching his arm out of an open window and shaking his fist at her.

Embarrassed, Wendy pressed down on the accelerator, and the boxy-looking station wagon jumped ahead with surprising agility.

Friends kidded her about it. Her retort was usually a simple one: "It may be dull but it's safe."

She knew they were thinking the same about her!

A woman pushing her large baby carriage had to hurry out of the way this time, the twins inside it oblivious to what could have happened.

Seconds later, Wendy slowed the car down, grabbing the steering wheel as though it was a life raft that she needed or else she would drown somehow, drown in the middle of traffic on a midday morning.

She nearly decided to pull over to the side of the street, and do what she could to steady herself.

And she began thinking about something that she had neglected for a long time: Angels.

I thought my angels would help in those days, she told herself. *But they were nowhere around.*

How Wendy clung to the belief that they actually existed, that they were by her side, that they would guard her and make sure that no harm intervened in the life she was trying so hard to lead.

How crazy everyone assumed that I was, she thought, *particularly Seth who had little time for anything spiritual. Or was it just that he wanted more control over me so that I would continue to put him at the center of my world?*

Wendy chuckled at the memory of what people had a habit of calling her angelic friends in those days, treating her, in the process, as though she was just a fanciful child and not the practical adult she had become, torn from days of naive youth to an adulthood that had started with so much anguish.

So near to me, she told herself, *so very near.*

Wendy never felt alone when angels seemed to hover nearby, for they gave her a sense of peace that she had assumed would always be just out of reach.

She had so much wanted to *see* them as well but that seemed impossible, and so she resigned herself merely to *feeling* their presence on a regular basis, or so it seemed, especially at night in her bedroom as she was shutting her eyes.

More than once she thought that she heard a sound, like some kind of ethereal *Good night, Wendy* but assumed that this was little more than her wishful imagination, and brushed the possibility aside.

Finally she awakened one morning to find that Seth had left, and the future that seemed to be unfolding before her was snatched away.

Gone.

He was gone, not taken from her by death but by deceit, dark, unholy deceit that exploited her desires. At least that was what she had assumed during the minutes, the hours, the days and weeks and months and years since that moment when she found Seth's side of their bed vacant.

Lies. Wendy had listened to what she had persuaded herself were all his many lies of one sort or another, tricked by a young man's "moves" that came not, she was sure, from pure love but, rather, lust.

My body, she reminded herself, *nothing more than that.*

Wendy decided that this was what happened, and no one, at least no one who was willing to venture anything new, seemed to be around to contradict her. Seth had wanted her body, she convinced herself, had wanted to brag to everyone that he had gone beyond simply bedding her down and had actually gotten her to marry him.

What Wendy assumed he did not tell anyone who listened to him was that she would not have sex *until* they were husband and wife, and, knowing that, Seth became so determined to win her over as a trophy that he would do whatever it took, speak whatever insincerities, wait whatever length of time until he had her in bed, and then he planned to throw her aside as soon as possible.

No one capable of pointing out the incongruities in this outlook was able to get through to Wendy, in large measure because Seth *had* disappeared. And her explanation, despite the problems, seemed no more impossible than any others, including a facetiously offered one that Seth had been kidnapped by aliens!

Wendy was intent on believing the worst, no matter how unfair this seemed to anyone the least bit objective. Even they could not deny that Seth's reputation prior to the marriage did little to quell her suspicions.

He's out there, alive, probably seducing other women, she would think over and over, almost on a daily basis, *and no one's punishing him, no one!*

The police could never find him. Or at least that was what they claimed. Wendy did allow herself to suspect that something else was going on, that some reason existed apart from Seth's cleverness or the ineptitude of the local authorities or whatever else she might have imagined. In the end, though, for Wendy, these "other" explanations lost out to the more personal one.

Even so, there *were* hints, the subtlest of hints, surfacing periodically during the course of their relationship—nights when he would return home later than he should have, or mornings when he left earlier than had been the case before—surfacing periodically during the course of their relationship.

Occasionally, Seth would act oddly nervous about a particular phone conversation that he conveniently concluded as soon as she entered the room. He mumbled an excuse and, because she loved him, she accepted whatever he said without protest.

Another woman. That should have been Wendy's first suspicion if she indulged any at all, the logical cause of a breakup so early on in a marriage, someone he had met with whom he became utterly infatuated.

However, Wendy refused to believe that another woman was the real cause. After he left, how many times had she run through what all the other possibilities were, concocting a mental list, and yet ending up with nothing concrete?

It became almost a game of sorts, she recalled. *And they all had to be cast aside because there was no way to prove or disprove of them. I couldn't hang on to each one without going bonkers.*

Eventually, Wendy no longer had any energy left, though she did not reach that point for many weeks, obsessed as she was by the need to *know,* to uncover the full story of what had happened. But human energy and determination could only go so far. She knew she had to stop or risk illness, serious illness.

I must not go on with this, Wendy told herself at last. *I must end it right now or there will be nothing left of me.*

And so she did end her "campaign" of hassling the police for scraps of information that they claimed were not available. And she apologized to them for being so unreasonable.

The detective who had been put in charge of the case involving Seth's disappearance was a bushy-eyebrowed middle-aged man named Stephen Watkins, someone who seemed altogether too distinguished-looking for the rough-edged profession in which he had been working for half of his fifty years. He had lost his temper more than once when Wendy kept after him and after him. But this time he was sympathetic as she sat in front of his desk.

"I can understand your pain," he told her. "I've said that before, but I don't think you believed me then. I hope you do now."

Wendy nodded, and said, "It's been so awful. You think you're with someone who will love you for the rest of your life, and then, suddenly, he deserts you. How could a man, any man do that to anyone?"

"Wendy..." he started.

"Yes, sir?"

"Never mind."

"But you were about to—"

"When you get past fifty, your mind starts to wander a bit," he told her but not very convincingly. "It was nothing."

She left his office more puzzled than ever but still determined to let go. But the release she expected from giving up the hunt she had been engineering did not manifest itself as she assumed it would.

Wendy had clung to the hope of finding Seth and punishing him, but now that she'd reached a dead end, along with the people best equipped to uncover his whereabouts, she felt—lost, at loose ends.

Yet always, after she left the police, she had the impression that they were withholding something, that they knew something about Seth and his whereabouts but perhaps felt that she was too unstable just then to handle it.

But as long as she persisted, she could feel as though she was *doing* something that would eventually bear fruit.

Even her angels apparently were absent, as though they had decided that she no longer needed them.

"How could you do that to me?" she said out loud. "How could you leave me alone at a time like this?"

Until an afternoon six months after Seth abandoned her.

Chapter Seventeen

Wendy had been sitting in the middle of a park not far from the high school that she and Seth had attended.

A stranger, a man, sat down on the bench beside her.

She could smell him, a not unpleasant odor of musky aftershave with the faintest hint of lime to it.

He sat quietly at first, apparently respecting her silence.

Or he might just want to think his thoughts, she told herself, *without anybody intruding upon them.*

Several minutes passed.

When the stranger spoke, he did so quietly, the sound of his voice curiously soothing to her.

"May I say something, miss?" he asked, a natural politeness to his manner that caught her attention at the same time she tried to ignore him.

Wendy muttered, "Whatever," remaining lost in the thoughts that were swirling inside her mind.

Out of the corner of her eye, she could see him staring at her but she refused to allow herself to be uncomfortable, and ignored him.

"You seem so sad," the man responded with a very slight English accent, and a tone that suggested the greatest amount of empathy that Wendy had ever sensed in another human being.

"I am," she found herself replying, surprised by her own candor.

Her initial reaction was to respond no further to him. Why should she feel obligated to do anything of the sort? He was the intruder, as far as she was concerned.

And yet, undeniably, she was becoming curious, just a bit, her curiosity colliding with her need for caution under the circumstances.

Wendy hoped that he would say something else so she could analyze that voice somewhat more, a gift that would be useful later when she talked with so many clients. Knowing that a large percentage of them would try to con her in one way or another, she had to separate the wheat from the chaff.

"But why?" he spoke enthusiastically. "It is such a beautiful day. The sky is clear, the temperature is just right. Birds sing. Flowers are in bloom. This is not a day meant for sadness, young lady."

Wendy did not answer the stranger but caught a glimpse of him out of the corner of her eye, a glimpse that she tried to connect with his voice to see if she could decide what kind of man he was.

Handsome. An older man, with streaks of gray through his full mane of black hair.

"Sorry..." she said.

"No need to apologize, young lady."

"I know you are just concerned, sir. I guess my feelings were way out in the open just then."

He nodded solemnly. "I encounter a great deal of sadness experienced by young people these days," he told her, sighing wearily. "It did not used to be that way. A hundred years ago, there was more hope, less encumbrance."

"You have studied this sort of thing." Wendy ventured, assuming that that was the only way he could learn about conditions of a century before.

"You could say that."

Wendy faced him as she added, "You sound like you meet kids a lot."

He smiled slightly. "I do," he acknowledged. "Here in the United States, Canada, England, so many other locations."

"You travel a lot."

"That I do."

"Are you some sort of diplomat?"

The man seemed to enjoy the implications of what Wendy was asking him, and chuckled briefly.

"Not as you are thinking, anyway," he told her, "but I do represent a certain government, I suppose you could say."

Wendy was frowning, something about the man's manner seeming a bit teasing, and she resented this.

"That sounds strange, does it not?" he admitted, acting as though he knew what she was thinking about him.

"It sure does."

"Then, please, accept my apology. I meant nothing by it."

Nodding, Wendy cleared her voice and asked, "What draws you to young people like myself?"

"Do I seem drawn, as you put it?"

"I would say so, sir."

"Their pain...primarily, it is the pain they are feeling, if not of body, then of mind or soul, sometimes all three."

"What does that mean? You just want to study them, for a report or whatever you're drawing up? Is that all?"

"No, it is not the whole story."

"There is more then?"

He acknowledged to Wendy, "Yes, young lady, there is."

"What is it?"

"I want to *ease* their pain."

The compassion Wendy sensed coming from him nearly overwhelmed her, and she began to feel a little less apprehensive and a little more interested. She asked, "How often do you get a chance?"

The stranger's sparkling blue eyes were particularly expressive then as he sighed and told her, "Hundreds of times, especially when they are dying."

"Dying!" Wendy gasped, a chill settling on her. "You have been with hundreds of dying kids."

"I hold their hands and I witness to them about what I know," he said, profound sorrow in that near-baritone voice.

Wendy was very uneasy then, not at all sure that she wanted to hear anything more from this stranger, whose manner was so perplexing to her, and she started to prepare herself to bolt out of the park given the slightest reason.

He smiled benevolently but said nothing.

"The Feds, I bet," she spoke. "You work for them. And you come upon a lot of kids dying from drug overdoses."

"You are right about that, young lady, perceptive as you are, but wrong about my employer."

"Then what *are* you doing here," Wendy asked finally, "sitting in this little park and talking to me like you're doing now?"

"Perhaps you could call it, shall we say, a chance encounter," he told her, though not very convincingly.

Perhaps...

She sensed that he knew more about that, sensed that he would only give her bits and pieces of an answer.

I can't stay here, she told herself. *Who knows what this guy is up to? He could be a kidnapper or a—*

Wendy was becoming more nervous than ever, that chill now spreading up from the base of her spine.

"I'm leaving now, sir," she said as she started to stand, though she was torn between getting away as quickly as possible and lingering just a bit longer.

"Go ahead," the stranger remarked, seemingly offering no reason for Wendy to stay any longer.

Is that it? she thought. *No attempt to persuade me to spend a little more time with you, because you find me so charming?*

Wendy chuckled at that, since she had never put herself higher than the bottom rung on any likability scale, her self-image in need of even more repair after Seth deserted her months earlier.

Go ahead....

That was all. Not quite sure how to deal with him, Wendy did exactly what she said she would do, and left the park.

Then behind her... One word. Just a single word. Nothing more. But so devastating.

"Revenge..." she heard him say behind her.

That was all he said but it was enough to freeze her steps, to cause her to sweat from head to foot.

Wendy faced him again. "What in the world are you talking about?" she countered, showing more than a little anger.

"You were thinking about revenge," the stranger repeated confidently, his voice quite calm.

"That's ridiculous!"

He waved his hand through the air in an abrupt gesture that was clearly one of rather curt dismissal. "But you were," he said.

"That's a lot of—" Wendy spoke, then cut herself off. Shaking her head in an exaggerated manner, she snorted contemptuously and resumed walking away.

He mentioned Seth then, a name and memories still as fresh as blood from a newly opened wound.

Suddenly Wendy's throat tightened.

"Seth is unreachable, you know," the stranger called after her. "You are only poisoning yourself. You may never see him again."

Seth is unreachable...you may never see him again.

Wendy stopped immediately, stunned by what someone she had not met before that moment had discovered about her personal life.

"You can't know that! *How do you know that?*" she exclaimed, ready to lambast him. Then she heard something...like the fluttering of— "And what about seeing him again? I *may* never see him again. Why would I ever—?"

Wings.

She swallowed hard several times, afraid of what she would see and what it all would mean.

Her stomach became unsettled, her vision blurry as she saw what she could not have anticipated seeing since only seconds had passed. The park bench. Empty.

The stranger was gone.

Wendy felt dizzy, had to lean against a nearby tree to keep from falling.

That sound, playing itself in her mind over and over.

Wings...

"Oh, God..." she spoke prayerfully, regretting that she had not been more perceptive about who the stranger was.

Chapter Eighteen

I'm so stupid, she berated herself. *Look at what I was sitting next to, and yet I drove him away with my unfriendliness.*

Now she was quite certain, now she knew what she had missed by treating the stranger as she had.

An angel...

"I was so close," she would admonish herself over and over and over. "What I might have said, what I—"

Later, as Wendy recalled that encounter, she never doubted that that was what he had been, the signs, in retrospect, so unmistakable.

I could have found out so much, she would say to herself, *I could have asked him about Seth.*

Suddenly a stunning truth hit Wendy less than a week after she had met the stranger. She was standing in the middle of the little apartment in which she and Seth had been living during the time they were married.

It felt empty.

It had a fair amount of furniture in it, as much as they could afford, a sofa with two built-in recliners. It was the pattern that had sold it to them both: a cascade of books of different colors designed in an abstract manner to look like a library gone wild. The love seat matched. The two pieces became the center of the apartment, understandably so as they were the most expensive.

"We do need to have everything look right when your parents come over at the end of the week," Seth told her.

And she loved him for that. Seth seemed to have adopted her mother and father as his own, and he gave the impression of wanting to please them.

"Look at the daughter they gave to me!" he exclaimed. "I owe them so much, I mean, don't I?"

Wendy giggled and pressed herself closer to him as they sat on the sofa, and pretended to be watching television, a twenty-eight-inch unit that was sold under the dealer's cost because it had a few minor nicks and scratches along the cabinet but was otherwise fine.

The rest of what they had bought was pretty basic: a no frills refrigerator that was smaller than ideal, and without an ice maker, but it had been on sale and they'd grabbed it; a bedroom suite they'd found at an outlet store affiliated with a department store in another section of the community, again with only minor blemishes; wall-to-wall carpeting but stitched out of remainders of the same color.

Money was tight for them at the beginning, but Seth's grandparents started them out with a helpful wedding gift: a checking account with a generous opening balance. And Wendy's own parents gave them a check that they immediately deposited.

After graduating from high school, Seth had no job, and Wendy worked at a hamburger joint.

Ironically, they were the happiest then.

Just a bit more than a month after their honeymoon ended—a honeymoon of a few days spent in San Diego, including slipping over into Tijuana, Mexico—Seth was hired as an errand boy for an Italian import-export firm where he made a decent amount of money, so decent in fact that both of them wondered why he was being paid three times the minimum wage.

They experienced so much happiness in that apartment.

And, suddenly, none of that was left, the memories taunting her.

Empty. Yet Wendy had refused to leave that apartment for a long time after Seth disappeared from her life. What else was she to do? She needed to cling desperately to the place, cling to it in a way that suggested she was subconsciously waiting for him to return with an acceptable explanation. How could she think otherwise of the man she had loved with great passion?

At times Wendy thought she could smell the odor of the aftershave that Seth used, could hear the sound of his voice as he told her how much he loved her.

Eventually, she flushed from her mind the delusion that her once-beloved would ever return. Yet, as long as Wendy lived there, walked from familiar room to room, she would never be able to break free, would never have a chance to leave behind the hurt and the shame.

Revenge. That was what the angel had mentioned. Though she scoffed at him then, she understood now that he was undoubtedly right, that revenge was chaining her to Seth, and as long she allowed this, she could not rebuild what he had torn down.

"The less I think of you," she spoke to the walls and the furniture and the very air and that oppressive emptiness around her, "the less I will allow you to dominate me, and the sooner I will recover."

After that, Wendy gave up any quest to find him. But she did not immediately find her life go back to normal. She would pay a price for giving up her need for vengeance.

He had been everything to her. She'd gone to bed with him, she'd woken up with him, she'd thought of him day and night. She had to have something to replace him, to fill the portion, the major portion of her life that he had ripped from her. So, she reached out to other people considerably more than she could ever have predicted she would.

At the diner where she continued to work—after a break of a couple of weeks after Seth left her—she was getting emotional support from the manager, the cook, the other waitresses and some of the regular customers as well.

This concern for her did a great deal to help Wendy reconstruct a new self-image out of a good many shattered pieces that constituted the old one, the image that had served her so well during her high school years. And she devoted herself to becoming what she had wanted to be since she was barely into her teens, her parents helping her keep on track, and not be diverted into something else, or nothing at all.

"I have been a housewife since I was your age," Wendy's mother acknowledged. "There is no shame in this, none whatever, my dear. But I did have some ideas years ago, some nonsense, I suppose, about becoming an interior decorator. I never pursued that, though, and all this time later, I find myself wondering what it would have been like, how nice to be able to earn my own money, and make my own plans."

Wendy felt the wave of regret that her mother was projecting then, and decided that, as long as it was possible to pursue her goals, she would do exactly that, rather than be forced into abandoning them, and then, years later, look back with the kind of wistfulness she was seeing in her mother's wrinkle-lined face.

Chapter Nineteen

Becoming an attorney had been Wendy's dream since grade school.

I was always interceding on behalf of one student or another, she recalled. *Defending a classmate became a signature behavior for me.*

Tabling that desire while she was married to Seth was one of the subsidiary reasons the breakup hurt her so much.

"I was willing to give up or at least delay everything for him," she said, glad that no one could overhear her.

But once Seth was gone, and once she had emerged from a long period of grieving—it could not have been more so if he had died instead of deserted her—she was free to pursue that dream of becoming an attorney.

And it changed Wendy in any number of ways because studying law made her refocus her attention on a redeeming pursuit that, if successful, could carry her through most of the rest of her life. She felt a new sense of freedom, and she became more outgoing as a result of her work in that profession.

I was forced into a new approach, she told herself. *Meeting with clients demanded this—as well as standing up in court and passionately defending them day after day, judge, jury, prosecutor and so many more focused on me. And I had to meet with the families of victims of the accused.*

Her sigh was not of weariness or regret but of thankfulness.

It all changed me, Wendy admitted, *forced me to involve myself with lives other than my own.*

She had been giving so much of her attention to Seth, with little energy left over for anybody else, but this was no longer the case. And she was free of him for the rest of her life.

What a relief, she thought. *Praise God, what a relief!*

Wendy smiled not infrequently, especially as she worked with several charitable causes that ranged from providing dying children with their last wish—the culminative moments producing a mixture of tears *and* smiles—to bringing comfort to elderly people in nursing homes by using cats, dogs and other animals to form a bond with men and women—a practice she pioneered.

Losing her own pain in that of others was a convenient route Wendy traveled obsessively in the early days after Seth walked away, when she was moving toward her career goals.

She was able to build some approximation of a new life and it rose like a welcome phoenix from the ashes of the old one. And her old life had been shattered so completely that at times it seemed she had no hope whatsoever of pulling through without expensive, heavy-duty, long-term psychiatric help.

To which Wendy did submit for a short period of time, contending, whenever the subject arose, that it was angels who guided her to the right office, and angels who stayed with her during every counseling session, nudging the psychiatrist by implanting insights that he could use to lighten her emotional and psychological burdens, so that the shrink did not have as much to do with her rebirth as might seem so to anyone prone to questioning the very existence of God's messengers.

"My angels!" she exclaimed to the emptiness around her. "That was nearly the last time they helped me, nearly the last time I felt their presence."

Actually that help never left her, but Wendy was not aware of this, for she did not realize that angels often worked through *other* means than direct contact.

And in Wendy's case, that meant she had had a "connection" since the age of eight.

Animals. She had always felt at ease around virtually any kind: cats, dogs, birds, monkeys, horses, other creatures. It showed, this sensitivity toward them, and childhood friends dubbed her "the female Francis of Assisi," because she seemed able to win over *any* creature, whether once wild or domesticated. And animals must have trusted her without reservation because they showed an extraordinary amount of devotion.

She remembered bumping into a man outside a video store. He had on a leash one of the most wonderful Irish setters that Wendy had ever seen. She complimented the owner.

"Are you a dog lover, too?" he asked pleasantly.

"Big time," she replied, "but I do prefer cats just a bit more."

"Cats?"

"Great animals."

"But are they are as loyal as dogs?"

"Just as much."

Wendy could tell that he was not convinced but smiled anyway, said goodbye and hurried off.

She stood quietly for a moment, thinking of the seven cats that she had had over the years since she was eight years old.

So fine, she recalled, *every last one of them.*

Some would sleep with her at night. Others were like having dogs. Would walk with her around the house she and her parents had lived in since she was born.

How I wept when they died, she thought. *We made them members of the family, and their deaths affected us greatly.*

That devotion between Wendy and her cats had often carried her through low periods in her life.

When she was eleven years old, a close girlfriend was killed by a school bus when its brakes failed, slamming it into a truck just ahead and the two vehicles tumbling over and over, ending up on top of one another. Her friend died along with a dozen other students.

I would have been on it with her except for Melody being sick, Wendy recalled. *Mom knew that I was concerned, so she agreed to drive me to school a bit later so that I could have a few more minutes with that dear cat.*

Later, after school sessions were finally over for the day—a day that Wendy found almost impossibly difficult to endure after learning what had happened—and her mother had picked her up and taken her back home, she fell down on the three-cushion sofa in the living room and started sobbing. In an instant, Melody was on her lap, and stayed like that, curled up, her warmth and gentle purr soothing.

How could that cat have known? Wendy would wonder periodically during the ensuing years.

And there were other occasions when a cat or a dog would sense her distress, and attempt to comfort her.

"Mother," she asked one of those times, "do you think pets are sometimes angels in disguise?"

Her mother smiled with complete tolerance, and replied, "I don't know much about angels, dear child. I just feel that we should never limit what God is able and willing to do for us in this life."

As an adult, Wendy would ponder such matters, and came to the conclusion that if an angel could appear to her in human form as did that stranger in the park, then could not God allow angels to assume the form of pets and minister to people in that manner?

Dear Boy-Boy, she thought, *sweet, sweet friend.*

When Seth disappeared, she had a male cat named Boy-Boy.

I might have done something very, very drastic, Wendy told herself, *if it had not been for him.*

Boy-Boy sensed when Wendy needed comforting, and he would jump up on her lap and start purring, and within a short while, that soothing sound and the warmth of his body would lull her to sleep, giving her body a chance to calm down.

"You're an angel," she said to him again and again, sometimes meaning that figuratively, other times half-believing that he was an angel in the form of a cat.

Wendy's angels were guiding her, these guardian angels, showing her at least a short-term detour from the self-destructive path she seemed destined to travel.

These creatures of light and glittering color helped her in ways that would seem inconceivable to any cynical "outsider." But help they did. And unselfishly, it seemed.

Knowing about them, knowing the *reality* of them, gave Wendy a source of relative peace and a sense of protection that was a central part of the foundation of her gradual recovery, a recovery that pulled her back from the brink of suicide, and enabled her to go on living, however imperfectly.

"I've loved animals since I was a child," she said again out loud. "Cats, dogs, birds, almost any kind. I thought they were better than people so much of the time. Now I know how true that is."

Unconditional love.

Closer to work now, embraced by memories, Wendy sighed as she spoke out loud, "If only you, Seth, had been like that...if only you had loved me unconditionally as I thought you did, if only—"

Before seeing that teenage couple, Wendy had convinced herself that Seth no longer had any control over her, but then, maddeningly, she knew otherwise, that fragments remained, propelled back from wherever they had been hiding in her mind, and she felt a little sick, felt that years of distancing herself from one of the great tragedies of life seemed brushed aside and rendered pointless.

"Where are you, angels, when I need you the most?" she whispered, some bitterness showing up, as she conveniently overlooked the comfort she used to derive from what she imagined to be angels hovered around her.

Wendy shook her head a couple of times, managing to clear it but not sure how long this clarity would last. In a few minutes she would be at her office where she had spent so much of the years since Seth had cut himself out of her life.

Goodbye, she whispered sweetly. *Goodbye, dear lovers.*

The teenage couple were long gone from view but Wendy sensed that she would be thinking about them the rest of the day.

Chapter Twenty

"*M*any lives have been changed because of you, Wendy, and more are constantly being added to the list here on earth as well as in heaven. The greet committee up there will be a large one, you can be sure of that."

Words of warmth and recognition, spoken with utmost sincerity, followed by sustained applause.

Just a couple of years ago. A leading Baptist preacher identified Wendy accordingly as he presented her with a special plaque in recognition of her public service work. The occasion was a banquet bringing together church leaders from a variety of denominations.

"There is one thing I could never say about you," he added.

She waited patiently for him to finish.

"That you're so heavenly minded you aren't any earthly good," the preacher spoke deliberately. "That actually is the trouble with many of us, concerned so much about often obscure spiritual matters that we succeed, unintentionally, in distancing ourselves from helping others in *this* life."

He cleared his throat, beamed from ear to ear, and said, "Not you, Wendy MacPherson. Truly you *are* a twinkle in God's eye. For Jesus was a Man of the poor. He felt great empathy with them. And that is just one way you carry on in His footsteps.

"Your feelings are grounded in love, my dear, love for the underprivileged, love for poor mothers and fathers and their helpless children. Wendy, if we have not love, every act is meaningless, like clanging cymbals being struck by someone without the foggiest idea of how to play."

She was typically embarrassed but gracious.

"I do not feel that I deserve this," she said, "but it is wonderful to learn that some folks think that I do. I will try my hardest never to disappoint any of you."

That declaration took center stage for Wendy, giving her career pursuit an edge that bordered on the fanatical, from law school to her first job in a legal firm to what she was doing at present.

At the age of thirty-one, Wendy MacPherson had become the youngest and one of the best public defenders in her state's recent history. She did not arrive easily at this stage in her career. Working hard was a necessity because she realized how complex the various laws were. At the same time, she realized how much "ordinary" people needed help if it took lawyers so many years to get a grasp of American jurisprudence.

Nearly five feet eight inches tall, Wendy was big-boned, thin-faced, fit, her long red hair crowning her as though it was a fiery declaration of who she was. But she never possessed the self-confidence that someone else with her attributes might have shown. After Seth disappeared, pulling the underpinnings of her world right out from under her, her emotional reservoir was drained.

Seth had helped me to turn away from self-doubt, and I began to think I could handle anything or anyone, Wendy reminded herself as she sat behind the large oak-finish desk that a former drug addict had hand-crafted for her, someone whose life she had been responsible for reconstructing. That was a large part of the good that Seth had brought into her life while he was yet part of it.

For months, they had been happy, happy since the day they were married, twenty-four hours after they graduated.

But where Seth was concerned, Wendy realized later, *I might as well have been blind and deaf!*

Seth might as well have been a wrecking crew, leaving behind rubble in place of what Wendy once had been.

She glanced at the plaques that lined one wall, plaques given to her by state and local officials to honor her work with the underprivileged. Four trophies rested on a credenza behind her. To the right of them were a red leather-bound Bible and a novel dealing with the subject of angels from the viewpoint of a guardian angel who told stories about people he had helped over the centuries.

I walked the only road I could see, she added, *except maybe jumping off a bridge or fatally overdosing on pills.*

Suicide was an option that she fleetingly considered, but felt ashamed at doing so, and brushed it aside.

Though Wendy's recovery took a long time, she did not give up, determined not to let Seth come anywhere near having the final victory. In time, the way to a life of reasonable satisfaction was the profession she chose and the opportunities it presented for losing herself in the problems of other people.

This happened by gradual stages, the first life touched and redeemed followed by another, the number of instances accelerating as Wendy gained more experience and greater proficiency.

The list of her successes grew. Along with her self-confidence.

In a majority of instances, she went beyond being merely their public defender, though attorneys with more experience cautioned her that this could sap her objectivity and drain her emotionally.

"You've got to be careful," others would say. "They are often very adept manipulators, forced into such behavior in order to survive. It is not judgmental to recognize that this is the case. You have to be aware of the pitfalls."

Wise advice that Wendy did not take seriously enough at the start. During that initial learning period, she did tend to disregard any possibility that she could ever be deceived again by another human being. But she learned quickly enough after losing money to a couple of clients who had no intention of moving into better apartments but wanted only to leave town so that they could buy drugs elsewhere, in a place where they were not known to the local police.

She felt bitter afterward but the successes she had with other teenagers and older clients who deserved the benefit of her ability wiped that away.

"I will not let you go down the drain," she told most of her clients. "You will *not* be sacrificed on the altar of someone who has more money, more connections, a bank account to hire some slick lawyer. What do they care about you? They enter your life and then leave you behind to sort out the rubble."

Anyone who knew Wendy well understood that she would direct those last two sentences primarily to young mothers who were pregnant by some well-connected young man, and everyone who heard her remarked at how understanding she was.

Including one very important man in her profession.

"You are amazingly intuitive," spoke Rolf Pedersen, president of the local chapter of the American Bar Association, an autocratic individual who seldom complimented anyone. "I envy you. You probably do not realize how much of an inspiration you are to people who meet you or even just hear about you. You should be well aware of who and what you have become."

Wendy had just given a speech at a jammed summer convention in Chicago for public defenders, and received a standing ovation. Many of those in attendance in the meeting hall were jaded by the strains they experienced on the job. Wendy represented a fresh face, a fresh approach and decidedly fresh enthusiasm that seemed to radiate to everyone present.

After the speech, Pedersen and she were standing in a corridor outside the main conference room.

"Envy me?" she repeated. "That's interesting."

"Interesting?"

"Yes. I don't find myself enviable at all."

"But you should, Wendy. You are intelligent, attractive, dedicated. From my standpoint, those are the ingredients for a noteworthy person."

"I appreciate what you're saying."

"But it goes in one ear and out the other, does it not?"

Pedersen seemed more like a graying bushy-haired college professor, down to the wire-rimmed glasses and slightly stooped posture. Wendy trusted him, felt, in fact, some affection for the man.

She did not know how to respond so she remained silent.

"I have been aware of your circumstances for some time," he added, "and if I could get my hands on Seth, well, I think I could not restrain myself." He lowered his voice. "Do not beat yourself emotionally bloody," he cautioned her, knowing that he could not push very hard.

Wendy shook her head and said defensively, "I stopped doing that, sir, a number of years ago."

Pedersen's smile was kindly. "But the wounds are there, my dear," he cautioned, "and I daresay they've not completely healed, despite what you have been pretending to yourself for a long time. They could break open at any moment."

Wendy flinched at that.

"Then it's something I need to work on, isn't it?" she told him.

"I would say so."

Some women would have been offended by the man's paternalistic attitude, evoking male chauvinistic images, but that was not Wendy's way as she tended not to make generalizations along such lines, finding these to be stultifying.

"I *am* grateful, sir," she told him. "I—"

"You *feel* it but find some difficulty in expressing it," he added knowingly but without presumptuousness.

Wendy blushed as she replied, "You know me well."

"After all these years, yes, I do."

Someone had been trying to attract Pedersen's attention, and so he patted her on the shoulder and left.

She stood quietly, thinking over what he had said, and felt very vulnerable, but tried to keep this from showing on her face since people she knew were passing by periodically, and she wanted to avoid having to offer any explanations.

...how much of an inspiration you are.

After a few years, comments such as that no longer had any impact on Wendy because Seth had been, at the beginning, full of compliments, and she no longer trusted nice words from anyone.

"Thank you, sir," she said simply in each case, and that was that, polite but in a reserved way. Nothing more.

While others would have reacted with a great deal more outward appreciation—after all, Rolf Pedersen was one of the most powerful people in her profession—Wendy had convinced herself that she had to hoard emotion somehow, as though it was some valuable commodity, and so she showed just a little in order not to seem impolite. But that was where any such display usually ended.

A phone call took Wendy out of that reverie.

Some weariness showed in her voice as she said, "Hello, Wendy MacPherson here. Can I help you?"

She listened for a few seconds, then added, "Grace, how are you? Lunch, today, are you sure?" She was embarrassed at her forgetfulness. "An early one? At eleven-fifteen?" Wendy glanced at her watch. "Wow! It's...it's ten-fifty now, Grace. Can I be a little late? Say eleven-forty-five? At Dominick's, right?"

Grace indicated that this was all right, that she would be able to change the time of the reservation.

"Great!" Wendy replied. "See you then."

As she was about to hang up, she heard Grace ask, "Are you okay, my dear?"

Wendy hesitated, not sure what it was that her friend had picked up on. "Just a little tired," she replied.

"Rough caseload?" the other woman asked.

"Not that alone. Like you, I always have a rough schedule. But, today, well, I'll tell you over lunch."

The conversation ended, and Wendy hurried through some paperwork, while feeling increasingly guilty that she would go out to lunch early after getting to work late.

She felt secure in that office. It was her private world, one in which she set the rules and determined her own schedule.

"What a laugh that is!" she said out loud. "In here, rules are made just so they can be broken."

Unexpected cases could barge through the entrance at any given moment, with little or no warning, perhaps an unwed mother with a wealthy lover demanding that she have an abortion and willing to pay her extravagantly to do as he wanted, but who hated the idea and had come to see if Wendy or one of her associates could help. Or a father whose wife wanted to terminate a pregnancy but he did not!

Some of the cases were more compelling than others, especially those that seemed to suggest the probability of a disaster about to happen. Wendy was able to catch virtually all of these in time, before any tumultuous outburst occurred.

Except for one devastating failure. The case of the overweight man in his midsixties. Just months before retirement he was fired from a company where he had worked for nearly forty years of his life, and was being asked to take a lesser pension. Wendy could sense that if she sent him away without hope, he would either commit suicide, or find a gun and take out his anguish on innocent people.

I've had five like that, Lord, she prayed silently. *I was able to win justice in four of them but that fifth, that...*

A rampage. The man had been able to obtain a semiautomatic rifle, a few hand grenades and enough ammunition to storm an enemy fortress. To him, to this confused, troubled, hurt human being, his once loyal employer *was* the enemy, a betrayer of his trust who had to be executed.

"They *will* pay a price," he vowed.

And he went on the attack.

For nearly two hours, he tormented those he had not killed immediately after entering the corporate headquarters building. He kicked them, slammed their bodies with the butt of one of his rifles, cut several more with one of a number of hunting knives that he had brought with him.

And then it was over.

He seemed to realize what he had done. Perhaps his mind was clearing enough for him to survey the contorted bodies and the blood, the broken glass, the spent shotgun cartridges at his feet and whatever other debris he had created.

"God in heaven!" the man shouted hoarsely, whether as a prayer or a profanity no one ever knew.

He put the barrel of a snub-nosed revolver into his mouth, and pulled the trigger. Those men and women who were witnesses instantly turned away, unable to endure the grisly sight.

Scattered through the rubbish of the ground floor of corporate headquarters, ten bodies were found, with a dozen more wounded but still holding on. Among the dead were a pregnant mother, a minister and two police officers who happened to be in the building as customers when the vengeful former employee entered.

Wendy arrived just minutes after the man took his life.

What could I have done?

In her mind, Wendy again and again returned to what she had seen, again and again revisited those horrifying images at night as she tried to sleep. Truly an exercise in frustration, she tried by sheer act of will to drive them away so that she could rest, though her body was covered with perspiration.

The bodies. Images of those bodies—men, women and children—piled on top of one another, lifeless and battered, expressions of pain and terror and the approach of darkness frozen on their faces.

What could I have done?

This was a question that took a long time for Wendy to answer, and sent her into another temporary emotional tailspin.

I nearly quit, she recalled. *I didn't feel that I was strong enough to face the possibility that that man was one of many, that there were so many frustrated, embittered people out there, it was only a matter of time until someone else blew up, until someone entered a school yard and killed students as well as teachers.*

She was right.

The second time was no easier to face. But she was stronger by then. Her co-workers had helped her to crawl out of the abyss into which she had fallen, an emotional abyss that was similar to the one that had engulfed her after Seth had left.

It was, in fact, a school yard.

The killer was not a disgruntled middle-aged man, but a student, an insecure student who was kidded by the others because he was a geek and not some sort of teen idol, because he preferred computers to football, because he did not seem interested in girls.

"Faggot!" they would call him.

Once, in the boys' locker room, he was dragged into the shower area with his clothes still on and laughed at as he was soaked, laughed at and called other names by teenage boys who had no idea what this would do to him.

But he was not a homosexual at all. He was shy, and he stuttered a bit, providing them with another way to mock him, to imitate the way he talked, and, dripping wet, he stuttered so badly that day that the other boys taunted him all the more harshly.

He could have been saved, Wendy thought. *If only I had had more time with him.*

But, that time, she did not. When he was brought to see her, after he'd made a couple of attempts at petty theft, it was already too late.

The shyness had already, in its extreme form, turned into mental illness, and the mental illness was what drove him to desperation.

Wendy attended his funeral, and the funerals of the other children. By then she was able to face her failures better. And she listened to co-workers who told her that his case could *not* be counted as a failure.

"You are a public defender," Bret said. "He was brought to you because his parents are on the verge of bankruptcy and could not afford their own lawyer. You couldn't have known how far gone he was."

Wendy accepted that. And the next one after that.

Wendy was now thinking of her many successes more than the very few failures, and as she became more experienced, the failures virtually disappeared, and the lives she helped to reconstruct mushroomed in number until she was able to find some personal fulfillment that was long overdue.

Chapter Twenty-One

The woman sitting across the table from her knew Wendy so well that, at times, the connection between them seemed well-nigh eerie.

"If you were given a million dollars...well, I don't think even that would please you," Grace Schaeffer, a public defender in another office, told Wendy over a sumptuous buffet lunch at a restaurant named Dominick's. It had a decidedly upscale reputation but the two of them found it necessary just to let go and splurge from time to time after all the depressing cases they both had to wade through.

"Aren't you being a little harsh?" Wendy countered.

"You would go on as though it had never happened," Grace answered as she shook her head. "There is something to be said, I suppose, for avoiding emotional excess, but you take matters too far in the opposite direction."

"You mean I seem cold?" Wendy asked.

She had a self-image that veered in the opposite direction, accessible and friendly perhaps to a fault, but Grace could not have disagreed more.

"I don't think of myself that way," she added confidently.

"But, dear friend, sometimes you *do* seem quite chilly. It doesn't happen as often as it once did. But it's there, hanging on like barnacles on some ship."

Wendy chuckled at that description.

"Maybe for a while, I was defensive, not trusting anyone," Wendy acknowledged, "but I grew out of that."

Grace tilted her head slightly. "How long have we known each other?" she asked.

"Years...probably ten years."

"That's right, nearly a decade now, and so I think I see what's underneath that facade of yours."

Grace was a regal-looking black woman about forty years old—tall, thin faced, a bit like Sojourner Truth, the famed Civil War era abolition-ist—but with a rather charming weakness for frilly clothes.

Wendy felt closer to her than she was to most individuals. Occasionally she tried to analyze why this had turned out to be so but could never come to a conclusion about the bond between them, except to acknowledge that it had been forged over the most troubled years of her life, and Grace seemed always by her side.

Wendy frowned while choosing her words with care, not wanting to offend the other woman. "Grace?" she spoke.

"Yes..."

"You've also known pain before, and you've survived the very best way you could devise."

"Right on both counts."

"Surely, then, you have to realize that I, too, have chosen the only way I know of to survive."

Grace nodded sympathetically for some reasons far deeper than Wendy would ever suspect.

"Honestly, though, is that all you want for your life?" she asked pointedly. "Just to survive?"

That hit Wendy hard, since she had spent just about a decade building the mosaic of a new life for herself, a piece here and there, one after the other until that life was meticulously assembled. And as she took each step, she did so with hope, and in the process was convinced that what she had done was more than merely surviving.

Since she achieved her dream of becoming a lawyer, and so much more with all those awards and commendations and letters of admiration at the local, state and national levels, she was able to put to bed the old phantoms. At least that was what *seemed* to have happened. After a certain point, she could sit back and feel a degree of satisfaction, despite the psychological scars that were still there.

After all, she thought, *aren't scars nothing more than wounds that have finally healed?*

But now her best friend was looking at all this from quite another perspective, a perspective that Wendy found disturbing.

She sat up straight in her chair. "Now wait a minute...look at what I do!" she protested. "For a lot of people, well, you know...I've been a blessing to them. After all, you've seen a bunch of the letters I have in my files."

"True, and, yes, your awards are right out there in the open," Grace added without the slightest hint of jealousy. "For outsiders, you represent the greatest possible success, a role model of the best sort. People who helped you early on are very proud of you today, which is as it should be since you have an extraordinary amount of honest dedication to your job. Nobody could accuse you of being into it just for the money."

"Doesn't all that constitute the ingredients for a wonderful life?" Wendy pointed out, "a life that should be more than enough for any reasonable person. Why, don't I make even the Good Samaritan in the New Testament look a little like Mr. Uninvolved?"

Grace did not reply instantly but sat and studied her friend for a few seconds before saying anything.

"Helping others, feeling *their* happiness?" she spoke. "That sort of thing? Is that what you're saying, girl?"

Wendy pressed both palms down on the table, the veins pronounced on the backs of her hands. "Of course!" she acknowledged, "that *is* exactly what I'm saying. What makes you think otherwise?"

Grace leaned forward, lowering her voice.

"Is it for *you*, Wendy?" she asked.

"Enough?"

"Yes..."

Wendy hesitated, wanting to sound convincing, so that they could end that topic of conversation immediately.

She shrugged her shoulders as she said, "Well, *shouldn't* it be? What more is there for me? Can you tell me that? If not, then we should never walk this road again, okay?"

"I will do whatever you want," Grace told her.

"There's a *but* coming, isn't there?"

"Yes, Wendy, there is."

"Out with it."

"You sidestepped answering my question. But then I am sure you know that as well as I do."

Wendy sighed, genuinely tired, and more than a little irritated.

"After all that I went through?" Wendy said. "You need to ask if I'm happy? Why wouldn't I be?"

Grace stared straight at the other woman, her eyelids narrowed, the intensity of her gaze making Wendy a bit uncomfortable.

"Yes, I think what I am these days is more than enough," she replied. "I can't think of anything better."

"Is that an answer, or just an expression of hope?"

Now it was Wendy's turn to feel irritated. "Why are you so rough on me today?" she asked.

Grace winced, sorry that she was pressing too hard just then.

"We're all noticing," she remarked.

Suddenly, Wendy's palms were sweaty. She had tried very hard to keep her deepest feelings hidden from all the members of her staff, assuming that they might think she was weak otherwise.

"Noticing?" she asked, trying to be as nonchalant as she could force herself to appear, but a slight tremor in her voice defeating this effort.

"Yes. That's what I said."

"What? What are you and so many others noticing?"

"A breakdown...you are close to a breakdown."

Cold sweat trickled down Wendy's spine. "That's absurd!" she exclaimed. "Really it is, Grace. I never felt better. I actually get out of bed humming a tune many mornings."

"*Never* felt better?" Grace's expression was now that of unmasked skepticism as she waited for the other woman to answer.

"That's right," Wendy told her confidently. "I hardly ever think of the past, Grace. I feel so free now."

Grace was not willing to let it pass.

"You mean since Seth left you?" she asked, knowing how to provoke a reaction from her friend.

"Of course that's what I mean."

"Will you *listen* to me, my dear, I mean, really listen?"

"To every word, I promise."

Grace was drumming her fingers on the top of the table as she said, "Listen to yourself for a moment."

"All right..."

"Everything begins or ends with that moment, doesn't it? You might as well change A.D. to B.S. and A.S.—Before Seth and After Seth."

"Ridiculous!" Wendy exclaimed, dumbfounded.

"Are you so sure?" Grace persisted.

"How would *you* have reacted?"

"The same as you have but—"

"So you *do* understand then," Wendy interrupted. "Why in the world cross-examine me like this?"

"You didn't let me finish."

"Go ahead...."

"For maybe the first six months or so, even the first year, I would have been devastated every bit as completely as you were."

"Then what?"

Grace's voice was softer, lower, not accusatory as she added, "I would have gone on, period, never looking back, never letting it dominate me. Seth doesn't deserve that power over you."

"What do you think I *have* been doing all these years? Getting rid of his claim to my emotions! And I think I've done very well."

"Clinging. You're still clinging, whether you understand that you are or not."

"Clinging? To the past? Is that it?"

"Exactly, Wendy. Instead of leaving it behind, as you claim you are doing, you've brought it with you, year after year. It waits there like some serpent in the grass, ready to strike given the least provocation."

"You couldn't be more wrong."

"I couldn't be more right, Wendy, and you know it."

Wendy shook her head defiantly, and said, "It's gone, over, ended. What more can I do? Please, you must tell me what you expect, even if it's not what I can give."

"It's not gone for you," Grace told her slowly, "it's not over, it has never ended, as far as you are concerned."

"You've lost some loves, haven't you?"

"Yes, several."

"And the first?"

"The first was the worst."

"So what's the difference between us?"

"As I said, I felt as you do, for a while. There is something, though, with which I came to grips that I'm willing to bet you never have, and, Wendy, if you keep on the way you are going, you never will."

Wendy was unconvinced.

"What's that?" she asked, her skepticism right out in the open.

"In absentia Seth's still been in control of you all these years. Everything you do is because of him." Grace reached across the table and took Wendy's hand in her own. "Stop it, my dear," she pleaded. "Break loose from him. He didn't deserve being your master and you should never have been his slave, even when the two of you were together, but especially not now. You've got to see that. If you do, the truth will liberate you in a way you never imagined."

Wendy was staring straight ahead but not at the other woman, *through* her to someone else, a tall, impossibly handsome young man who seemed to be standing there, mocking her as he mouthed, "I've got you, babe, and I'm never going to let go."

"I reached out for him one morning, and he was gone," she spoke. "How could he? How could any human being do that to another?"

"It hurt, I know, the worst hurt you'd ever felt."

"Like a knife in my gut."

"It's still there, Wendy. Pull it out and throw it away, please."

"Is my life so bad the way it is?"

"You can't say that to me or yourself. You've got to ask instead, 'How much *better* could my life be?' "

Wendy's shoulders were slumped as she asked, "Better than helping so many with *their* lives?"

"Help yourself, my dear, and then see what happens. What you're doing now is only a hint of what you *could* accomplish."

"I...hated him so much."

Grace patted the back of Wendy's hand for a moment, and asked, "Hated? Past tense? As in no longer?"

Wendy's cheeks flushed. "That's been buried so long now. Why relive it? What's to be gained? I don't understand you today."

Grace dodged answering her. "You mustn't love him and you mustn't hate him, Wendy," she said instead. "As far as you are concerned, Seth no longer exists."

Wendy tensed, knowing that her friend was not deliberately provoking her, then asked, "Why now?"

"Now?"

"Why are you telling me this now?"

"I've been *trying* to do it for a long time."

"But you haven't. You mustn't feel it's too important."

"I suppose the Lord's own timing is what I've been dealing with, Wendy. Who can say? If He's got a timetable, what can I do about that? I just need to be open to His leading, as you do."

"But this is old—"

"Old news, right."

"That's what I was going to say."

She paused, and asked pointedly, "If it's old news, why are you listening so intently? Just tell me to change the subject, you know, that's all you have to do."

Wendy remembered what she had seen earlier that day, as she was driving to work.

"I saw—" Wendy started to say.

"Go ahead," Grace told her. "Take it slow. We can stay out longer for lunch if need be. The system owes us a lot of extra time, all the extra hours you and I put in year after year. As you know, there's no overtime in our profession, dear."

She told Grace about the young couple, describing them in detail and naming the school.

"Dear God..." the black woman said prayerfully.

"What's wrong?" Wendy asked.

It was Grace's turn to be silent.

"Grace..." she spoke again, concerned, wondering why her friend was reacting as she was.

"Praise His name."

"About what? Please don't act like this."

"I've been helping them," Grace told her.

"You—"

"What you see now is not what I saw a few months ago. They've both changed, changed until they are what you saw so clearly."

"Tell me, Grace. Tell me, will you?"

The black woman nodded.

"It's my turn to get my thoughts together," she said. "Give me a moment."

"Sure."

Then Grace told her about the drugs, the wild parties, the other aspects of a life-style that was out of hand.

"I found out about the two of them when both were brought in on cocaine charges," she recalled.

"*That* couple?" asked Wendy, incredulous. "They don't seem like any of that scene could ever—"

Grace held up one hand. "Now, yes, like the ideal boyfriend and girl-friend," she said, "but not at first, not back when I started with them."

"But they seem so—"

"Pure? That's what appealed to me when I saw them. I was able to cut through what had been layered over them, and I found that what they had used to be was still there. It had not died as yet. And it could be reclaimed."

Grace was talking with great passion.

"I managed to get them to go to church," she said, "but a special kind of church, actually."

"Special?" Wendy asked. "What was special about it?"

"Its ministry was single-minded, the members of the congregation with similar needs in their lives."

Wendy was fascinated. "Tell me more."

"I became involved with them nearly three years ago. The results of their approach have been wonderful."

"Everyone there was or is on drugs?"

Grace nodded. "Even the preacher."

"What?"

"He fought a drug habit, beat it, now is ministering to people on a personal and a spiritual level."

Wendy was touched by the mental image of a man reaching into the lives of people who were benefiting from his own experiences, experiences so similar to their own that he had no trouble convincing them that he knew how they felt.

"So he can talk their language then," she said.

"And get under their skin."

Wendy recalled the teenagers, which was hardly difficult for her, finding it nearly impossible to reconcile what Grace was telling her with the way they appeared as they crossed the street and lingered at the opposite corner.

"Are you so sure we're talking about the same boy and girl?" she asked. "How could they be so different now?"

"As sure as I can be, Wendy," Grace replied, nodding.

"They were having really bad problems?" Wendy needed to be convinced, needed to be shown the proof of what her friend was claiming.

"The worst you could imagine," Grace reiterated, "as severe as any you have dealt with among your own clients."

Wendy felt her illusions about the young couple dissipating in a flash.

"Don't feel the way you look," Grace admonished her.

"You know what I'm thinking?"

"I read your expression, not your thoughts."

"And my expression tells you what?"

"That you are letting another disappointment get to you. Which is a shame since you should be rejoicing instead."

Wendy wondered why she could be expected to rejoice after hearing the tragic history of a couple so radiant.

"Am I that obvious?" she asked.

"Every bit."

Wendy's shoulders slumped. "I guess I was putting them on some kind of pedestal."

"You wanted to go back to the days when you thought you were like the two of them, isn't that right?"

"I suppose so."

Grace bowed her head a bit. "May I say something that might upset you?" she asked.

"I haven't stopped you yet."

"Are you sure?"

"Yes, yes, come out with it, Grace, please."

"Wendy, you sometimes act like life *owes* you something because of what happened between you and Seth, perhaps a form of penance."

"That doesn't make any sense."

"Sure it does, Wendy. Whether you realize it or not, you seem to be expecting life to pay penance for letting you down years ago, and you expect this to go on until the day you die, I suspect. Because of that one awful tragedy, you want to be free of anything else that is bad from now on."

"That's just ridiculous. What a crazy bit of psychobabble! I really am surprised at you, Grace."

"Listen to me, okay? I am only trying to help. You can't expect protection from pain for the rest of your life just because you've already had a lot of it."

"But, truly, Grace, haven't I had enough? What more could the Lord ask of me? I am not superhuman, able to weather every conceivable storm, and then slip into the next one."

Grace looked at her with a mixture of pity and frustration. "That does it!" she exclaimed, throwing her napkin down on the table.

"What's wrong?" Wendy asked.

"You'll know soon enough!" she declared.

"Are we going somewhere?"

"Are we *ever!*"

Grace signaled for their waiter, and when he arrived, she asked for the check, but Wendy protested.

"Let me take care of this," she offered.

"No."

"Why not?"

"I asked you to lunch, remember. You don't have to please me, Wendy. You don't have to *please* anyone. If you were able just to be yourself, that would be okay for most of us. The real you is all any of us could ask for, *capisce?*"

"Okay..." Wendy answered rather unconvincingly.

After leaving the restaurant, Grace tipped the parking attendant generously and asked if Wendy could leave the station wagon in the lot for a short while. He assured her that there was no problem with doing this.

"You're going with me," Grace spoke commandingly, her manner suggesting that there was no use objecting, rather like a judge overruling a lawyer, or demanding that a defendant be quiet or else be ejected from the courtroom.

"But I have appointments," protested Wendy. "I can't just pretend that they aren't there, can I?"

"You can call from where we'll be," Grace said, adamant. "You've earned that right, I should think."

"But—"

"But nothing, my dear. This is too important."

"More than fulfilling my obligations to the people who need me most, the underprivileged who—"

Grace did not let her finish. "No speeches now!" she declared. "I know what I'm doing. Haven't you thought that in the past?"

Wendy had no idea what she would be confronted with but she knew her friend was only trying to help her, so she sat back in Grace's SUV that was far spiffier than the wagon she drove, and waited to arrive at what destination was ahead.

"Are you sure about this?" she asked.

"Very sure. Trust me, okay?" Grace told her.

Grace Schaeffer was the only person whom Wendy would have trusted with her life, and nothing more needed to be said.

Chapter Twenty-Two

It was an older building with which Wendy MacPherson had already become more than a little familiar.

Brickfaced, three stories high, near the outskirts of the Southern California community where she had spent all her life, a building she visited frequently as she was called in on cases by the local district attorney.

As they were getting out of the car, Wendy asked her friend, "Why here? I know it as well as you do."

"I want to introduce you," Grace told her.

"Introduce me? To whom?"

"That's part of the surprise."

They went inside where both were greeted by several staff members.

"Where are we headed?" Wendy asked.

"Second floor."

"The drug rehab unit."

"You got that right, girl!"

The entire floor was given over to such cases. Wendy cringed every time she walked down one of the corridors.

Moaning.

Or screaming.

From one side or the other.

Young lives squandered at the point of a needle or up bleeding nostrils or however else drugs were taken into their once healthy bodies, bodies now ravaged by sores or disease or simply shell-shocked by a constant influx of chemicals.

That day, for some reason, it was even worse, deplorably so, the scene more like that of a supernatural horror film than a real-life center for treating young people who were mentally impaired.

"The valley of the shadow..." Wendy whispered.

"That's right," Grace agreed.

"But what's your point?"

They came to double doors at the end of that particular corridor.

"You won't be prepared for this," Grace assured her.

Wendy steeled herself as her friend held open both doors, and the two of them walked through.

The large room was nearly empty except for three young people across from where they were standing.

A girl was in poor shape, alternately screaming and shaking.

"Watch this..." Grace whispered.

Wendy was watching, watching as though hypnotized, for she saw the same couple that had captured her attention earlier.

"You knew..." she started to say.

"It was more like a guess," admitted Grace. "Now sit down and observe them, will you do that for me?"

Wendy had no choice but to say yes.

And she witnessed, as a result, the same teenage couple calming down the girl who was about their age, touching her, holding her, whispering, crying as she cried, trembling as she trembled, saying nothing as she lapsed into silence.

Nearly half an hour passed.

That was the time it took for the couple to calm that girl down, for the three of them to be sharing tears, for a great deal of pain and hurt and bitterness and much else to pour out like poison from an inflamed wound.

"They are very good," Wendy whispered.

"You mean something more than that, don't you?" replied Grace.

"Yes..."

"Then say so."

"They seem to have done the work of a team of psychiatrists."

"I don't know about that, Wendy, but, yes, these two are remarkable. None of us have ever seen a team like them."

"A team?"

"They *always* work together."

"But how can they get away from school?"

"Lunch hours and evenings and weekends, my dear."

"When do they do their homework?"

"They manage it all. Both have B plus averages."

"In *every* subject?"

"No."

"Oh..."

"Kyle has an A in English. And Jeanne as well. It seems likely that both may be writers as the years pass."

The girl was ready to go back to her quarters. She walked away from the couple and past the two adults, turning briefly and smiling at her benefactors.

"Ready?" Grace asked.

"I can't," Wendy told her, her stomach tightening.

"Can't?"

"Meet them."

"What are you talking about?"

"I could have had a life like theirs now."

"But what about the valley of the shadow that both needed to walk through? What about that?"

"I had my own, Grace."

"But you don't have the life they do. You don't have their kind of relationship. Isn't that the point?"

"They got through what they needed to get through by doing it together, didn't they? I had to do it alone."

"Not alone, dear, not alone."

Wendy felt immediate shame then. Grace was right. She and others were by Wendy's side much of the way.

"Sorry," she apologized.

"It wasn't the same kind of intimacy that Kyle and Jeanne had, of course, but it was what you needed at the time."

Wendy sensed that the couple had been waiting for some signal to show them that they could approach.

"Hello..." she said a bit uncertainly.

But that was insufficient.

"They're still a little insecure," Grace whispered.

Wendy herself may have been more so. After driving beyond the location of the school, she had assumed that she would never come in contact with them again unless she sought the couple out, and she had not been about to do that.

"I've seen you before," Wendy confessed as they sat down on gray folding chairs in front of her.

Both were startled to hear that.

"You have?" the young man responded. Then he twisted up his lips and said, "Excuse me, please."

"For what?"

"For being so impolite."

"You were? I don't see how."

"We've not introduced ourselves. I'm Kyle and this is Jeanne."

"I saw you going to school this morning," Wendy remarked. "I was the driver who almost ran a red light."

Kyle blushed charmingly as he acknowledged, "I was thinking very dark thoughts about you." Then he added, "Sorry about that."

"No need to be sorry," Wendy assured him. "I have to tell you, Kyle, that you seemed to take it all in stride."

"Yes, I know. I was smiling instead."

"I thought that was rather charming."

"Charming? Are you serious?"

"Very much so."

"It's a good thing that you weren't about to read my mind!" he told her. "Your reaction would have been a lot different."

It was Jeanne's turn to speak.

"Why have you come here?" she asked in a friendly manner.

"Grace has told me a little about the two of you."

Jeanne seemed genuinely surprised.

"Us?" she said. "But why Kyle and me? There are other kids who manage to get through what we did."

"I think you're different, so completely different that I find it almost impossible to describe you both," Wendy remarked.

"A total transformation," Grace interjected.

"For you, that's what has happened. You have turned a nightmare into something wonderful." Wendy's voice became husky. "Beyond anything I have seen in nearly a decade."

"It's not us," Kyle told her. "It's not us at all. Give Grace the credit. She's the reason we both pulled through."

Jeanne glanced at Grace. "She saved us from hell," she added.

Grace shook her head modestly. "I was only God's instrument," she remarked. "That's all any of us can be, you know, His servants or those who cause Him grief. The choice is ours. What we do with the life He gives us can be our gifts back to Him."

"Whatever the case, we had been in a kind of hell for three years," Kyle spoke, his expression reflecting memories from that time.

"Do you mind talking about it to the kids you help, to strangers?" Wendy asked.

"We did at first but it happens all the time now. Every teenager on drugs is a stranger to us only for a while. We're getting used to it."

And so they settled down and described to Wendy what their hell had been like.

Chapter Twenty-Three

Wendy was pale by the time Jeanne and Kyle had finished.

"I..." she tried to speak but could not force out any words. This embarrassed her, and she added a moment later, "So sorry."

"Yes, we know, it affects everyone like that," Jeanne acknowledged. "They see the way we are now, and they wonder how we could ever have gotten through what we did."

Stealing. The couple robbed people for money to buy drugs. Both sold themselves as prostitutes. They did without food in order to put every last dollar into crack or heroin or whatever else they could ingest.

"We were dying," Kyle confessed. "And there was no one we could talk to except Grace, no one else at all. She was like an angel to us."

"But you have no aftereffects, it seems," Wendy pointed out. "That is really something! I have never heard of anyone living the way you both did who wasn't marked up somehow, who wouldn't carry the burden visually for the rest of their lives."

"That's part of the miracle," Kyle added. "Outwardly there are no scars, no blemishes of any sort."

"We are drug-free and disease-free," Jeanne said.

Grace was frowning. "I need to add a few words," she said, her expression serious.

"Go ahead," Wendy told her.

"There is a danger here, though," Grace went on.

"Danger?" Kyle spoke. "What do you mean?"

"It just hit me, as I was listening to you both. Wendy has never had a drug problem. And the story *is* compelling about how awful it was when you were shooting the stuff or snorting it up your nose or however else you got high."

They waited for her to continue after she had paused for emphasis.

"The way you look now, virtually untouched, is remarkable," she told them. "After all, look at how Wendy reacted to you, though she had her own reasons for doing so. You went through hell, and now you seem so flawless. Are you beginning to get my point?"

Nobody responded, fascinated by what Grace was saying.

"It's as though you seem too good. It's as though you paid a price *once* but now you're off the hook. There's nothing you can do about this but I think someone who has suffered physically and looks the part is in a little better position to be convincing."

Kyle was appalled.

"Someone might think we were lying?" he asked.

"That *is* a possibility," Grace agreed.

Kyle stood and started pacing. "But what about *inside* us?" he said. "What about how our emotions still haven't fully recovered? Maybe they never will."

"And conscience," Jeanne added. "Every so often we go back over in our minds the long list of people we hurt, and it ties us up in knots, it really does. And what kind of examples were we? How many other teenagers experimented with drugs because they heard that *we* were doing it?"

Kyle was weeping. "And the money we put into the pockets of criminals, the pushers who were supplying us!" he said. "That could have gone to charities which deserved it. We could have fed starving children!"

Wendy stood and put her arms around him. "The 'could haves' can be killers," she spoke softly. "I know about that sort of thing. Think of what the character of Oskar Schindler said in the movie *Schindler's List.* No one can deny that he had done so much to save hundreds of Jews during WWII. Suddenly he looked at an expensive car he had ordered, which was driven up to his front door, and he said, 'How many *more* Jews could I have saved if I had used the money *that* cost?'"

Her own eyes were shedding tears again.

"We do our best in this world," Wendy said. "We fight against sin and corruption, and sometimes we are successful. But alongside the victories are the defeats. We fight the good fight. We are not angels, we are not devils. We are somewhere in between, I think, with some qualities of each. All God expects is our best. All He needs—"

Wendy's emotions were surging. As she held Kyle tighter, Jeanne and Grace joined them, and they all hugged one another.

"Can I speak?" they heard a voice ask.

Jeanne muttered yes to the girl whom they had been trying to help minutes before.

"I want what you have in your life now," she said, her voice barely audible. "I can't go on the way I've been doing."

Her gaze went from the teenagers to Wendy to Grace. *"Please don't give up on me!"* she cried out.

Wendy reached out and held her tightly. "None of us will," she whispered. "I'm a stranger to you now. But if Grace doesn't mind, I'd like to help out any way I can...if you'll let me."

"I was hoping you'd say that," Grace Schaeffer said in the background.

"God bless you all," the girl said as she pulled away, smiling.

"He does," Jeanne and Kyle said in unison.

Wendy sensed that she would not remain a stranger to this troubled young woman for very long.

Chapter Twenty-Four

Grace was frowning, obviously concerned.

"Did I do wrong?" she asked as she drove back to the restaurant where Wendy would switch to her own car, and return to her office.

"No..." Wendy replied, her voice husky, "no, you didn't."

She was lost in a whirlpool of memories, and had forgotten exactly where she was for a moment.

"But you're so quiet."

Grace knew about Wendy's mood swings, having witnessed these many times over the past decade.

"It's not because I'm upset with you. I know why you arranged for me to meet that couple. How could I be angry about that?"

"God does work in mysterious ways, Wendy."

It was not the most original comment Grace could have made but Wendy tried to be patient.

"That's been said so often it's become a cliché, of course," Grace added, "but the truth behind it is never out of date."

"I agree, dear friend. Please believe me when I say that my silence has to do with something else than what you set up back there." She smiled at the black woman. "Truly," Wendy added, "I'm not upset with you."

But Grace was not satisfied, and asked logically, "Then what's wrong? Can you tell me that?"

"I'm upset with myself."

"I see."

"You were trying to get me to confront the truth about myself, and you were wildly successful."

"I'm glad. I thought you needed something. Do you know that some members of your staff have seen your hands shaking lately?"

"They—!"

"That's right. It's happened more than once. And all of them are deeply concerned. They think a great deal of you."

Wendy was quiet for a few seconds before saying, "Look at what those kids have been through, and look at what they are today."

"I admit there is *one* difference...that you certainly did not ask for what Seth went and did to you."

"And they were asking for trouble the minute they started with drugs, right?" Wendy added.

"Exactly what I was going to say."

"But, otherwise, the comparison is valid, Grace. They were in a nightmare that threatened their lives far more than anything he caused in mine."

Grace asked, "May I speak freely?"

"*Now* you ask permission?"

"They don't beat themselves up over it by revisiting it over and over again. It's behind them, and it must *stay* behind them if they are to recover. They have to remember, they have to talk about it with each young man or each young woman they counsel. But they've already learned the kind of detachment they must have at this stage if they are to continue to survive."

Detachment was an interesting word. On the one hand, it described a group of soldiers being sent on a military mission, usually an attack force. On the other hand, it meant pulling back, becoming disengaged, holding at arm's length.

For Wendy, it was definitely the latter that was as important to her as it was with Jeanne and Grace, and as it would become with the young woman who had been so plaintive about needing their help.

"Grace..." she spoke as they neared her office.

"Yes, my dear," the black woman replied expectantly.

"I did think that how Seth treated me no longer had any effect, that I had put it all where it should be, in some mental trash can."

"I know you did."

"But...but how could I have fooled myself for as long as I did when...when I can spot similar rationalizations in client after client of mine? I've got the reputation of being one broad who can't be suckered into anything."

"Except early on," Grace said, chuckling. "when you were an easy touch for anyone with a sob story."

"I think I still hear my bank account singing the blues!"

"I used to be the same way. And there are times when they fool me all over again. They have to be clever after a fashion, you know, in order to survive on the streets, especially the barrios."

"You, Grace. They pulled the wool over *your* eyes?"

"Yes, indeed. I'm not as tough as I think sometimes," Grace added.

"You and me are a lot alike in some ways." She turned her gaze to Wendy. "Has this helped, dear friend?" she asked.

"It has."

"Are you sure? Please don't just humor me. You have an annoying tendency to do that with me and others."

"I am very sure. But I have to say that I'm a little depressed."

"Why depressed?"

"How different would the years have been? How much happier? How much better the relationships? I might have remarried."

There was a quaver in her voice. "And I can blame no one but myself, not even Seth."

Abruptly Grace steered her SUV over to the curb.

"It's not *those* years that need to concern you," she said, her expression one of pleading. "It's the ones that are ahead of you."

"I see that now. But I can't help thinking about what I have missed."

"Listen up! If you keep on that way, girl, you're just substituting one nightmare for another. What you need is a kind of selective amnesia. From now on, as far as you are concerned, Seth never existed. Can you handle that, can you *really* handle that?"

Wendy was unable to answer.

Chapter Twenty-Five

*T*wo *angels were listening with great interest to the conversation between Wendy MacPherson and Grace Schaeffer. Unseen and unheard.*

They waited until Grace had finished, and then communicated between themselves about Wendy's plight.

"She is trapped by her emotions," spoke Darien, having seen countless numbers of men and women going through life in a similar state of being. "She thinks she has escaped the pain of the past but it is still there, ready to confront her again and again. Otherwise, she would not have reacted as she did to that young couple."

Stedfast, the other angel, could not have agreed more.

"And yet those emotions have been repressed because that was what she felt she needed to do in order to survive," he added. "Instead of facing how she felt, she pretended that they no longer influenced her."

"She is so fine a person," Darien said. "But it is a bit like the story of the little child and the dike in Holland."

Stedfast was familiar with that.

"All it takes is pulling a finger out," he recalled, "for so much misery to come rushing in over her."

They liked Wendy, liked her a great deal.

"If she were an angel," Stedfast remarked, "she would be an extraordinarily successful one helping people live properly or die properly."

Some human beings had the characteristics of angels, such as Madame Curie, Louis Pasteur, Joan of Arc and another, one who seemed an angel to countless numbers of men, women and children...

Mother Theresa. Both Darien and Stedfast were present in Calcutta when she left her tired, sick, old body. They had greeted her and lifted her spirit from that ancient frame. At first she was aware of nothing but the lack of pain, of stiffness, of aches from the top of her head to the bottom of her foot.

"I feel so young," she said, using the only word that occurred to her, and then she saw them, saw these most beautiful creatures of light and color and iridescence.

"You are—" she started to say in awe.

"Yes, dear one," Darien told her.

"Am I going to my Lord now?" Mother Theresa asked expectantly.

"He and all the hosts of heaven await you," Stedfast said.

Mother Theresa listened, listened to something so sublime that she wondered if her imagination was somehow substituting fancy for reality.

Then she smiled, as she spoke, *"I hear...song."*

"Ten thousand angels," Stedfast said.

"Singing for me?" Mother Theresa asked, uncomfortable with that notion after practicing humility for the better part of a century.

"Yes, for you and you alone."

"But I am so unworthy."

Stedfast was nearly overwhelmed by the spirit of this woman. *"So many live today because of you,"* he reminded her. *"So many are in heaven because of what you told them about redemption."*

"But how could I do less?" she asked. *"How could I live a life always facing the accusing cries of those from whom I would turn away in indifference? They would rise from the flames of hell itself to condemn me. I had no choice but to help, to succor, to be at their side and speak the very words of life to each of them."*

Suddenly she ceased talking, turned and looked down.

"I am looking—" she started to say.

"Down, yes," Stedfast agreed.

"The world is shrinking."

"You are ascending."

"Oh, my..." She seemed momentarily sad.

"Rejoice at last," Stedfast added.

"I know...."

"But what is wrong?"

"I could have helped so many more."

"You helped thousands," Darien reminded her gently, his voice a whisper inside her. *"You were an example to millions."*

"But how many more of the dying need comfort? How many more of the hungry need food and milk and—"

"Blessed one?"

"Yes..."

"Be still. Be at peace. Others carry on in your place. Our kind will be at their side, helping."

"It has been so long," Mother Theresa told the angels, *"most of my life, caring for others."*

"Now we will be caring for you, beloved."

Just ahead were the gates of heaven.

Just ahead were those ten thousand upon ten thousand angels forming a choir that sang her name.

Just ahead were the risen, redeemed souls of men and women and children whom she had hugged in their death throes, whispering to them, reassuring each one, loving not less than all of them.

Just ahead...

Boundless streets of gold. Light the brightness of which was greater than the incandescent sun but it did not blind.

"Mother, Father!" she exclaimed, seeing them for the first time in decades.

And other nuns like herself, those whose bodies had been left behind before hers.

And so it was, the day of Mother Theresa's death, not a death of the spirit, but only the body. For her spirit was eternal; her spirit would live on in a state and in a place where there would be no more hunger, no more sorrow, no more pain and suffering.

Part Two

*A*ngels know well the reality behind an ancient truth, the one that says that all things work together for the good of those who know and love God.

All things.

No exceptions.

Even the greatest of tragedies would produce something good along the interlinked chain of human events.

That did not always seem the case to those in the midst of that very suffering. How could death or disease produce something good? How could a flood or an earthquake or a fire be the seed of something of benefit, something of healing rather than hurting?

The answers were not always there for us this side of heaven. The answers that seemed apparent were seldom the answers that really were behind some age-old questions: If God existed, and cared, why did He allow so much suffering? If God existed, why were children subjected to abuse in or out of the womb, by mothers who were drug addicts or alcoholics or both, by societies which forced them into the cruelest of labor or the most fatal of neglect?

If God existed...that in itself was the question in countless numbers of minds over the centuries.

Angels were proof.

If there was no God, there could be no angels. Or if there was no God but there were angels, then they could never be trusted as honest, for they spoke of Him regularly. Belief in the creations mandated belief in their Creator.

Why did the good suffer?

A question Wendy MacPherson was to face, and ponder, her search for the answer one that would change her life.

Chapter Twenty-Six

Wendy was shaky after she returned to her office, not speaking to anyone, which was completely contrary to her usual manner, since she would usually come in after lunch and cheerily wave to the dozen people with whom she worked. She had been working with them for up to eight years, and they had their own share of problems, problems that most would take to her for what they had come to trust as wise counsel.

So many depend on me, she once told herself, *but to whom am I going to turn when the time comes?*

Noticing that she seemed troubled, they did not descend on her right away but allowed the boss some time alone before they reminded her about the first meeting that afternoon. It would be with curly-haired mayor Robert Friedl, whose last name meant "friendly place" in the original German language, which was appropriate in view of the fact that he had managed to keep racially oriented confrontations minimized thus far in his first term. Lately, he had been mentioned as a possible gubernatorial candidate.

"It has nothing to do with politics," he had told Wendy previously. "It is a matter of honor and decency to me."

And Wendy believed him, as did hundreds of millions of other constituents, his job approval rating extraordinarily high.

"When I first started this job," the mayor had added, "I was told that I was so popular I could get away with anything as far as the voters were concerned. Most of those whispering in my ear had in mind something altogether different than I did. They wanted the same old pork barrel projects, the favoritism over city contracts, the pay raises. When I refused to go along, they tried to sabotage me."

Oh, did they! Wendy exclaimed to herself as she sat down behind her desk and glanced at the appointment sheet for the day. *They tried to get the election results nullified on charges of vote tampering, sexual im-*

morality and anything else they could throw at you. But you stood up to them, and they had to issue more than one public apology, retracting all the implications and actual charges.

A genuinely decent man.

Wendy could not lie to herself by claiming that she did not feel attracted to Bob Friedl, that the fact he was divorced and very much eligible gave her some incentive to see him as often as she could, though she had not as yet gotten up enough nerve to try to find out if he was interested in her.

And it would have to be discreet, she thought. *The media could have some fun with this one.*

Yet she was still inclined to hold back, still inclined to be suspicious of the motives of any man.

He might be like so many others, Wendy told herself, *just interested in getting me in the sack and nothing more!*

But there was a chance, however fragile, that something might be in the making regarding the mayor, something more substantial than a few hours of sex, something finer and more beautiful, something upon which to build a significant part of her future.

So, no one had to tell her how important it was to be on time for the meeting at city hall, and to avoid the risk of offending him.

She took care of some paperwork, dealt with a few issues that staffers raised, and then said goodbye. "You know where I'll be," she told them.

She left the office, hurried down the corridor to an elevator at the end, and waited without much patience for it to reach the fourth floor. The door opened, and she started inside, pressing the button for the ground floor.

Suddenly the elevator lurched, and Wendy was thrown off her feet, hitting the railing that was attached to three sides. And then, whatever the cause, the elevator started to run naturally.

Wendy got to her feet. "So dizzy..." she said out loud. She blinked her eyes several times.

As the elevator stopped at the ground floor, and the door opened, she walked forward slowly, afraid of falling again.

Be strong.

A voice. For the first time in years. Very much akin to the one she had heard after Seth left her, but even sadder.

Your world is about to end....

Wendy gasped at that, her eyes darting from side to side, wondering if she should return to the office and rest for a bit. Surely the mayor would understand, surely he knew what kind of person she was.

"My world is about—" she repeated.

And begin again.

"Are you an angel?" she asked.

A short, balding man in his late forties who had been about to pass by in the lobby stopped, and spoke, "Ma'am, were you talking to me?"

Wendy shook her head.

"You are so pale," he observed. "May I be of any help?"

"No, I'm fine," she told him. "I just hit my head but not seriously. I'm beginning to feel better."

"Really, now, you might be hurt. Perhaps you should hurry on to your doctor."

"I'll try."

"Good! You seem very nice. The best of luck!"

She thanked him for his concern.

And as soon as she reached the entrance to her office building, and was outside, she did feel stronger, no longer unsteady.

You will never be alone, dear, dear Wendy. Remember that during every minute that follows this one.

"Yes..." she said. "Where are you?"

The voice in her mind did not answer.

Wendy started to cross the street to get to the parking lot on the other side. The dizziness hit again. And she became disoriented, unable to ascertain the direction in which she should be walking.

"Hey, look out!" she heard someone scream.

She did not see the truck that was just a few feet away from her nor make much sense of the persistent honking. Instead, she was fighting just to stay on her feet.

She did not see the truck....

Or hear people screaming, screaming, screaming, "Get out of the way! You're going to be hit!"

Abruptly, someone knocked her down and aside, rolling over twice with her.

Wendy screamed in pain and fear, cold, awful fear, not knowing exactly what was happening.

Pain. Oh, the pain! As something incredibly heavy rolled over the lower end of her body, and she heard the sickening sound of muscles being squashed and bones breaking. Whether she actually heard these or not, she *thought* she did.

A man! So familiar, even through her deteriorating sight. A man bending over her. Shouting. This man was saying something, words she could not understand at first, words spoken by a voice of desperation and anguish.

Who are you? Wendy tried to ask out loud, but everything about her body seemed paralyzed, her jaw frozen.

The man's face was close to hers. Wendy strained her eyes, trying to see, trying to remember who he was, his strong features familiar to her. And then, for an instant, but only that, her vision cleared.

Mayor Robert Friedl!

"We'll move heaven and earth to help you!" he exclaimed.

To someone else, he screamed, "Did you call an ambulance? I want an ambulance *now*. Is that *understood?*"

She wanted to ask him what he was doing there but she was fading rapidly.

The sound of an ambulance coming closer.

"Stop the traffic!" the mayor was shouting. "Get the police to barricade, if necessary. I want a clear path."

Then complete blackness reached out and overwhelmed the conscious world of Wendy MacPherson.

Chapter Twenty-Seven

Something bright...she had to turn away. It was too sudden—her eyes could not adjust quickly enough.

"You'll make it, you will. Everybody will be helping."

Bret!

He leaned down and kissed her on the temple.

"We love you, dear friend. You've never believed that but we do."

Wendy wondered how he could have known because she thought she had always been friendly toward her staff members, and never meant to seem distant, to seem as though she was apprehensive about committing her emotions to them at the same time they were committing their own to her.

If I committed to anyone, I ran the risk of being hurt by them, she thought amidst the jumble of images that were now competing for her attention. *How could I open myself up to yet more pain?*

Other voices. Some familiar. The voices of men and women.

Some were devoid of emotion, but most were *filled* with it. Talking at the same time, trying to help but mostly only adding to the confusion.

Wendy heard those voices, one after the other, and wanted to reply, wanted so desperately to scream out, to scream again and again, and ask what was happening, ask where she was, but could not be certain who was speaking since they were merging with one another in an incomprehensible blur.

A hand. A hand touching her, so suddenly that she felt herself jumping for an instant but with no strength to go anywhere else but back against the hard asphalt.

"Be still...."

Another voice.

"Do not try to move. An ambulance is coming."

Familiar.

"Who are you?" Wendy thought she said out loud but could not be sure of that or anything else.

She strained to recognize it.

"I am getting a full police escort over here immediately...."

Yes!

"You will be given specialists around the clock."

Now she knew!

"Whatever your insurance plan does not cover will be paid out of a municipal emergency fund."

Bob Friedl!

"Just don't move...and don't worry. Please don't worry."

Normally more self-assured than most men she had met, he sounded vulnerable then, curiously vulnerable to what was happening to her, his emotions poking through that well-rehearsed political facade.

"The ambulance is pulling up now, Wendy."

She heard the siren.

Pain hit her then. Wendy wondered if she had broken an arm, a leg, her hip, if—

"And I am going to have my own personal physician take over. Nothing will be left to chance."

A pause.

"Wendy, many will be praying for you...and you mustn't forget about those guardian angels of yours."

She could not remember ever having talked to the mayor about angels, could not remember hearing him raise the subject.

More pain. *Help me, sir, please...it hurts,* her mind cried out but he could not hear the words because they never reached her lips.

This time excruciatingly intense, ripping its way through her body, every inch of her protesting. Wendy screamed, the pain unbearable.

Something being stuck in her arm. And then the pain faded as she was being lifted up.

For a moment, she saw the face of the mayor bending over her, frowning deeply, his eyes bloodshot, as he whispered to her.

And then darkness that had been threatening now took her within itself.

Chapter Twenty-Eight

Wendy would need to go through the first of a series of operations less than an hour after she arrived at Cedar-Sinai Hospital. No time could be wasted, especially dealing with any injuries to her spine.

"A great deal will be determined over the next hours, Mayor," one of the paramedics told Robert Friedl as the ambulance raced over a freeway already beginning to choke up with rush hour traffic. "We have to make sure that she remains absolutely still, and that moving her is done with extraordinary precision."

"I know...." Friedl muttered. "I have been at the site of so many accidents during my term as mayor."

And that he had. Relatives, friends and associates had been hit by cars, in trains that derailed, on airliners that crashed, one killed by fumes inhaled at a toxic waste dump.

"It got so bad at one point," he said out loud, "that it just did not seem safe to be related to me, a friend of mine or working with me."

He was not being facetious.

"And now look at this dear woman," he moaned.

Bob Friedl was a pragmatist. He did not believe in fate or anything of the sort. The overwhelming coincidences he had mentioned were just that to him, yet he had to sit back and ponder periodically the significance of such cumulative tragedies.

"After a while, there are no tears left," he added.

"We can understand how you feel, Mayor," the second of the two paramedics agreed. "We see death every day, you know. But death in itself isn't the worst part, sir. I mean, those who die are beyond pain, beyond fear, beyond so much of the negative part that the living must experience."

"What is then?" Friedl asked, glancing at Wendy briefly, frowning, as he saw her so helpless then, cuts on her arms and legs and elsewhere, barely breathing, it seemed. "I mean, the worst part, as you just mentioned?"

"The impact on the families and the friends left behind."

The mayor nodded sympathetically.

"I can see that," he said, remembering moments that broke through the tough-as-nails political facade he was supposed to maintain. "I have had to console scores of wives, husbands, parents, children."

"Do you believe in an afterlife, Mayor?" the first paramedic asked, apparently out of the blue.

"Yes, I suppose I do."

"Suppose?"

"Who among us can say for certain? No one has been there and come back, at least anyone whose story can be believed."

"And angels?"

"I have much more difficulty with that."

"May I ask why, sir?"

"The idea that invisible spirits are floating around all over the place seems impossibly fantastic and...and delusional."

The paramedic was silent.

Ever perceptive, Bob Friedl spoke pointedly, "You think you've *seen* an angel, isn't that the case?"

The other man, tall, red-haired like Wendy, and also, like her, roughly a dozen years younger than the mayor, was genuinely taken aback. "How could you suspect that?" he asked.

"When you are in politics as long as I have been, you develop a sixth sense of sorts, frankly."

"What tipped you off, sir?"

"The tone of your voice, the expression on your face, little clues like that. You seemed to be saying, as a subtext, 'Now, Mayor, I'll listen to your response and then I'm going to tell you the truth, truth based on experience, not supposition."

The paramedic blushed. "Exactly what I was thinking!" he exclaimed.

"Well, what are you waiting for?" Friedl asked. "Will you tell me what happened that *proves* to you the existence of angels?"

"Just today, sir."

"Not before then?"

"No. Only a short while ago."

"But that means—"

The young man nodded.

"Exactly, sir. It has something to do with Wendy MacPherson."

"Tell me the rest."

"I was getting into my car about an hour ago and as I was turning on the ignition, my hands started to sweat, sir, I mean, *really* sweat. So, I stopped for a few seconds, sat back and closed my eyes."

"A hypoglycemic attack."

"I thought that at first but this was different."

"How different?"

"It was more intense, more, I guess you could say, *persistent.* I thought I might be in the early stages of a stroke."

"And then what?" Friedl asked.

"A knock on the car window on my side. I turned and saw a man was standing there, tall, middle-aged, dignified-looking."

"Hardly an angel."

"I would never have thought him to be one myself but, listen, Mayor, listen to what he told me."

The paramedic glanced at Wendy to see if her condition had changed, then continued retelling his experience.

"This stranger told me that there was an emergency at the dispatch station. I scoffed at this, and said, 'Sir, I would have heard about it. Besides, how come you know and I don't?' He smiled tolerantly, and said, 'That doesn't matter. All the other ambulances are out on call and the one you and your partner use is all there is left.'"

After recalling that, the paramedic shook his head in amazement, and admitted, "I can't believe that I'm telling you this."

"I'm glad that you feel you can," Bob Friedl replied. "Go ahead. I really am quite fascinated."

"Anyway, this man was becoming insistent. And I was on the edge of calling him a nut and driving off. Then he added, 'I've already spoken to your partner. He tried to reach you but your radio is malfunctioning.'"

"I told him that that was nonsense, and intended to prove this by getting through to my partner here—" he gestured to the other paramedic in the ambulance "—and checking out whether someone he had never seen before had warned him about a shortage of ambulances."

Despite his natural cynicism, the mayor was intrigued to the point of hanging on every word this young man was telling him.

"Sir, the radio was dead," the paramedic went on. "I couldn't send or receive anything. So I looked at the stranger, my mouth hanging open, before I asked, 'How in the world did you know?' His reply was odd, really odd. He said, 'It is what I do, young man. I have *been* doing it for centuries.'"

"For centuries?" Friedl repeated, wondering if he had understood what the young man was saying. "He actually said that?"

"He did, Mayor, and went on to add, 'Believe me when I tell you that you must hurry. Please do that. Do whatever is necessary to get to your station as quickly as possible. Your partner is on the way now. The sooner you arrive there, the quicker you will be able to answer a call that will be coming in the very moment you arrive.'"

The young paramedic had to stop and swallow several times.

"I remained skeptical, of course," he continued, "but he was well-dressed, rather distinguished-looking, not like a typical nutcase. Some of his urgency carried over to me, and I said, 'All right, all right, I just hope you're not a practical joker.' He shook his head vigorously, and told me, 'My kind have no sense of humor, only a sense of duty. A young woman's life is at stake. Please, please hurry!' I found myself thanking him, and on my way racing to the ambulance station."

Friedl cut in, asking, "He said that a young woman's life was at stake?"

"That's right."

"What time was this?"

"It was 3:47."

"Are you quite certain?"

"Yes, I am. As I was speeding up the street, I happened to glance at my watch. It read 3:47."

"Young man?"

"Yes, Mayor."

"That was at least five minutes *before* the accident occurred!"

The color drained from the faces of both men.

And the other, slightly older paramedic, overhearing the conversation, reacted in precisely the same way, exclaiming, "What in God's name?"

"Mayor, that's not quite all there is to tell," the young one added.

"What more could there possibly be?" Friedl asked numbly, not especially looking forward to any other shocks.

"Less than a minute after I pulled up in the parking lot, my partner here came in behind me. He had also been approached by a man who had claimed there was an emergency, and he had to leave right away." He sighed, trying to calm his own nerves from the assault on them over the past hour but only partially succeeding. "Apparently no one had been able to reach me," he added. "But there I was, getting ready at the same time, and we were on the road in minutes."

"My goodness!" Bob Friedl exclaimed.

"Mayor?"

"Yes, my friend."

"One more thing, sir."

Friedl waited, having no idea what to expect next.

"Listen to this—no emergency message had been sent by any of the dispatchers from the station to my partner. And none of them had tried to contact me. None of us could explain what had happened."

"What in the world?" Friedl remarked.

"And, sir, it was my partner's day off and mine as well. We both were heading in opposite directions. If that stranger had not contacted us minutes apart, we would have been too far away to get back to the station.

Who knows what would have happened to this young woman in the meantime?''

Friedl mused over what he had been told, then his eyes widened as he thought of a final question to ask.

His expensive Italian hand-crafted clothes were sticking to him as he asked, ''You said that the stranger, as it turned out, had contacted you and your partner minutes apart?''

''That's right.''

Friedl could hardly speak. ''How far away from you does he live?'' he asked, almost dreading what he was sure the answer would be.

''You know, don't you?'' the paramedic spoke.

''I think I do, I think I know exactly what you are going to say but I need to have you actually tell me. I need to *hear* it.''

The young man nodded, impressed that this political veteran was willing to be so open with him.

''Twenty-five miles,'' he replied.

''Twenty-five—!''

Even so, the mayor nearly choked.

''How could the same man have—?''

''My thought as well, sir.''

''Are you *certain* it was he?''

''Down to the handlebar moustache, the thick eyebrows, the scar running across one cheek, and the fact that he was almost completely bald.'' The paramedic smiled cryptically as he added, ''Yes, Mayor, I am absolutely sure that it was the same man.''

Chapter Twenty-Nine

Finally the ambulance had arrived at the hospital but getting Wendy MacPherson inside and prepared for surgery was not so simple, complications arising as soon as the ambulance approached the emergency entrance.

Traffic. Outside the famed hospital, the lanes were severely tied up because a famous actress had had a disastrous fall, broken several bones and had a punctured lung. Her ambulance was arriving just ahead of the one carrying Wendy. Everyone else had to wait.

"Get moving!" Robert Friedl shouted to the paramedics as he sat beside her in the ambulance.

"It's not only vehicular traffic, sir," the driver told him, "but there are so many reporters and photographers, and a very large crowd of bystanders. I've never seen anything like this, sir. See for yourself."

"For what reason?" Friedl demanded.

The driver mentioned the actress.

"How does *she* rate this kind of—?" he started to say, then stopped as someone banged a fist on the side of the ambulance.

Friedl opened the door and got out.

A well-known television news commentator named Marlene Dixon whose long red hair was her trademark noticed him. "Do you have any statement to make?" she demanded rather than asked.

"About what?" Friedl replied, playing dumb.

"About the condition of—"

"Quiet!" Friedl told the commentator.

"I beg your pardon?"

"This is ludicrous, Ms. Dixon. The world does not begin and end with over-the-hill actresses, no matter how completely their celebrity status had been maintained by hacks overpaid for the job."

"You're calling—"

"Exactly what I said."

Someone else came over to the two of them, a burly-looking man who easily could have played the part of a mobster in some television miniseries.

"I hope I didn't hear correctly," he snarled. "I didn't, did I? Tell me that, Mayor Friedl, okay?"

Friedl had to admit to himself that he was enjoying the moment despite the urgency of getting Wendy into the hospital.

"Every word...and I meant them all."

"I'm her manager. That will cost you votes."

"And if we don't break through this mess, the delay could cost the life of someone much more important to this city."

The manager looked defiant, hands on his hips, his lips curled in an obnoxious snarl, a thick cigar to one side. "Who could that possibly be?" he demanded.

"Someone you couldn't possibly know."

"An unknown is more important than one of the leading actresses of our time? You *are* joking, Mayor, aren't you?"

"Not at all. Now get out of my way."

The manager stepped aside reluctantly.

Friedl walked ahead of the ambulance, demanding that everyone step aside. He was instantly recognized, and reporters and photographers started to gather around him.

"What's going?" one of them yelled.

"Wendy MacPherson has been struck by a truck and may be dying," he told them. "I need your help."

The reporters and photographers glanced at one another.

"We hear you, Mayor!" several shouted in unintentional unison. "If it's for Wendy, we'll do anything."

Friedl knew that she had had extraordinarily good relations with the media over the years, the various newspapers and television stations periodically featuring some fresh aspect of her work with young people as well as the attention she devoted to barrio cases. More than one journalist had a relative or a friend whose life had been touched by Wendy. At least one had been helped directly by her, narrowly escaping from a life that would have ended in the city morgue or in prison.

"For Wendy's sake!" someone yelled, all that was needed.

The crowd of them not only cleared the way but most offered to help out any way they could.

"Thank you!" the mayor exclaimed. "What you can do is to leave her alone. I promise to let you know about her progress."

"Anything else, Mayor?" someone shouted.

"Pray..." he told them all. "That's what you can do...pray."

A minute later, Wendy was being taken out of the ambulance and rushed inside, the operating room already prepped for her.

Someone grabbed Friedl's arm. The manager.

"Mayor?" he said, the arrogance gone.

"I can't listen to you any longer," Friedl told him, pulling away, too concerned about Wendy to waste his time listening to anything trivial by comparison.

"I am very sorry." His voice was breaking.

"About the way you acted?" Friedl asked the obvious.

"Yes..."

"Why this sudden contrition?"

"I had a son who was getting into heavy drug use, and started committing robberies seven years ago. I tried to help him but he gave me the finger and turned his back on me and his mother."

Friedl saw that the man was showing some genuine emotion, not make-believe for the sake of gaining sympathy.

"Wendy MacPherson got ahold of his case and...and..."

"And he is a different young man today?"

"Completely, Mayor. But, without Wendy's intervention, I think we would have had to bury him." He took Friedl's hand in his own. "I'll handle my client," the manager said. "She's got to understand that there must be occasions when she isn't the center of the universe."

Friedl smiled appreciatively, not accustomed to such an admission. "Perhaps you can come to see Wendy later," he suggested.

"I would like that...I would like that very much."

And then Robert Friedl hurried inside to be with Wendy.

Five hours later, she was still in surgery.

Chapter Thirty

Wendy had no so-called out-of-body experiences while she was in the operating room at Cedar-Sinai Hospital, hovering in a spiritual form above her flesh-and-blood body, nothing like that at all.

But she was not rendered into complete oblivion either.

Wendy heard, yes, and she felt, yes. She heard and felt and was quite aware of whatever she could be in such a place, a place that was somewhere between life and death, heaven and earth.

Voices. Many. From every direction. Voices that were not singing but which sounded musical just the same. Voices in a chorus so filled with the most sublime joy that Wendy thought she could listen for the rest of her life, and never become bored, listen to the beauty of harmony beyond mortal ability to fully comprehend.

Then, in addition, she felt…something. Something being wrapped around her. Something so soft that she surrendered to the comfort of it.

Pain that she had been feeling was now gone.

"Don't let go," she pleaded with whoever and whatever the presence was. "I beg you…don't let go."

My kind has been with you before. You must sense that, Wendy. Believe that we have been assigned by God.

"You're an angel?" Wendy asked but with little surprise. "And God sent you to be with me?"

I am as you say.

"Am I dying?"

She thought she was prepared for that, but upon speaking the very question, was not so sure.

You are not dying. It is not your appointed time. There is much for you to accomplish, dear one.

"Much for me to accomplish?" she repeated. "How can that be? I have been injured. I am sure of that. Surgeons are operating on me now."

Yes, that is true. But you must not question, my dear. Have faith. Trust. Faith is the substance of things hoped, the evidence of things unseen. Believe, Wendy MacPherson, just believe, and be at peace.

"But what will happen to me?" she persisted, fearful as she considered what the answer might be, as she waited for this angel to speak the truth, no matter how unnerving it was.

As your Creator wishes.

Flashes from the accident came back to her.

"I was hit!" she screamed though somehow sure that no one except the angel could hear her. "I could feel bones being broken. I could—"

Dizziness overwhelmed her in that empty abyss where she felt herself enfolded by the wings of an angel.

Yes, you are now very, very badly injured, Wendy, as you suspected a moment ago. You must not be deceived into thinking otherwise. The surgeons will be working on you for many more hours.

She gasped upon hearing that, repeating numbly, "For many more hours? How bad my condition must be!"

She had seen numerous accident victims since she became an attorney and then a public defender. Some were *in* cars. Some had been hit *by* cars. The pain on their faces! More than one were missing limbs, and had been covered with blood. Others had arms or legs or both completely paralyzed.

She had thanked God often for keeping her safe.

And yet, now, what was there that she should thank Him for after He had removed that protection she had enjoyed for so long?

Paralyzed. That word froze on her lips. It was far too terrifying, unspeakably so. And Wendy tried to erase it from her mind. Tried to but failed.

"How will I be able to go on?" she asked, her natural tendency to worry starting to take control of her. "I won't be able to walk, will I? You have said nothing about this. You have ignored it, not wanting to—"

The angel interrupted not harshly, not even impolitely, but with a kind intent that she was not capable of appreciating.

Like an eagle, you will soar.

Wendy wondered if she was being delusional, a result of trauma and anesthesia, and whatever fantasy she was living just then.

"I...I feel nothing," she said plaintively "I can't move. How can I soar if I can't even walk?"

The angel seemed to hug her more tightly.

The peace that passes all understanding will be yours, Wendy. Ten thousand angels are waiting for God's command should you need them.

She started sobbing. "But I am nothing. I am—"

You have thought yourself as nothing for too many years.

"I must be," she went on, drudging up sad, sour images. "Or...or else Seth would never have left me."

Forget him, Wendy. There is much that you do not know. Only God Himself, your Creator and ours, knows what is in store.

"I thought I *had* forgotten Seth," Wendy spoke, close to not paying attention. "I thought I had *buried* our relationship a long time ago."

You did not.

The angel had merely told her what her earthly friends had been trying to impress upon her. To a degree, Seth was still in control of her life.

"What can I do?" she begged.

Seth no longer matters.

She tried to tap her forehead but was unable. "He's still here in my mind," she said, her voice trembling, "even if I have gotten him out of my heart."

That will change.

"If I live," she remarked, "if I *want* to go on living. I might not, you know. I have been active all my life. To be so badly injured that I—"

A part of her wanted to ask the angel to let her die rather than be crippled after the surgeons were through, and the anesthetic had worn off, and she was eventually told the truth.

The angel interrupted.

You will live, Wendy, you will live many years of great happiness, greater than any you had known before.

She was not convinced. "Is that what God has told you?" she half snarled, an edge of sarcasm in her voice, her weariness overtaking her good sense. "Is that what I am supposed to believe? You seem to be saying that I should be grateful for this."

You will be, dear. Oh, you will be.

Wendy felt an abrupt compulsion to make a comment that was nasty, truly obscenely nasty, perhaps close to being irredeemably blasphemous but did not, did not because she knew, even in that place of nothingness, that some roads should never be traveled because they led in only one direction.

"But what about my work?" Wendy insisted. "You surely know that there are so many people depending on me every day."

Of that I and the rest of my kind are well aware.

"*All* angels know about me?" she asked.

There is not one who would think you a stranger, and would have to ask your name, sweet Wendy.

"So many lives could go down the drain if I am not able to follow through, to help them. What can I say to those people? Go ahead, you've got to make it on your own? Forget about me doing anything for any of you?"

You have much more to be concerned with, Wendy. You will soon have a wholly new life ahead of you.

Wendy snorted and refused to say anything for a moment or two, trying to contain her anger.

Finally, controlling herself, she spoke again.

"But what will that life be like?" she demanded. "How could it be anything but miserable as a result of these injuries?"

Finer than you could ever have guessed, richer, fuller, more beautiful, a life beyond expectation.

If it were not an angel speaking that way, Wendy would have tuned him out, would have rebelled at his cheery assessment of her future, would have accused him of delivering meaningless platitudes.

She repeated those words out loud.

"Richer, fuller, more beautiful," Wendy said. "Do you mean that? Do you *really* mean that?"

Yes, Wendy, we truly do. And it will be through time and eternity. You need never ask again.

A voice of calm.

A voice so filled with love as well that she felt her fear melting away like a block of ice under an August sun.

Wendy began to cry, to pour out feelings that were kept repressed too long, too needlessly.

Since she was a child, Wendy had had faith, vibrant faith, faith that was utterly unassailable. But never enough trust. She had faith in God regarding the life to come, which helped to sustain her after her parents died because she had no doubt that she would be reunited with them, and never again be separated.

But Wendy's level of trust about the life she was already living ebbed and flowed, sometimes stronger, though often much weaker.

And now she felt ashamed, deeply, awfully ashamed. She bowed her head and asked for forgiveness.

"I must...oh, Lord...I know that...I must put myself in Your care with all the trust of which I am capable," she said slowly opening her eyes, clarity rushing in on her like the sunrise of the rest of her life.

It cannot be any other way.

"Will you...will you be with me, angel?" Wendy asked, desperately needing some reassurance.

Wendy, believe this. I shall never leave your side. We are bonded, you and I.

"What is your name?" Wendy inquired of the angel, remembering well how the other two angels in her life had identified themselves.

Guardian, that is what my Creator has called me, that is my destiny.

Wendy smiled. "Such names..." she spoke. "Darien. Stedfast. Guardian."

We are comrades, Wendy.

Her smile broadened. ''One for all, and all for one,'' she said, with no intentional mockery, finding the notion exhilarating.

It has ever been that way...since before the beginning of time. It shall ever be so, dear, dear Wendy.

Chapter Thirty-One

It has ever been that way...since before the beginning of time. It shall ever be so, dear, dear Wendy.

Those words stayed with Wendy even as she was coming out from under the anesthesia hours later.

She had felt so secure in that "other" environment that returning to the one she had known for thirty years was unpleasant.

Pain. That was why. *There* she felt none of it. *Here* it was taking charge of her.

"I hurt so bad...." she muttered.

"This is only the beginning, Wendy," a male voice told her from nearby. "The pain *will* lessen in time but not now. Be prepared. But also know that we will be there for you. We all will."

"I hurt...." she repeated, as though not hearing whoever had spoken. "And I am going to be sick...*help* me!"

The gentlest of hands, soft hands, held Wendy's head up at a slight angle. But nothing happened.

"I can't feel...." she moaned.

"Be still now, Wendy," the same voice told her ever patiently. "You have been through a series of enormous shocks."

"I can't stand it...." she tried to say, not really paying attention. "I...I can't get the sickness to...to..."

"I know, Wendy. But it can't be helped. We had to—" He cut himself off, deciding that she should be given any information in the smallest dosages possible.

"Don't go!" she begged.

"I'm staying right here," the voice assured her.

"Are you a—?"

"A doctor? Yes, I am."

That was not what she meant. She knew that he was a doctor. What she wanted to know was whether he was something else as well.

"An angel?" she asked.

The voice was laughing. "Thank you for the promotion."

"*Are* you?"

"No, Wendy, I'm not an angel."

"I was just with—" She felt dizzy.

"You need to rest," the voice spoke soothingly. "Do not be concerned with angels or anything else."

"But I want to tell you about them...about my...angels," Wendy insisted, sensing the disbelief in that voice.

She was given a sedative then.

"My...my angels," she persisted. "I need to—"

Asleep.

Welcome sleep came quickly and took her.

Mayor Robert Friedl wanted to know the facts.

"Tell me everything," he demanded.

He was sitting in the wood-paneled office of chief surgeon Wilkins Howe, short, stout, in his late fifties.

"You aren't family," Howe reminded him. "My hands are tied. As much as I would like to tell you—"

"There is no family left," Friedl spoke in his most authoritarian tone. "But she has many friends. Would you like to have me bring in someone else? Perhaps the president of the American Bar Association for starters?"

The other man shook his head.

"Of course not, Mayor," he replied. "I was just repeating what is applicable in most other instances. After all, we do have procedures, you know, and—"

"Red tape," Friedl interrupted incredulously. "Do you honestly think that I don't know about red tape?"

Howe took that as an attempt at humor and chuckled. "Touché," he said.

"I am not playing word games."

"Nor am I. You can't imagine, Mayor, how difficult it is to hold back the truth when you are talking with loved ones as I do so often. Sometimes you are forced to lie, which is unfortunate."

Howe closed his eyes briefly, thinking of some of those instances when he faced a man with a bad heart who asked about the condition of his wife who had just been in an automobile accident. He mentioned this to Friedl.

"If I tell him the truth right there, that she is dying, and we can do absolutely nothing to help her, then you can be certain that this decent man, this loving, devoted husband will have a heart attack immediately or very soon afterward. But the dilemma is that he will *have* to know at some point. Therefore, I must ask myself, should I let him find out just after she's actually dead? Or should I prepare him somehow, so that he can be at her side when it happens? But how do I do that in a manner that minimizes the possibility of a heart attack or a stroke? Tough issues, Mayor. And, sometimes, lying may be the only way."

Friedl cringed at the truthfulness because he was not accustomed to it, and recognized the *reality* of what the other man was saying. But he still abhorred the use of lying on what might be called pro forma basis.

"I appreciate your candor," Friedl told him. "Now spit the rest out. What is going on with Wendy MacPherson?"

"She will never walk again because she is permanently paralyzed from the waist down," Howe spoke. "I cannot be more direct than that."

Robert Friedl had had years to perfect a special ability, the ability to respond in an instant to anything that anyone told him, which served him well particularly at press conferences and city council meetings where he had to be constantly "on." But unlike so many other politicians, he never responded with patently devious comments, with half truths, with double-talk expertly camouflaged as a direct answer.

But, now, he could say nothing.

"Mayor?" Howe asked. "Are you feeling—?"

"Yes, I *am* feeling," he mumbled.

"I mean—"

Friedl turned and gave the other man a look that spoke loudly of his need for keeping quiet.

"Would you like to be alone for a bit?" Howe asked.

The mayor nodded.

Howe left the office, closing the door behind him.

Friedl bowed his head and wept.

Darien and Stedfast were in that office with the veteran politician, a man accustomed to plastic smiles and backslapping and all the clichéd phrases that men like him trotted out to make his constituents feel that he understood them, that he really cared.

"This one is not the same, though," Darien commented, himself a longtime observer of the personal lives of dozens of governors, senators, secretaries of defense, vice presidents and presidents.

"I agree," the other angel said. "He shows character."

"That he does."

"And behind the platitudes, he does care."

"Especially about Wendy."

"Quite right."

Darien wanted to reach out and dry those tears but God had not given him that act as part of his mission.

"He has much power, this man," Stedfast observed, "and he seems to be quite wealthy but neither his innumerable political connections nor his considerable financial assets can bring about a cure."

"Knowing this has left him feeling helpless."

"Before the will of God, all human beings are helpless."

Robert Friedl was unaware of the angels standing next to him.

Nor should he have been, for he would only have begged them to do what they could not, and then gone away bitter and resentful.

"Humans think we can do so much," Darien observed.

"And there is a great deal that our kind surely does accomplish," Stedfast interjected a bit defensively.

"But healing is not one of them."

These two angels left Mayor Robert Friedl alone but it would not be the last time they would visit with him.

Chapter Thirty-Two

The operation had lasted just short of ten hours.

It would be followed during the weeks and months to come by four others, none of these shorter than four hours apiece.

Wendy was not to be allowed visitors for the first ten days of her recuperation. The only exception was Robert Friedl.

"This is a critical time for her," Dr. Howe told the mayor as they both stood in the corridor outside Wendy's private room. "When my team and I operated, we had to excise numerous bone fragments which had been broken off from her spine but, principally, off other bones of her body." He did not hide his concern. "The internal bleeding was extraordinarily massive, Mayor," he went on. "She was close to drowning in her own blood. Only your prompt response saved her life. Otherwise I would be shipping her body to a funeral home."

Friedl's shoulders were slumped. "But, Dr. Howe, what sort of life will she have?" he asked, his voice breaking. "This is a woman for whom activity is—"

The surgeon rested a hand on the other man's shoulder. "I know all about her," he said. "So do a great many other people in this region. Wendy MacPherson could have run for political office a few years from now, and won quite handily, Mayor, even *your* job!"

Could have... Robert Friedl had spoken those same two words to himself over and over during the past week.

"I think she will be tormenting herself with 'could haves' for a long time," he said. "Undoubtedly she will consider where her career was heading, and then reality will hit her. That guarantees some additional trauma."

"No one could hope to make it on their own," Howe told him, "but then she won't *be* alone, will she?"

"Absolutely not. I will stay with her whenever I can."

"And your own career?"

Friedl hugged himself. "I can manage," he said a bit uncertainly.

"Can you? Being mayor of so large a city is a full-time job, but now you have another on your hands. Wendy MacPherson will require a degree of commitment that you may not have anticipated."

"Being Wendy's...protector?"

"Exactly that. Are you ready for this? After all, you cannot be with her every minute. Once she comes to depend upon you emotionally, she might expect you to be by her side more often than you are prepared."

"I know she will understand that I can't be with her every second. I don't think that Wendy is a demanding sort of person."

"Yes, I am sure that she's not. But what about the millions of men and women who swept you into office?"

Friedl had been thinking of potential voters for the better part of his adult life, from his late twenties in his first elective office to the present. While basically a rare breed, an honest politician, he was nevertheless a follower of polls and sound bites and the rest. He had damage control staff members, finance committee wizards and more—the same as any other political figure.

"I am endangering what I have achieved, is that what you're saying?"

"No, I'm not. It's just that you will have to be careful. When word leaks out about you and Wendy, you will have to deal with accusations of, on the one hand, between freezing the public out and, on the other, seeming to use what has happened to your political advantage, you know, the old sympathy routine that FDR used so well."

"Why are you being so helpful?" Friedl asked because of an old cynical streak that made him always want to dig deeper.

"I...I adore this woman as well," Howe replied. "She is one of a kind. Neither of us wants Wendy MacPherson to have less than the best possible opportunity for as meaningful a life as she can have under the circumstances."

"I think there's more to it than that, Dr. Howe."

The surgeon's eyes widened. "You are too perceptive," he acknowledged.

"No, sir, you are too transparent."

Dr. Howe smiled with some appreciation. "I don't often allow my feelings to seep out so nakedly as apparently has been the case with you just now."

"Nor do I."

"Wendy prevented my son from committing suicide. Please don't ask me to tell you more than that."

"I won't."

"Thank you for respecting my privacy."

"We seem to be partnered in a way, you and I."

That thought seemed to please the surgeon.

"That we are," he replied. "Yes, that we are. I thank you for pointing it out to me, Mayor Friedl."

"Whatever you and the doctors who work with you need is a given. The cost is irrelevant, Dr. Howe. Either the city will pay or I will."

"How generous!"

"How necessary. She is not wealthy. She may have some savings but hardly enough to pay for long-term care."

Dr. Howe looked at Friedl knowingly as he asked, "You have feelings for Wendy, don't you?"

"Yes...I do."

The surgeon lowered his voice, and added, "I am truly sorry that things turned out this way." He paused, frowning, obviously reluctant to say something.

"Tell me the truth," Friedl said. "That's all I expect."

"You know, of course, that she will never be able to—"

"Don't say anything more, please, Dr. Howe, please. Respect *my* need for privacy this time."

"Indeed I will," the surgeon replied.

The two men shook hands, and Robert Friedl left the surgeon's office to return to his own where he found staff members clamouring for his attention. There were more than fifteen phone calls that needed to be dealt with; some "emergencies" that had cropped up in several city-wide departments; and several reporters and photographers demanding to know what was going on between him and Wendy MacPherson.

Chapter Thirty-Three

Though Wendy MacPherson had a tendency to belittle herself, other people looked at her differently. And when news of her accident and the probable aftermath spread, it seemed that no one whose life she had touched was unaffected.

Grace Schaeffer was at the top of the list.

She had already gone home for the day, to a house filled with pets of one sort or another. She was the guardian of three Siamese cats, a German shepherd, an iguana lizard who had been adopted by practically every other creature in the house and a potbellied pig. Her next intended addition was supposed to be a cockatoo but she had not found one that would fit her personal budget.

A loner like her friend Wendy, she lived in a bungalow at the very edge of the Watts district, hardly a low-crime area but she had never been robbed, molested or been the target of a drive-by shooting.

For good reason. The word was out. And street gangs and other punks heeded it: Do not mess with Grace Schaeffer.

She was a guardian angel to many, many street kids and others. And she was always available to give help to anyone who needed her, especially help of a legal sort.

And so Grace could sit in her modest but well-kept home on her rundown little street, and be safe.

"The Lord blesses," she told another public defender.

"What if someone doesn't believe in the Lord?" came the reply, an honest one if a bit awkward to answer.

"That's *their* problem, not yours!" Grace insisted.

That night, she was tired, more so than usual because her workload had been heavier since morning, and some of the cases proved even more draining than she was used to during the past ten years or so.

Grace sat down with the iguana on her lap, after feeding the other pets, and stroked the top of his head. He looked at her, then closed his eyes, calm as always, and the two of them went to sleep together.

Until the phone. Its insistent ringing awakened her.

But not the iguana—nothing ever shook it out of that placid manner that made it either boring to some people or reassuringly steady and uncomplicated to others—and as she grabbed for the receiver, he stayed where he was.

"What's happening?" she asked as always before learning who the caller was.

One of her male co-workers at the office spoke. "Wendy's been in an accident," he practically shouted, his voice trembling.

Grace swallowed several times before demanding, "How? Where? I want to know everything."

He told her those details of which he was aware.

"I'll head right over to the hospital," she added, already starting to hang up. "Cedars-Sinai, right?"

"Wait, Grace!"

"Why? I need to hurry."

"Please, don't..."

"Why?" she repeated. "No time to waste."

"Everyone is being urged to hold off. There are vehicular traffic jams outside and human traffic jams inside."

Grace smiled slightly. "All because of my dear Wendy?" she asked but anticipating what the only answer could be.

"You got that right!"

"Thanks for letting me know."

Grace hung up the receiver.

"Something needs to be done!" she exclaimed.

She stood before an open window in her Early American-styled living room, and looked up at the darkening sky, noticing that a comet was streaking across the heavens, and remembering what it was like to ride it from its birth to its final place of rest as a burnt-out piece of rock in the middle of a desert somewhere.

"Lord, this is serious," she said softly, knowing into Whose presence she had come, the Person before Whom she was standing.

Yes, it is.

"May I summon the others?"

You must do that. Throughout the city. Do not hesitate to get them all to listen and be at your stand.

"Why, Lord?" Grace asked respectfully, pleased but curious as to why the response was immediate, without some need for deliberation, and the scope of it, the scope that seemed so vast, so total.

Because of what she will become.

"Forgive me for not understanding," she spoke prayerfully, "but that is the truth. I do not understand."

To serve, that is what you must do. Comprehension will come. My Father is not of darkness but light.

"Lord?" she asked.

Yes, dear one, what is it?

"Will You tell the Father that I love Him so very much? Will You do that for me, Lord, please?"

Tell Him yourself.

In an instant that room was filled with divinity.

My Son has said that you need to tell Me something. I stand before you now that you may do so.

"Father..." Grace spoke haltingly, overwhelmed, as ever, by being in the presence of Almighty God.

Go ahead. You were one of the first I created right after Lucifer came into being. Later, you refused to go with him and ten thousand others who have been duped by him. I love you for that, and for a great deal more.

"Father, I was going to say how much, how very much I love *You*," she added, driven to her knees by God's declaration of love for her.

I have known that since before the very beginning of time.

For Grace, love of the Father was love felt and expressed during the worst of times, the best of times, and even during a darker period when God had chosen to manifest Himself, a period that had begun with the worst hurricane, the most destructive natural force in the history of the world.

"There is something else, God," Grace ventured.

Tell me.

"I felt the greatest joy, the most invigorating sense of relief," she went on. "Even in the midst of the storm, when lives were being lost, when the destruction of the world seemed about ready to take place. Even then, heavenly Father, I had no fear, only love, because my kind and I are under Your protection. Nothing can hurt us. And rushing through was the experience of being loved by You without the encroachments of sin. We cannot sin, my comrades and I, and the lack of sin never felt so reassuring than in the midst of the chaos of those hours.

"As I stood before the tomb," she said, "I never loved You more than at that moment. I knew what You planned to do. I saw so clearly the next great moment in the history of civilization."

I remember well. It happened just before I rolled the stone aside and presented Him to you, to your comrades, even to the minions of hell and their leader so they would know that, ultimately, they were to be doomed, that they had no hope no matter how fiercely they continued to rebel through the ages of time to follow.

"Yes, until then, until then, Heavenly Father, I wept greatly, wept until I thought I could never stop!" Grace exclaimed as the memory of that tragedy grabbed hold of her. "How foolish of those You created to do this to the One Who wanted only to give them peace and joy...and eternity."

But then cometh your joy.

"At the resurrection, I rejoiced with all of my kind except—" she said, remembering the others, the others who shouted with jubilation at the death and burial that had preceded that moment but then shrieked in anger and fear, especially fear, as the stone was rolled aside and they saw who came from within the tomb. It was He, the One Who had endured so much agony before death temporarily claimed Him, but who now was resplendent as the hosts of heaven came from above to gather around His unspeakably magnificent form.

She looked directly into the very center of divinity. "I need to help Wendy MacPherson," she spoke with an earnestness that was its own message.

Go...do what you must.

"You will allow me to help her then?" Grace asked.

How could I do less? And I shall come to be by her side should you need Me. Just think the thought, and I shall heed it instantly.

"Must Wendy, this dear, dear woman truly be left without the ability to walk, Father?" she ventured. "Would you reconsider her destiny?"

God paused for a millisecond.

Yes, I have deliberated upon that, and a great deal else in Wendy MacPherson's regard. As you know, she is remarkable.

The light that was God shone brighter.

Let me give you a glimpse, and then tell Me whether this young woman's fate is a just one or not.

Suddenly, Grace saw it all, saw it all from the accident that late afternoon to that final moment later when Wendy MacPherson would breathe for the last time and then shed her body of flesh, to assume a new body of pure spirit.

Do you now see why?

Grace smiled, her feelings bordering on ecstasy. "Yes, Father, I see, and I know, and I truly, truly understand!" she shouted, unable to contain the sublimity of her feelings.

Now go and do what you must. She needs all the help that can be mustered. Go everywhere. Bring together any others of your kind that you see fit. You are in charge, blessed angel. Call on me if you need help.

"I shall never fail my Creator," she said, standing quite straight, even as her body was changing.

Nor will I fail you.

And Grace took flight.

Chapter Thirty-Four

Wendy was fully conscious for the first time in a week. Earlier, she would face a pattern that involved her coming to, then drifting away, back and forth, until everything seemed part of a kaleidoscope. A natural consequence of the trauma undergone by her body.

"It's instinctive," Wilkins Howe told Wendy, "I have seen many, many patients go through the same syndrome, believe me."

He was sitting in a chair next to her bed, and holding her hand as he spoke, occasionally giving it a gentle pat.

"What is to become of me?" she asked. "Am I completely paralyzed from the waist down?"

"Yes, you are," he replied.

She gasped though, days before, she had decided that that was the only answer she could expect from him as, repeatedly, she would awaken, try to move, try to *feel* something and then, crying, she would fall back into nothingness yet one more time.

"No therapy can help me?" she asked dumbly, grabbing at whatever feeble possibility she could.

"None, I am afraid," responded Howe.

He tapped the back of Wendy's hand with his fingers, and asked, "But you can feel that, right?"

"Yes."

He touched her shoulder.

"And that?"

"I can."

Then he brushed his fingers against her forehead, as he added. "And no trouble feeling my touch there, either?"

Wendy's reply was the same.

"Then you are very fortunate," he told her.

"Fortunate?" she repeated. "How can you say that?"

"Because, believe me, I do have more than a few patients who are paralyzed from the neck down, men and women cursed with no use of their arms and having to be fed every bit of food that they consume. They are the ones who have become quite helpless. But not you, Wendy."

"Am I supposed to be grateful for being a cripple? Are you trying to tell me that?"

"If I were you, I would be reacting in the same—" he started to say.

Wendy interrupted him. "Yes, Dr. Howe, I agree. I should be grateful," she said seriously.

Normally a rigidly controlled man, almost military in his bearing, Wilkins Howe was nonplussed and unable to conceal his reaction.

"I...I...never..." he tried to say but ended up saying nothing.

She smiled weakly, still the captive of sedatives and a body wracked by pain despite the medicine. "Be at peace, Doctor," Wendy said as she closed her eyes, unable to stay awake any longer. "I will be fine."

Howe watched until she was asleep, and then nearly stumbled from her room. Once out in the corridor, he leaned against the wall.

A nurse, seeing him, hurried to his side.

"Dr. Howe, is there anything wrong?" she asked with great concern.

"I am fine," he said. "No need to worry."

Though he was anything but fine, he invariably had conducted himself among the members of the hospital staff as though he was never given to overwhelming feelings of any kind because, in his view, people who were prone to acting that way could not be altogether counted on in a crisis.

"You look as though you've seen a ghost," the nurse persisted, noticing that the color had drained from his face.

"Not a ghost, my dear, not that at all but something else, something that I can scarcely believe."

Howe looked from side to side, then asked her if he could take her into his confidence, and she assured him that he could.

He told the nurse what Wendy had said.

"How *could* Ms. MacPherson be reacting that way, sir?" she asked, as astonished as he was.

"I think..." he said, scrambling for an explanation, "that this patient may be heavily into denial."

"Sir?" the nurse ventured.

"Yes. Go ahead. I don't bite."

She did not want to add to the mystery but knew that he needed to hear anything that concerned his patient.

"She was mumbling something earlier."

"About what?"

"Angels, sir. She was talking about angels."

Dr. Howe had been an agnostic most of his adult life, reluctantly admitting the possibility of God but not hopeful that He actually did exist in any form. Believing in angels would have taken even more of a leap of faith for this man, and he automatically dismissed any chance of their existence.

"Delusion," he replied.

"In other words, it amounts to something she has created in her mind to help her through all this?"

"Exactly, nurse."

She was nervous about detaining him any longer but as the primary nurse attending to Wendy, she thought she should be fully informed.

"Sir, may I ask why you reacted as you did? Denial is not uncommon among patients who have had a heart attack or paralysis or something else equally traumatic. You've seen countless cases like that."

Howe was feeling uncomfortable, and muttered a nearly indistinct, "I can't say," before excusing himself.

He walked a bit unsteadily down the corridor, stood quietly a moment.

...she was talking about angels.

"What is happening to you, Wendy?" he wondered out loud, suspecting that Wendy was in the midst of a postoperative nervous breakdown. "You have never seemed the type to fall for such nonsense as thinking that you had angelic companions. What rubbish, my dear lady, what rubbish!"

Then he turned right down an adjoining corridor, approached his own office suite a few seconds later, and stopped again.

I must get myself together before I can hope to help that poor woman, he thought. *And a great deal of help is precisely what she is going to need.*

Unfortunately, everything he believed told him that Wendy Mac-Pherson had entered a stage that, if she did not pull out of it, would mean trouble for her during the weeks and months ahead.

"No one can build a lasting recovery or any kind of meaningful new life on a foundation of fantasy," he muttered, "regardless of how seemingly pious."

As he entered, his secretary looked up and started to greet him but he ignored her, and went into his inner office, sat in a well-stuffed burgundy leather chair behind his desk, and tried to control the shaking that had started throughout his entire body.

"Will this one ever be reached with the truth?" Stedfast asked, concerned that such a dedicated and otherwise principled individual could be so blind.

"He has heard the truth often," Darien remarked, *"but he has always rejected it quite resoundingly."*

They were in the surgeon's office but, of course, beyond his ability to comprehend their existence.

"If we were flesh and blood," Stedfast said wistfully.

"I know what you are thinking but the Father has not instructed us to do this, as you know."

"Yes, I know. He seldom does. His thinking is that belief should be based upon faith, or it means nothing. If people believe in only that which they can see, what is the point? There must be a leap of faith."

"You have spoken with wisdom."

"Thank you. Is that so surprising?"

"Not to me."

The two angels left that office just as Dr. Wilkins Howe hugged himself and muttered something about a breeze, but then he turned and saw that the window was closed, and assumed he was coming down with a cold.

"What else could it be?" he reasoned as he reached for some cold medicine he kept in his desk's middle drawer.

Chapter Thirty-Five

W endy soon required fewer injections of sedatives. Her recovery was slow, but without relapses or complications. No one who came in contact with her was less than astonished at the unhampered recovery she was experiencing.

Nurses began talking about her.

"She's getting along so well!" more than one would exclaim.

"I've never seen anything like it," another would add.

But, still, there was no question about her paralysis from the waist down, so *recovery* was a relative term.

"How can she be so happy?" the nurses would say among themselves. "We've never seen another patient as badly off as she is respond so well, as though she is expecting to get better eventually."

Early on, that was the reason for Wendy's upbeat conduct. She had deceived herself into thinking that she would be miraculously healed.

How can it be God's will that I remain like this? she would ask herself periodically. *He helped me survive losing Seth. It can't be that I would get beyond that only to face this. Surely not!*

So, she clung to the certainty that, someday soon, she would be able to get out of bed and walk, that she would have *feeling* below her waist, and other than the pain during a period of rehabilitation, she would never have any more.

However, that remarkable dream she had had, that actual experience, that angelic encounter seemed geared principally toward preparing Wendy for something else, a life of confinement, yet at the same time, a life of unfettered growth and the kind of deep-down happiness that had eluded her since Seth had disappeared.

I must...oh, Lord, I know that...I must put myself in Your care with all the trust of which I am capable.

Nevertheless, there were moments, even knowing what she had said and to whom she had said it, that Wendy thought that if she could just appeal to God, and present the facts, then He would surely alter her fate and give her back the use of her lower body. She had always believed Him to be a God of mercy and grace, and, because of that, how could He resist her entreaty?

Wendy seemed to be on a hypocritical track, feigning complete happiness and adjustment with the doctors and nurses while, inside, her emotions were different.

Fearful. Yes, she was that.

My legs! her mind screamed. *I shall never be able to walk or run, never dance, never—*

She would be completely dependent on the help extended by other people, some of whom would have no personal interest in her, since for them she would merely be part of a job they had been hired to do.

Completely dependent. That thought nearly unhinged her.

How can I exist like that? she thought. *I've seldom fully trusted anyone except perhaps Grace Schaeffer.*

Now, though, she would need people round the clock. She could not have a bowel movement without help.

How can I stand the embarrassment of that? she asked herself. *My complete helplessness!*

Of course, nurses in hospitals and home care providers had been faced with such duties for centuries.

"We've learned long ago not to become disgusted by anything," nurses would say when asked.

It had been that way with them since the days of Florence Nightingale. And the messiness would continue for as long as people became ill or were injured. Nurses were special people called to a special mission.

In time Wendy realized that. In time she came to admire what they all had to put up with for the rest of her life.

Wendy gasped as she envisioned the significance of those simple words. *For the rest of my life.*

She would not be better in a few weeks or a few months. Years would pass without a change in her condition, a decade, two decades, three decades.

"I might have forty years left," she said out loud to one of her hospital nurses, Emily Wighton. "Isn't that a horrible thought? Forty years *or more!*"

"That's true," the bone-thin veteran agreed. "You might have a very long haul ahead of you, my dear."

"Can I take it?"

"Do you have a choice? After all, I don't get into assisted suicides, you know. They're an abomination."

Choice. That was the harshest of words for someone in Wendy's situation, because for her there were no choices. She could refuse to eat, perhaps, but then there were now ways to force her to do so, to keep on living.

She pondered how some patients were kept alive only with the help of life-support systems. The thought of being little more than a human vegetable seemed far worse than confinement to a wheelchair.

Yet Wendy still had the use of her arms, still could see, hear, was still able to feed herself, to wash her face, even, later, to do a little cooking of her own if she got hungry.

"Half of me can still move," she told Emily.

"You *can* last," the nurse replied. "Remember how amazed we have been by your cheerfulness." She smiled with great tolerance. "Is that all a lie, dear?" Emily added. "Is it perhaps possible that you have been deceiving the lot of us?"

"No..." she said uncertainly.

"Then why are you acting like this now?"

"I look at what's ahead and I feel so weary," Wendy finally acknowledged, having to say that to someone. She was weeping.

Emily sat down on the edge of the mattress, reached out and held Wendy as firmly as she dared. "No one will desert you," the nurse spoke.

"But I don't deserve any of this," Wendy protested, not thinking of her condition but the extent to which she would have to be looked after for the rest of her life.

"You don't deserve help and love and whatever else all of us are able to give to you? How can you say that?"

"I deserve nothing."

"Look at the people you have helped."

"Anyone else could have done the same thing," she retorted morosely. "I happen to have been the one."

The tears were coming faster now.

"No, Wendy, what you have done is your accomplishment and yours alone," Emily said.

"But all that's over," Wendy interrupted her.

"*Over?*" Emily repeated. "Listen, and listen good because it's apparent that you haven't thought this through very well."

"But I think I have. I haven't been able to do anything else, confined to this bed and unable to move."

"Thoughts clouded by self-pity are hardly reliable."

"Am I so unusual?"

"In that regard, no. You seem very much like everyone else. All of us succumb to the same emotions periodically. We are not superwomen, after all. And this life is often hard to take. It is only natural that self-doubt hits us every so often."

Emily pushed away from Wendy, holding her shoulders and looking at her without blinking. "Have you noticed that there are no flowers in your room," she asked, "and there haven't been?"

Wendy had, which, subconsciously, may have precipitated her melancholy, equating the lack of flowers with the likelihood that people were showing their true colors now that it seemed she was no longer able to help.

"And you're assuming that it's because nobody cares. Out of sight, out of mind, that sort of thing?"

"Yes."

"There's a reason. It's been deliberate, you know. People have been *asked* to please hold off."

"*What?*"

"Sounds strange, doesn't it?"

Wendy nodded as she wiped away her tears. "Why?" she asked, the reason escaping her. "Why in the world would simple flowers be banned?"

"One reason," Emily replied.

"Go ahead."

"Allergies, Wendy. Some people are violently allergic, not just to pollen and ragweed but, also, roses, carnations, scores of other flowers."

"I have none."

"Are you sure?"

"I think so."

"Thinking so doesn't cut it, Wendy. Dr. Howe and his associates have no intention of playing Russian roulette with you."

"If I am allergic to any flowers, then I could very well..." Wendy tried to reason it out for herself. Her eyelids shot open wide. "I could injure myself by sneezing or coughing violently!" she exclaimed, the wisdom of the ban now obvious.

"Exactly that!" Emily assured her. "And the kinds of foods you are given will be carefully monitored. We've taken many blood samples, and we know pretty much what your allergies of that sort are."

"Has anyone called or...or...?" Wendy asked, her own insecurities returning in a fresh surge.

Emily stood, and left the room without answering, and for a moment Wendy was alarmed and offended.

"What's wrong?" she called after the nurse.

Seconds later, the answer was apparent.

Two very large and completely stuffed mail sacks. Emily had these dragged into her private room by two hunky interns, both of whom winked at Wendy, making her blush.

"What in the world—?" she said, dumbfounded.

"I would put it another way," Emily replied. "In this world, this part of the world anyway, are countless numbers of people who adore you. And they have written letters and get well cards, sent presents and—''

''Presents?''

Emily turned toward the doorway.

The same interns were each bringing in an armful of packages that had been sent to Wendy care of the hospital.

''How could this be?'' she asked. ''I don't understand.''

''That is your curse,'' Emily chided her. ''The Bible says that we are not to think of ourselves more highly than we ought. But, I think, the Lord intended for us to look at the opposite end of that admonition also— we are not to think of ourselves as less than we are because this only means that God created us as inferior. Unless we think of ourselves as worthwhile, we are not honoring Him.

''Some of the sects bear the responsibilities for that, Wendy. They berate self so much, they batter the human ego so thoroughly, that people who have been a part of their group spend a lifetime in the grip of recurring bouts of insecurities and melancholy and outright clinical depression.''

''Is that what has happened to me even without some off-trail religious sect being involved?'' Wendy asked.

''It's what you have allowed. You allowed circumstances to dominate you rather than the other way around.''

''Do you know about Seth?''

''I do.''

''How could you?'

''During your periods of unconsciousness, you would mumble about him, alternately loving and hating him. You were pretty specific, I have to say, Wendy.''

''After all this time...''

''Nothing that is traumatic in our lives *ever* really leaves us. It slips down into our subconscious, which becomes the scrap heap of our memories which we can never truly empty of its contents.''

''Just before the accident, my friend Grace was telling me that I seemed to be on the verge of a nervous breakdown.''

''That's possible.''

''That scares me. Couldn't it still happen?''

''I suppose so, Wendy, but, ironically, the accident *has* relieved a lot of the pressure that was building up inside you.''

''Have I forced God to do this to me for my own good?''

Emily scoffed at that. ''I doubt it.''

''But why not?'' Wendy persisted. ''I know it sounds bizarre.''

''And I couldn't believe in a God given to ordering the bizarre in order to somehow help people.''

"But you *are* saying that, in one respect, I am better off than I was before that truck hit me."

"Not in just one respect."

"Don't beat around the bush, please."

"You have a devoted man in your life now."

"A devoted—?"

"Yes...Bob Friedl. The mayor comes here pretty much every day, checks up regularly on your status, pledges his and the city's full cooperation, tells us to let you know never to worry about medical costs. And he's offered to fly in any specialist from anywhere in the world, if necessary."

"Every day? I've not seen him yet."

"As soon as you got your faculties back, he let up a bit."

"Where is he today?"

"That's the other reason why I'm here. He is waiting in the corridor right down. He wanted me to ask if you would care to see him."

"I must look a mess!" she exclaimed, momentarily panicky as she felt her hair and ran several fingers across her face.

"Give me ten minutes, and I can transform you," Emily said grandly.

She had no argument from Wendy on that score.

Chapter Thirty-Six

Mayor Robert Friedl generally had reporters and photographers trail him wherever he went. And he seldom objected, for how he treated them was part of the formula for his political success.

But not this time.

After the initial frenzy at Cedar-Sinai Hospital prior to Wendy's arrival by ambulance weeks earlier, the media coverage changed perceptibly. For one thing, there was less of it, not because she had become yesterday's news but due to a phenomenon that no one anticipated, though it hardly came as a surprise. The media decided to give Wendy McPherson a break. Over her ten years as a public defender, she had helped hundreds of people, young and old, and *they* had families and friends, which meant that five hundred cases ultimately touched at least fifteen hundred to two thousand lives.

All in all, the effects of Wendy's superior performance of her duties had reached throughout that region, and connected with men, women and young people in every community. The only exception were the very affluent communities where lawyers were kept on retainer, and spoiled kids got away with anything. But teenagers from the barrios were not so fortunate. Wendy proved to be the only hope many of them had for justice or, at least, leniency.

Friedl recalled the first meeting he ever had with her. "What I am concerned about, Mayor," she said, "is that, since they have never known anything else, and have been trapped in a cycle of poverty, violence, crime, all the rest, they have come to feel that this will *never* change for them, that they might as well go on selling drugs, stabbing or shooting rival gang members because, for them, *their* gang represents a kind of family, a center of stability, however careless it might be. They think they literally have no other choices."

"Do they?" he asked. "Have any of them other choices, I mean?"

"It might be no for a large percentage. How tragic that so many are being written off, by the authorities, even by the churches. I mean, getting involved in barrio ministries involves an element of risk that is unacceptable to many."

He liked Wendy by the conclusion of the thirty minutes he spent with her that afternoon, sensing that "liked" might be too mild a description for what he was beginning to feel about her.

She was attractive, strong-minded, articulate, he remembered, *and utterly charming, and I made the mistake of telling her how I felt.*

She avoided him after that for as long as she could. In Wendy's mind, that was the only response she knew to a stranger who seemed to be "coming on" to her. Before Seth rearranged her psychological makeup by deserting her, she might have been flattered, but now so much damage had been done that she was conditioned not to trust any man who was as forward as Bob Friedl had been.

I blew it, he told himself, without knowing exactly why she reacted as she did. *She would have nothing to do with me after that.*

Until the evening of a special banquet set up to recognize men and women who had served the community to an extent that the quality of life was improved for a wide range of citizens. It was held in the grand ballroom of the Beverly Wilshire Hotel, with more than five hundred people in attendance.

A fireman was honored who had nearly died rescuing the elderly from one of the fires that Johnny Perez had set. And then a nurse came to the podium to accept her award for helping AIDS victims get better conditions during their final days of life.

"According to some," she said, "certain people who have contracted AIDS deserve their agony because they brought it upon themselves by disobeying God."

The nurse had to stop, fighting back tears. No one spoke during those few seconds, nor coughed, nor moved impatiently in their chairs.

"I won't argue the moral aspects of one life-style or another," she continued. "That is between these patients and their Creator. What I will say is that, as a nurse, I believe the Lord called upon me to ease the pain of anyone who is afflicted, no matter how they were infected. Am I supposed to gauge the morality of an individual patient before I do what I can? Drug addicts, adulterers, homosexuals need not apply!"

The only sound apart from her voice was that of handbags being opened as tissues were retrieved.

"That is not what God has asked me to do. I am not to deny mercy but to *extend* it. I am to treat the repentant as well as the hard-nosed unredeemed spouting the worst blasphemies. I am to be a nurse to the mob boss guilty of murdering scores of people as well as the born-again Christian dedicated to saving souls...to the Catholic, the Protestant, the

Buddhist, the Mormon, the member of the weirdest of cults. I am to treat the despicable, arrogant, hateful neo-Nazi in the same way as I do the self-sacrificing Franciscan priest. There are no differences for those of us in the nursing profession. There are only hurting people who need us as they are dying or as they are undergoing the worst physical and emotional traumas imaginable, although they are not destined to die."

She held up the statue that had been presented to her. "I accept this in recognition not of any special worth that I have but as a tribute to the profession which I have adopted as my own, and the mission to which I have dedicated myself until that day when I join my heavenly Father in His Kingdom."

And then she left the podium.

Wendy had no idea what was to happen next. After what the nurse had said, the ceremonies seemed to stop in midstream, her impact still being felt by everyone in the audience that night.

A child, just twelve years old, stood and walked on crutches from the back of the grand ballroom to the stage in front. One or more offers of help were rebuffed. Wendy recognized her immediately.

Amy! she exclaimed to herself, her throat tightening with emotion as she recalled this child's circumstances.

Amy made it to the podium, which had to be lowered. Someone took her crutches as she leaned forward, and with amazing grace, spoke, "I don't speak too well, you know. So I won't say much." She seemed to search the hundreds of guests. "There is someone here who saved my life," she told them, "and my mother's, and my father's, my brothers and sisters, too."

Wendy was starting to sweat.

"She got me out of drugs...." the twelve-year-old told them.

Several gasps could be heard.

"Drugs was eatin' my brain away," she continued. "I had to rob stores to get money for my habit. My father caught me stealin' from his wallet. He threatened to call the cops on me. I was mad. I decided that I wanted to kill everyone at home, then take my own life."

She pointed directly at Wendy. "She stopped me!" the youngster said, her affection showing. "She knew I was plannin' somethin' because of the way I acted durin' one of the sessions between me and her. I was supposed to be at a court hearin' the next day. I knew I couldn't go on any longer, so I figured that I had to do what I had to do that night."

Wendy had sensed that something was going to happen. She had been with Amy through so many sessions that she probably knew her better than the parents did. So, she had alerted the police to stand by, but she was going to try to handle everything herself.

When she arrived at the family's house, which was right in the center of the Watts area of Los Angeles, Amy was already threatening everyone, telling them that she had no will to go on living.

"We did some good, that night!" Stedfast exclaimed.

"Things do not always work out that way, do they?" Darien spoke. "It is quite true that we win some, we lose some."

The two angels could not take over a human being the way demons were able. They could not possess. But they were able to influence, a whisper in the mind, a tug at the conscience, an appeal to righteous emotions.

And that was what they did.

The words that Wendy spoke had their impact, aided by what unseen angels did that day, sending images into Amy's mind, images of love and peace and joy, the hope of better days ahead.

Another child was saved. Another family was spared the shedding of blood.

As Amy finished what she had to say before that elite audience, Mayor Robert Friedl stood, and started clapping. And so did hundreds of other guests.

In fact, everyone in the plush grand ballroom of the Beverly Wilshire Hotel gave Wendy MacPherson the recognition she deserved. They did not know that she was being helped by angels but that did not lessen what she had accomplished, for there were many Amys that she had worked with since becoming a public defender, and angels were absent from the majority of these cases.

As she made her way to the podium, she felt very inadequate to say anything of value to people who would be attentive to every word that she uttered.

Lord, she prayed silently, *I truly need Thy help yet again.*

And He gave it to her.

Without having prepared a word, Wendy nevertheless spoke compellingly. And by the time she was finished ten minutes later, the audience stood and clapped again, even more thunderously this time. But she held up her hands and raised her voice over the loudspeakers in the ballroom. The applause stopped.

She asked the band that had been hired to provide music for the evening if they knew Andrae Crouch's "My Tribute: To God Be the Glory." Surprisingly, everyone gave her a thumbs-up.

"This is the way I would like to close," she said. "This is the reason why I never give up, why I keep on going."

The band started to play, and she sang for the first time in public.

"'How can I say thanks for the things You have done for me?'" she began, her voice melodic, with power that surprised even Wendy.

Seconds later, she closed her eyes, and sang, "'The voices of a million angels could not express my gratitude...'"

And then she asked the audience to join her in the chorus.

Memories of that night months before flooded his mind as Robert Friedl entered Wendy's hospital room, praying for wisdom as he began to tell her what the next few months and the rest of her life would be like.

Chapter Thirty-Seven

During those early weeks after the accident, if it had not been for her angels, Wendy would have started on a downward slide emotionally. But this did not signal that she had a weak personality. If that had been the case, she would never even have recovered from the breakup of her marriage.

Not many men or women would have faced what Wendy was forced to confront without being initially devastated by the reality of what the rest of her life promised to be like, her mind screaming words that would have been unthinkable days earlier.

I will never walk again!

Stark and real, the finality of that.

After years of relative peace, she had fallen into the rut of thinking that losing Seth was such a wrenching catastrophe that, surely, a merciful and gracious God would not send another into her life. But now that was exactly what had grabbed hold of her, another nightmare at a time when she was doing everything she knew to please Him.

While Wendy had convinced herself a decade earlier that she would be able to get beyond *that* nightmare, the new one, by its very nature, was destined to stay with her for the rest of her life.

Whatever lessons He wanted me to learn, she told herself, *surely I have learned. And there can be little else He can teach me.*

The slide was starting despite what the angel named Guardian had told her. That "high" had lasted only a little while because it had seemed so ephemeral. And the nurses had begun to whisper that her so-called "spirituality" was perhaps nothing more than a facade.

One night, as she was half-asleep in her hospital room, these thoughts tumbling around in her mind, Wendy was startled by a visitor, someone who had entered her room without being noticed until he wanted to be.

He stood by her bed without saying anything, and, initially, she had no idea that he was there.

"Wendy?" he finally spoke, startling her. "I need to speak with you, my dear. Is that all right?"

She mumbled a yes without thinking, then opened her eyes wide, starting at the figure half-visible in the darkness relieved only by thin slivers of moonlight through the venetian blinds on the room's one window.

"Doctor?" she mumbled, thinking he was either a doctor or a male nurse. "Is anything wrong? More results from tests you've taken?"

"I am not what you say," he answered.

"You aren't—"

An intruder! Her solitude had been invaded by a stranger.

"But you know whence I came," he went on, no element of intimidation in a voice that could not have sounded less dangerous.

In an instant, that one statement told her everything. If it were written instead as volumes of type, it could not have been more explicit.

"You're an angel!" Wendy blurted out, perspiration sticking her flimsy hospital gown to her body.

"I am."

The voice was not much different from that of other angels who had spoken to her since the first time so long ago, leading to the suspicion that they were perhaps doing so with a human representation of the voice of God Himself.

Angels were created in the mind of God, she recalled. *And then He called them out from Him. But how far from Him are they ever destined to go? Or will they always be nothing more than extensions of—*

The significance of that had stunned her at the time, and she closed off considering it again because it was absolutely overwhelming.

Angels were but God in another form! Separate yet part of Him!

Suddenly, something...someone...else.

"Another?" she asked, not really doubting that she knew the answer without it being presented to her.

"Yes."

"Two...angels."

"Yes, there are two of us with you now," the incarnate angel told her, "as God has asked us."

"God sent you directly to me. Both of you?"

"He did."

"Why can't I see the other one?"

"It is not yet time for you to do so. My comrade has been with you for many years, Wendy."

Silent. Invisible. But there. That was what Wendy assumed but she did not perceive the truth, and neither angel volunteered it to her.

"Since the accident?" she asked.

The reply was a simple one. "Before the accident," the angel told her.
"How long before?"

"Years, Wendy, many years. Please believe that that is all the Creator
feels you need to know just now."

She could not resist returning to an old issue, for she was desperately
trying to justify the self-pity now beginning to surge.

"Why was Seth allowed to run out on me then?" she demanded. "If
an angel attended my way, as the hymn says, why wasn't I protected?"

"Free will. Seth's free will. If it were otherwise, human beings would
be a race of marionettes, with the Creator pulling the strings."

"Where is Guardian?"

"He is elsewhere."

Fear gripped her then, cold, hard, like a physical hand around her
throat, making the simple act of swallowing difficult.

"But why?" she pleaded. "I thought Guardian was looking out for
me. That was what he promised."

"He is."

"But how can he be doing that when he is not here, by my side, so
that I may talk to him?"

The angel interrupted. "Your future does not begin and end in this
room, Wendy."

"But until you came, I was alone. Yet Guardian told me that I would
never be alone, that I need not be afraid at any time."

"Guardian was correct. That you cannot always see us does not mean
that one of us is not sitting on the edge of your bed."

She was startled by that. "Every moment?" she asked.

"For the rest of your life."

"Can I be *sure* of that? God knows I need to be certain of that, else
how can I hope to survive?"

"Unfallen angels cannot lie."

"But what about the fallen ones, the demons?"

"Yes, Wendy, what about them?"

"Can't they pose as angels of light? At least that's what I understand,
according to the Bible."

"Yes, they can. But you *will* know if that happens, Wendy. You will
know, and be able to resist."

She fell silent, thinking of what this angel had just told her.

"Guarding me?" she finally spoke again. "You and your comrades
will be at my side, safeguarding me then?"

"Then. Ever."

"I am so tired, weary...."

"You have reason to feel that way. Only angels have endless energy,
Wendy. For human beings, there is an end to it."

"When I die, could it be...could it be that I...I will become an angel?" she asked innocently.

The stranger shook his head emphatically. "That will not happen."

"But I have read—" she started to say.

"None of that speculation is true. When you die, you are changed, yes, but not that way. Any such notion is not of God, Wendy."

"Please tell me more."

"Angels were created once and for all, in a single instant, by the heavenly Father. Our ranks are not added to as deserving men, women and children die, their souls going on into eternity."

"It's all false then, that sort of thing."

"Entirely false, and dangerous."

"Why dangerous?" Wendy asked.

"A human soul is born, my dear, sheathed in a flesh-and-blood body, in and out of the womb. When that body deteriorates and, after however many decades, dies, it is no more. But the soul goes on, to heaven or to hell. The soul is as it ever was. It does not become something else, Wendy."

"When Seth dies, is he heading straight for hell?"

Silence.

"Angel?" she asked.

"That is not for us to know," the angel told her. "Only the Creator can answer that question."

"Will you talk to Him for me?"

"I will not, Wendy."

"But why?"

"Because there *is* more that I *do* know, more that I am not allowed to tell you, for it is that which you must experience."

"Is Seth dead already?" Wendy persisted.

Part of her would have relished an affirmative response. But another part would have grieved, because as long as he was alive, there was a chance that—

She brushed away that thought, that wistful longing from her mind, and repeated her question to the angel.

"Is Seth dead now?" she asked.

No answer.

"Sorry..." she added, embarrassed that she was being so impudent, but hungry for information.

"You are asking normal questions," the angel assured her. "Others have done so throughout the centuries. You are the same, Wendy, because you are human."

"Others feel the same way about moments, about people in their lives?" she asked. "The same as I do?"

"So many millions that they are beyond counting over the ages of time, Wendy. You are not unique in this way."

She sighed again, increasingly weary. "Forgive me for all this," she spoke, pain poking through the sedatives, her voice strained. "I mean nothing disrespectful."

"You are one of God's special people, Wendy."

"You know I can't believe that. It's not that I think you're lying but I just feel so ordinary, so commonplace, and, now, so helpless. What is there that is so special about me? Can you tell me that?"

He could not. He did not. Instead, this incarnate angel reached forward and touched her on the forehead.

"Sleep, dear Wendy, sleep," he whispered, his voice soothing enough to calm her in an instant.

And she did.

Chapter Thirty-Eight

Three days later.

My poor charge, my dear, dear charge...

Grace Schaeffer was now home, her earthly home.

More than ever, she had seen just how fragile Wendy was at the hospital, and how much the most tender care would be needed. Knowing what she did, Grace had spent much of the time that had passed in the deepest prayer.

I must be with her physically even more than spiritually for the time being, she thought. *I need to hold her hand, and talk to her, and look into her eyes, and reassure her moment by moment.*

Grace felt the beginning of tears.

What poor Wendy will have to face, she told herself, *month after month of grueling rehabilitation. She has no real idea of what is ahead. She can only imagine.*

Grace sucked in her breath.

"I love her," she exclaimed out loud, the tenderest of emotions in her voice. "I truly love that dear, dear child of the King."

Angels were not supposed to become particularly attached to those human beings for whom they served as guardians or companions.

"But how can we avoid that?" Grace, in her angel form, asked of the Creator during a visit to heaven.

"It will be difficult," acknowledged Almighty God Who was always sympathetic to those He created.

This angel looked with eternal love at the One to Whom she owed everything, especially her very existence, an existence without illness, an existence that gave her entrance to the wonders of heaven itself.

"Father?" It was a word spoken with love, the most sublime love of all. And motivated by that very love, the angel wanted and needed to show respect, for that was the way of unfallen ones, respect for the One to Whom they owed everything.

"Yes?" God replied. "Speak freely."

"Without offense?"

"Without offense."

"I have found that human beings have more need of deep and lasting attachments than we do," the angel spoke, having had centuries of experience, "but my kind never developed that way."

"And you know why, do you not?" observed the heavenly Father with wisdom that was typical of Him, wisdom that was for the benefit of human beings who had originated from Him.

"Because angels had to be able to go from child to child, adult to adult, in one place or another, one time period or another, without any kind of entanglement, without being held back by the bonding process."

"Can you tell Me the reason?"

"Because there have been so many humans who needed us, and there will continue to be through whatever time remains before earth and all the rest of creation become as one with heaven. We are not omnipresent as You are, heavenly Father, so if we are with one girl or boy, man or woman, we cannot be with another who perhaps might be needing us just as much."

"You have spoken wisely."

"But Wendy MacPherson is different from some."

"She is."

"And I have spent ten finite years with her, occasionally breaking away to visit others but centering my guardianship on her."

"And you are wondering why."

Without fail, God had known what this angel's concerns were, had known because the minds of every unfallen angel were open to Him.

"I am, Father."

God had dealt in the past with many angels like the one before Him then, and He never regretted giving them the emotional characters of human beings.

"You will know soon," He spoke.

"May I ask something else?"

"Of course."

"Since I have spent all this time with Wendy, is it possible for me *not* to have been bonded with her more completely than usual?"

God was silent briefly.

Grace knew enough to wait. No one—spirit being or flesh and blood— could ever rush God.

"My dear angel," He began, "Wendy MacPherson *is* an exception, as you have alluded. And as a creation with emotions, you cannot always keep them under control. I created you as I am."

God loved, how deeply He loved, throughout the centuries of history He loved with a consistency that no human could match. God felt righteous indignation. God knew sorrow, despair. And hatred. The God of Love knew scalding hatred, yes, hatred of evil, sin, corruption, hatred of greed and deception, hatred of those despicable angels who rebelled and had to be exiled permanently from heaven. God knew all of these emotions. All except the petty ones, the selfish emotions. He knew nothing of greed, the need for power ever increasing. But the rest, yes, He knew these because they had *originated* from Him.

And so did the unfallen angels, tens of thousands strong. As well as the humans He brought into being. This emotional link was part of what united Creator and created, part of what He gave them. It was also central to the tragedy of separation between the two, when humans rebelled by acts of sin. *Separation from God.* That was the definition of sin in the original Hebrew language. Anything that caused this, anything at all was sin.

Grace shook her head as she stood in that place she had called her earthly home for so long.

"How many times have angels met here?" she reminisced. "How many times have we exchanged stories as the guardians we are?"

There had been successes and failures. Angels were not all-powerful. They could not transform a practicing alcoholic into a recovering one. They could not rip from a drug addict the compulsion to inject or snort or smoke their poison.

Fallen angels could move in when invited by word or deed, inhabiting the victim's very soul. It was also true that angels such as Darien and Stedfast, Guardian and the one whose earthly name was Grace Schaeffer could whisper, could plant a thought, could nudge, as it were, but never dominate.

And something else. They could rebuke demons. They could stand between a demonic entity and a human soul and ward off the onslaught *if* the human being let them.

Grace shuddered at some of the images that periodically disturbed her mind, images from the recent past as well as ancient times, images of creatures so foul that they disgusted themselves.

"Lord..." she said, looking up toward the heavens. "How I covet the day when sin and evil are no more."

That *would* happen, according to the wisdom of the ancient prophets, wise ones who spoke with the voice of God Himself.

"Let it be soon," she prayed out loud, "let it be soon."

Then the phone rang. It was Wendy.

"Grace," she spoke, her voice joyous, "I am going to be moved out of the hospital by Friday, and into rehab. Isn't that wonderful?"

"Hallelujah!" Grace shouted, ecstatic at what this still-young woman had said. "Praise God!"

"That is what I am doing. And some of the nurses are also. It's wonderful. People really care about me."

They talked for a few more minutes. Grace promised to go to the rehab center with her. Wendy closed with a prayer, and then the connection was broken.

Grace sat with the phone receiver against her ear for several minutes.

People really care about me. For Wendy to have done such extraordinary good so often for a large number of people since becoming a public defender and yet never fully realize how deeply many of them *did* care about her...that was one of the greatest of personal tragedies.

Nearly twenty years before, this incarnate angel had been with someone else who went through life like that. A celebrated writer, he wrote books that touched the lives of millions of readers, books that helped them with problems that frequently threatened to send them into terminal despair.

You blessed men and women, boys and girls more than most clergymen did in their lifetimes, Grace thought. *You kept a large percentage of them from suicide. You instilled joy and hope.*

But he couldn't pull himself out of his own troubles.

He was phenomenally successful, and became a millionaire soon after his books started to be bought by television and movie companies, a dream he had nurtured for almost four decades. The demand for his services as a screenwriter was increasing by the month.

One of the scripts he wrote was nominated for an Academy Award, forcing him to compete with four other writers. This sent him into a tailspin of depression from which he never withdrew, thinking that he was not worthy of winning anything, and certainly could not be compared to others who were far better than he.

The Sunday night before the awards were presented, he was found dead in his luxury apartment in a plush building on Wilshire Boulevard.

Twenty-four hours later, the winner in each category was announced. And he proved to be one of them, for best original screenplay.

"Lord, Lord, Lord!" Grace exclaimed prayerfully.

She had failed. Though she had tried her best, the writer's shattered self-image destroyed him, not from suicide but from self-inflicted stress that caused a massive coronary. Just before the ultimate triumph of his career.

"I can't let that happen to Wendy," Grace said out loud. "She's not as bad off emotionally and psychologically, at least she wasn't before the accident, but now her stability might be more tenuous than ever."

She bowed her head.

"Father, what do I do?" she asked in prayer so profound that beads of perspiration suddenly seemed as thick as blood across her entire body. "Show me the way, Holy One, I beg of Thee."

And the answer came like a chorus of ten thousand angels.

Chapter Thirty-Nine

In her finer moments, Wendy was an inspiration to doctors, nurses, patients and visitors at the hospital. That there were occasions when she slipped back into self-pity seemed understandable, and other people made allowances for her.

Sometimes, alone in her room, she would succumb to a fit of crying. But she was an emotional woman, and those emotions did not stay at one level each minute of the day. When she dozed off, and then awoke a short while later, she might have been dreaming about horseback riding or swimming or competing in the Olympics as a runner, which seemed a possibility, however remote, during her high school days.

And waking up meant returning to reality, the reality of seeing the lower part of her body in a brace.

"I hate to go to sleep," she told Bob Friedl one afternoon.

"Sometimes I do as well," he said.

"Why? You have everything going for you."

"Because when I do awaken, it is often because of the phone ringing at home, and whoever is calling is trying to reach me about one municipal crisis or another."

Wendy nodded as she said, "I can understand that, Mayor."

He jumped to his feet in exasperation. "You must stop that!" he exclaimed.

"Stop what? What am I doing?"

"You mustn't call me mayor when we are alone," he explained. "That is only for public use."

He was looking at her with such affection that she blushed.

"Is something happening here...Bob?" Wendy asked, not entirely uncomfortable with the notion.

"It's *been* happening for a while."

"You—"

"Yes, Wendy, that's right. I've been falling in love with you. Obviously you've never noticed any clues."

She was genuinely surprised.

"The look on your face tells it all," Friedl told her. "You're so accustomed to hiding your real emotions behind some kind of psychological wall—"

"But I show my feelings all the time," Wendy protested. "It's not fair to say otherwise. I'm not putting on an act with my clients."

"Not all the time, no. Nor do I. But is *everything* you express to them genuine? Be honest with yourself."

"Yes, yes, it is! I don't turn plastic for anybody."

He was looking irritatingly smug.

"You think you're right about this, don't you?" she said.

"I *know* I am. That's why you can't believe that I have fallen in love with you. You're not sure what's real anymore, what isn't."

"You mean I have lost contact with reality? Is that what you're implying?"

"Not the way you put it. You've faced more of *reality* than most people ever will, the grim reality of the people who are your clients. That's a reality that would shock middle-class folks sitting in their safe little homes."

"Then what are you talking about?"

"You've become a public defender, the very best, but you've lost yourself."

"Bob, Bob, that *is* what I am."

"There is more, Wendy. You are a beautiful, passionate woman. Otherwise you couldn't understand the pain of others the way you do. But everything goes out to them. There is nothing left for yourself." He smiled warmly. "It's like somebody in a desert who has plenty of water for travelers and their animals but when he wants some for himself, the water is suddenly dry."

Wendy seemed, then, like a rag doll that had sprung a leak and all the stuffing was abruptly gone. "Oh, God..." she muttered, though not profanely.

Friedl could see that she was trembling, and bent down and wrapped his arms carefully around her. "Forgive me," he said. "I love you more than you know."

"How could you?" she asked. "How could you love me?"

"Damn Seth for doing this to you! Damn his soul to—"

She pressed a finger to his lips.

"No..." she said. "Don't, Bob. I've been doing it to myself for a long time. I just don't know how to stop."

"I'll help. Oh, Wendy, please, I'll help if you'll let me."

The phone rang. Friedl grabbed the receiver.

"Yes..." he said.

"Tell them to handle it for themselves," he barked. "I'm not in the mood to baby-sit anyone right now."

Pause.

"Look, everything's a crisis these days," he added. "I'll be there in an hour but not now, not this moment. *Capisce?*" He slammed down the receiver.

"My people await me," he said.

"Hurry," Wendy said, concerned. "It does sound serious. You can come back when you have more time."

"Ego, dear. Arrogant people who are unequivocally demanding *their* share of the mayor's time."

"Could you get into trouble over this?"

"Who knows? Who cares except those guys? I care about no one but you now. They're a faraway second, Wendy."

She cupped his cheek in her hand. "I think..." she started to say.

"What do you think?" he replied. "I'll listen to whatever it is that you want to tell me, no matter how long you take."

"I think I could be starting..." Wendy went on but, blushing, cut herself off, unable to finish.

"Starting to what?" Friedl asked, sounding more like a teenager, "Starting to love me? Is that what you were going to say?"

"Yes. I think I am. I think I actually am."

A bit hesitantly, Friedl kissed Wendy then, a gentle kiss, a kiss of the most infinite tenderness.

The ring rang again. Three times. Four. Five times.

It was never answered.

Chapter Forty

Wendy was feeling well enough to be transferred to the rehab center which was not in Los Angeles but part of a secluded ranchlike estate nestled at the base of the Santa Monica Mountains. Grace Schaeffer rode with her in the specially equipped van that the hospital had had outfitted for someone in Wendy's physical condition.

"You look comfortable," Grace told her just after the doors were slid shut and the driver had started the van.

"I am," Wendy said quickly, not wanting to worry her friend.

That was not entirely true. She was as comfortable as she could expect to be, strapped in a bed, the upper part elevated, braces on her body from the hips down.

She blushed as she added, "Sorry, Grace. I shouldn't have said that."

"Said what?" the other woman repeated. "What do you mean? And what in the world could you be sorry about?"

"I should have told you the truth. I'm not all that comfortable."

"Should I have them stop? Make adjustments?"

"I don't think they could make me feel better," Wendy replied though she appreciated her friend's typical willingness to try to help out.

Grace placed her hand on Wendy's wrist.

"Why don't we pray?" she asked.

Both shut their eyes, and Grace prayed out loud.

Interestingly, Wendy had never really heard her pray before. Grace continually seemed rather like a walking prayer, always putting her needs last while helping other people, never once showing the wrong kind of anger. Any time she let loose with some display of temper was against drug dealers, rampant HMO corruption, lying and deception in Washington D.C., a righteous anger, but never the sort that spouted off against traffic congestion, waiting in line at airports, and other aspects of modern life.

But now Grace was *speaking* a prayer, and Wendy could not stop the tears that started to flow seconds later. It was a prayer of supplication to Almighty God that was so beautiful that she gasped more than once. And when it was over, she found herself wishing that it could have gone on for a great deal longer.

"Grace?" Wendy said, barely able to say anything but wanting to tell her friend how she felt.

"Yes, dear friend?" the other woman responded.

"You talked to God!"

That was what that prayer was, according to one definition...*direct* contact with Almighty God.

"I did," acknowledged Grace.

"It was as though you were standing directly in front of Him."

"Prayer happens to be a conversation with God."

"But—" A fresh surge of tears. "I don't know how to express what I felt but I have to say something, Grace. Your prayer was wonderful."

Grace seemed the embodiment of loving patience as she spoke, "Do your best, dear, dear Wendy."

"It was almost as though you were able to carry me into His presence as well. I know how that sounds but I have to tell you honestly how I felt."

Grace smiled. "You never know," she said.

"But I've never felt that way before. I've never felt so close to God. You did that for me, Grace."

"We did it *together,* Wendy. Remember that He is present where two or more are gathered together in His name."

"No, no, it was you. I have been in groups of twenty people, fifty, a hundred people or more, people praying. But none of those prayer times were ever like this one. You...you seemed to be able to lift the veil between the infinite and the finite, and enable me to *sense* a little of heaven."

"There's a reason," Grace said, thinking that perhaps it was time to tell Wendy what she was.

"A reason? Tell me what it is."

The van lurched.

Wendy's bed was anchored to the floor, so she did not shift at all. But Grace was thrown off her seat.

Screeching... The van's tires protested. And then it came to a sudden, wrenching halt.

"I'll be back," Grace said. "You're safe. I need to help. Someone is dying right now, Wendy."

She slid back the door on her side and jumped out.

An accident. One of the worst on that road in years.

The van was not involved in it but clearly would have been if the driver had not acted instantly.

"What's happening?" Wendy asked, feeling every bit as helpless as she was, trapped without being able to move, and having no idea what was going on.

Someone is dying right now.

As she was waiting for someone to come to her, she asked herself how Grace could have known that. She had not even seen the extent of the accident!

How did you know? she thought, just before one of the two paramedics poked his head through the open door.

"Are you all right?" he asked.

"Yes, I think so," she told him.

"If you need me here, I'll stay with you."

"No, I'm okay. Just come back as soon as you can. It's scary. Being alone. Not able to do anything."

He fully understood. "I think I should stay with you," the good-looking curly haired, dimpled young man remarked.

"Someone may be dying," she told him. "Go, please. I can make out."

He looked at her oddly. "Wendy?" he asked, since everyone who had been involved in her treatment had come to call her by her first name. "How did you know that?"

She started to blurt out an answer but stopped herself. "Just a guess," she said. "That's all."

"I'll be back as soon as I can." He smiled, and left.

Grace was right! Wendy exclaimed. *And yet she couldn't even see what had happened. I've got to ask her later. I've just got to!*

At no time since her own accident had her disabled condition left her feeling more frustrated. "Oh, Lord, help me here, please!" she begged out loud.

Just a few seconds later, a stranger stuck his head in the doorway.

"Were you calling for help?" he asked.

"Yes," she answered without thinking. "I need to get out of this van and see what is happening ahead."

"Let me help you," the tall, aristocratic-looking middle-aged man told her, the tone of his voice the essence of kindliness.

"God bless you," she said.

He smiled curiously at her as he was pushing the bed into two ridges on the floor of the van.

"Now we need to lower it," he told her.

"I don't know where the control is," Wendy said.

"I do, Wendy," the man assured her.

He found it beside the doorframe, operated it properly, and she was outside in less than a minute.

"I'll take you as close as I dare," he said.

The accident involved three cars. All of them seemed so battered and crumpled that she could not imagine anyone being alive.

"I don't know if I want to see this after all, sir," Wendy said as she turned her head slightly.

Gone. The stranger had disappeared. "How could he—?" she questioned. And then she knew. "Another one!" she exclaimed. "God sent me another angel!"

She saw Grace kneeling before one of the accident victims. Her friend touched the man's bloodstained forehead, and then bent over him to whisper something in his ear.

Something happened then. He stood up a few seconds later, a bit wobbly but seeming to strengthen soon enough.

Then Grace went to another of the victims, and the same thing happened. But with the third one, a small child, it was different. Wendy could not take her eyes off what was happening. Grace wrapped her arms around the little boy, and sobbed, then placed his crumpled body back on the asphalt.

As she looked up, she saw Wendy looking at her, and slowly walked over to the wheelchair.

"You saw?" she asked, seeming a bit annoyed.

"I did," Wendy acknowledged. "What happened with the first two? You seemed to give them life."

"Not me."

Grace's manner was proving quite strange, perhaps a bit evasive, which was not like her at all.

"But I saw you," Wendy countered.

"God, Wendy."

"God?"

"God gave those people life because it was His will to do so. He gave them recovery through me."

Wendy was astonished. "Are you a faith healer of some sort?" she asked, her prejudices colliding with what she clearly had seen.

"No, my dear, I am not."

"Then what?"

Grace was not eager to continue the discussion. "Could we talk about this later? I am feeling a bit weary now. Let's get you settled into the rehab center."

"Fine..."

She could see that Grace was indeed exhausted. It seemed as though life had partially gone out of her and straight into those two other individuals.

Wendy started to speak, trying to change the subject, but Grace held up her hand, and it was obvious that she wanted to be quiet. Her normally aggressive manner seemed changed, if only momentarily.

Once, during the remainder of the ride, as Wendy glanced at her, she could see tears rolling down those beautiful ebony cheeks.

Chapter Forty-One

The rehab center seemed more like a sprawling country club.

"The reason is simple," one of the nurses told Wendy after she had been taken to her quarters. "The better patients feel, the more they respond to treatment. It seems simple but is often forgotten, which explains why, more often than not, rehab is done in dreary buildings that smell of antiseptic and seem to be well past their prime."

A beautiful fountain spraying water upward, with a rainbow forming, graced the exterior, just in front of the entrance. Lining the circular driveway were tall narrow Italian cypress trees, ten on each side. People were sitting on the lawn or in wheelchairs, enjoying the clear air, nurses or male interns hovering nearby for their protection.

"So beautiful..." Wendy whispered as the nurse who had just spoken left the room. "Can I stay here for the rest of my life?"

It was not a serious comment but some wistfulness was attached to it as she considered what the rigors of the future surely must be, and how isolated and protected this new environment was.

"No," Grace told her. "Here, Wendy, the purpose of all this is to prepare *for* the real world."

"It isn't real here?"

"Of course it is. It's real for the moment. But it's a planned reality, a little like the inside of a cocoon before a butterfly is released."

Wendy thought of her Olympic hopeful days, days when she could run like a winner, and hear the cheering of an enthusiastic crowd.

No longer.

God help me! she cried out in the privacy of her mind. *God help me and forgive me for the blackness of my heart, my soul just now.*

She seemed particularly vulnerable as she spoke, "But, Grace, I'll...I'll never fly...or walk."

"Just an expression, Wendy," her friend pointed out. "Don't make of it anything more than that."

Wendy nodded. "I'm all right now, Grace," she said. "But...I do have spells, terrible, dark moments lurking like some beast ready to devour me."

Grace was hardly unsympathetic. "That's to be expected, my dear," she said. "We can't deny that your old life is gone, and the new one is radically different."

"And as always you continue to be a part of it."

"That's what I'm here for."

Wendy looked at her friend curiously. "You sound as though you mean that literally."

"I do."

"But you have other friends, and you have clients of your own. Despite that, you have always spent so much time with me."

"You're right. And I'm tuned into each one. I care about each more deeply than even *they* realize."

"But—"

Grace anticipated what Wendy was about to say by adding, "None of them, though, concerns me as much as you do."

"I'm so ordinary."

"How can you honestly say that to yourself and to me?"

"You mean the awards, all that?"

She envisioned her wall at the office, with photos of events involving dignitaries, the plaques that hung on it, and the statues on the credenza behind her desk.

"That's *exactly* what I mean." Grace was becoming irritated. "Don't they mean *anything* to you?" she asked. "A lot of good folks got together and expressed their convictions about you."

"Of course they do," replied Wendy. "And, yes, I know that. But they honored someone who could do what I was *once* able to do, get around the way I did, be active for them. But, now, I won't be of any use to them ever again."

"Is that why you treat them in such a cavalier manner?"

"It's something I can't help. You think anybody will give a hoot about what happens to me now?"

A knock on the closed door of Wendy's private room interrupted them.

"May I come in?" Robert Friedl asked.

Grace opened the door wider and he walked over to Wendy's bedside.

"You're looking really well!" he said.

"I feel pretty good, Bob," she told him. "I'm not sure what the next few weeks will bring, though."

"Everybody here is going to do everything possible to make things less difficult," he assured her.

"Bob?"

"Yes, my love?"

Wendy blushed as Friedl said that.

"The money to pay for all this," she asked, "where is it coming from? I know we've discussed this a little before but, now, I can see what's going to be involved. The cost of this rehab center must amount to a small fortune in itself, not counting the hospital and all the nurses at home when I get back there. What's going to happen?"

"Your insurance plan *will* cover virtually everything."

"But to this extent? And isn't that unusual?"

"Yes, and yes. But public defenders are a special case. Even the bureaucrats recognized that there are many high-risk situations that you all face, the neighborhoods you have to enter, the danger even in your own office downtown if someone goes berserk. Insurance is expensive but in a rare burst of wisdom, my colleagues realized that they couldn't get quality people if they didn't provide quality medical and related protection."

"Every penny, Bob?" Wendy pressed. "Every last penny? I don't have a bank account big enough to pick up the shortfall."

Bob Friedl never got a chance to answer as Wendy's gaze momentarily shifted through the open door to the corridor.

Wendy's attention was riveted by a familiar voice, a voice that she never conceived of hearing again, a voice she recognized the first second she heard it.

Recognized it, yes, and froze, the upper part of her battered body nearly as numb as the rest.

"What's wrong?" Grace and Friedl said at the same time.

"I thought I heard—I mean I *did* hear—" Wendy started to say, then stopped, her lips quivering.

Grace sat down on the bed. "Heard what?" she asked.

"Not what...who."

"Who did you think you heard?"

"Dear God, I did!" Wendy exclaimed, pressing the back of her hand against her mouth. "I hear...him."

"Tell us," Friedl pleaded.

"Seth."

Friedl was startled but Grace registered no reaction whatever.

"So help me," Wendy continued desperately. "I...I...heard Seth. God knows I didn't want to."

Grace took her hand and held it gently. "Wendy?" she spoke.

"All right," Wendy said. "Go ahead. Go ahead and tell me I'm crazy. Tell me that. I *need* to hear you—"

"I can't," the other woman acknowledged.

"You can't tell me it's not Seth."

"That's right."

Wendy was sweating, her temple pounding. "Are you saying—?" Her blood pressure was shooting up. "It *might* be him?" Wendy demanded. "Is that what you want me to know? Is that it, Grace?"

"It's not a question of that," Grace replied, trying to be as gentle as possible, trying to keep her friend calm.

"I...I don't know what you're saying."

"Wendy, my dear...that *must* have been Seth. It could not be anybody else, not here, not now."

"How could that be?" Wendy protested. "He's gone. He might even be dead by now. I *want* him dead."

"He's here. Recuperating."

"Recuperating from what?"

"Gunshot wounds."

"My G—!"

"The Mafia has had a contract out on him," Grace said. "If they find him again, he's a dead man!"

Wendy could not process easily what she had just been told, could not withstand the shock to her system.

"Take me away from here!" she nearly screamed. "I don't want to be anywhere near...anywhere near him."

"There are reasons for almost everything," Grace told her.

"But this? How could this be a part of any plan, God's or anybody else's. How could it? Seth ruined my life once. Is he going to be allowed to come back and do it again? Is that what God wants?"

Grace turned to Friedl. "Mayor, would you please leave Wendy and me alone a moment or two?" she asked politely.

"Surely," he replied without hesitating, and left the room, closing the door behind him this time.

"Wendy, there is something you should know," Grace spoke, "something that you *have* to know."

"Did you expect something like this would happen?"

"I did. I was the reason for it. I found Seth and made sure you were to have your rehab here."

Wendy shook her head disbelievingly. "But you *know* what he did to me! You know better than anyone else except me. Why did you do this to me?"

"It is time."

"Time for what?"

"Time for you to see."

"See what, Grace? What else am I supposed to see?"

Dizziness hit Wendy. The room seemed to have been hit by an earthquake.

And she saw, in the midst of her confusion, a being of such profound beauty, so invested of color and shimmering radiance, that she could not feel other than instantly at ease in the very center of her soul.

"Grace?" she spoke weakly. "Are you...are you...?"

"Yes, dear," her friend said. "I *am* an angel."

Immediately, a comforting darkness grabbed hold of Wendy, taking her momentarily away, and she felt such joy that the prospect of returning to the room and the reality it represented seemed a forlorn prospect to her.

"Dear Grace..." she begged. "Please take my hand. Please stay with me. I need to know that you will be with me, no matter what."

"I shall...for all time, for eternity."

The last sensation of which Wendy was aware, before a seeming oblivion joined the encompassing darkness, was not sight or taste or touch, not any of those, but hearing, sweet, sweet hearing.

A sound. A voice yet not a voice. In her mind, bypassing her ears altogether.

"Grace, is God—?" she tried to say.

"Yes, Wendy, God is."

And she was at peace.

The two angels were relieved.

"At last!" Stedfast remarked.

"Yes, my comrade," Darien spoke. "Two truths have been revealed."

"If only Wendy is able to take those truths and apply them."

"I suspect she will. God never begins a plan that He does not complete."

"Hallelujah!"

And the two beings joined together in praising their Creator.

Chapter Forty-Two

When Wendy awoke, she remembered the encounter but assumed it was a crazy dream, and told Grace what she had seen.

"Strange..." Wendy said, not at all frightened by it, her emotions stirred in other profound ways.

"Quite," her friend agreed, "judging by what you've told me. I can see why it really got to you."

"Seeing you as an angel!"

"Wild idea, that one!"

"And I even dreamed that Seth—" Wendy swallowed hard. "That wasn't a dream, was it?" she asked, reality separating from fantasy and coming back to her.

"No, dear, it wasn't."

Wendy was trembling, her cheeks temporarily pale as she asked, while dreading the answer, "Here? Now? All of that's true."

"Yes, Seth's in this same center," Grace replied, in no way wanting to deceive Wendy about what has transpired.

"How could that have happened?"

"You never know...." her friend spoke evasively.

Wendy was frowning. She knew Grace well, or so she thought, and sensed that the other woman was holding back on some of the details.

"Was God behind it?" she asked.

"You can safely assume that He was."

"Why, Grace?" Wendy pleaded. "Why would God want this to happen? He knows how much I—"

"Hate Seth, right?"

"Yes, I did, I do."

"What if hate is no longer called for?"

"How could that be?" Wendy asked. "Look at what he did, with no warning, no explanation."

"My dear friend, what if hate was *never* called for?"

Wendy paused, that possibility completely alien to a mind-set that had been in place for many years.

"You've been right often before," she said, "but this time, you're way off base. What was I to feel about my husband? One day he is holding me, we're kissing, and he's pledging his love. The next morning, he's gone, no note, no phone call, nothing, just gone, Grace, as though I was an old toy of which he had tired, and could be thrown away without an afterthought. I should *not* hate him for that?"

"Having him here stirs up everything again, doesn't it?"

"Of course, Grace! What would you expect? You've known me for all these years. Surely you're not surprised by my reaction?"

"I'm not, that's true," Grace acknowledged. "But there is more here than you ever knew, much more."

"When Seth was gone, after all that time, I could start to forget about him. I could start to deal with what he did to me."

Grace stood and started pacing the floor. "Wendy?" she asked.

"Yes?"

"You said, 'what he did to me.' Isn't that right?"

"You know the answer as well as I do."

"Could it be instead something else?"

Wendy tensed, wondering what new revelation was going to be flung at her by someone whom she had trusted so long. "What are you getting at?" she demanded.

"Is there any chance in the world that you should have said, 'what Seth did *for* me' more accurately?"

Wendy lashed out at that possibility. "He did *nothing* for me," she said, incredulous. "Seth almost destroyed me. Why do I have to repeat all this?"

"Because you assumed that he had walked out on you."

"What else would you call it?" Her cheeks were flushed with rising anger. "Not once did he try to contact me!" Wendy exclaimed.

"That you know of," Grace interpolated.

"You're bothering me with all this stuff. You've never talked like this before. You've always supported me."

"I am doing no less than that now," her friend pointed out.

"Is that what you call it?" Wendy blurted out. "You sound like an apologist for a wife deserter."

Grace smiled as she asked, "Would you let Seth explain?"

"What could he *ever* say that would make me think differently about him? I see nothing at all."

"I can't say. I don't read minds, Wendy."

Both women were silent for a few minutes as they sat in quarters that seemed more like someone's living room, with a plush sofa, well-stuffed chairs, a twenty-seven-inch color television, fresh flowers twice a week.

Oh, Lord, what is happening now? Wendy prayed to herself. *I don't want to displease Thee by doubting Thine involvement in all this, but I just don't understand what is going on, and why.*

Every so often, Wendy would glance toward the doorway, catching her breath as she half expected Seth to pass by and, seeing her, stop and—

"No!" she exclaimed finally.

"No what?" asked Grace.

"I don't want this."

"Why not?"

"Isn't that obvious?"

"It isn't. Wendy, give it a chance."

"A chance for what? That Seth will tell some lies, yes, *that's* obvious. That, somehow, after more than ten years, he and I are destined to get back together. No, that's not obvious at all. It'll never happen, *never!*"

"Never say—"

"Cut the clichés," Wendy interrupted the other woman. "You're expecting me to forget all the pain, to forgive him, aren't you?"

"Forgiveness is a part of your belief system," Grace countered, "or have I missed something?"

Wendy shook her head. "Not this, Grace," she said. "I could forgive anything but this."

"Even if that's what God wants?"

Wendy looked at her friend with disbelief. "You won't let this drop, will you?" she asked.

"No, I won't."

"Then I want to go to another rehab center. I *demand* that you make the arrangements. I can't face the burden of my therapy *and* knowing that Seth may be right next door at any given moment."

"He is."

"Next door?"

"No, but Seth *is* in the same building...at the other end."

Wendy was beginning to sweat, a headache pounding at her temples and nausea commencing. "I feel sick," she said.

"You *could* feel a lot better, if you allowed this to happen."

"By embracing him again, by pretending that—?"

"It's not entirely what you're saying, is it?" Grace interrupted.

"Of course it is. What else could there be?"

"You are afraid that Seth will reject you *again* if he sees you in a wheelchair, if he learns that you will never walk again. The Wendy he knew when you both were teenagers was young, athletic, vibrant."

"That's ridiculous. I don't *want* him to *accept* me so how can I be concerned over Seth's *rejecting* me?"

"Ridiculous, Wendy?"

"Yes, yes, that's right. That's—" Wendy cut herself off this time.

"I want you to confront Seth soon," Grace told her. "I want you to confront the past ten years, and be free of them when you learn the truth."

"I already know the truth."

"You know only what *appears* to be the truth."

Something about Grace's manner just then stopped another protest before it was ever uttered.

"How could the truth be so different?" she asked.

"What if the *reasons* for that truth change it altogether?"

"I can't—" she said before sobbing.

Grace sat down again on the edge of the bed, and, leaning over, kissed her once on the forehead.

"Cry as much as you need to," she spoke. "The truth, Wendy, is very special here. Please believe that it *will* set you free."

Wendy pulled away from her. "I'll do this," she said, her voice breaking, "but, you know, it may end our friendship, it *may* do that."

"I'll risk everything that we have had between us, Wendy."

"Go ahead. Set it up. Give me a few hours."

As Grace was leaving the room, Wendy asked her, "Does Seth know?"

"He doesn't. He will be as surprised as you are."

"He may not want to face me."

"What would you say if I told you that that's something Seth has been praying for all this time?"

Grace closed the door quietly, and Wendy, sitting upright in the hospital bed, tried not to admit that her heart was pounding so fast that she wondered if she would have to call in a nurse to quiet her down.

Chapter Forty-Three

Wendy knew that she could not avoid confronting Seth forever. Grace would not let her get away with that. But she desperately wanted to postpone that wrenching moment as long as possible.

"I need to feel more confident about myself," she told her friend after a relatively brief water-based therapy session. It had involved being in a pool along with a well-trained, rather good-looking therapist named Richard Gilardi, who seemed gentle enough, but who pushed Wendy to her limit.

"I can understand that," Grace replied.

"I need to show Seth that I'll...I'll never have to be dependent on him again, regardless of where he is."

"Wendy, Wendy, does that include the hold this man's had on your emotions all these years?"

"Yes..."

Grace was in a folding lawn-type chair as she sat outside with Wendy, a bit uncomfortable, but no other chairs were available.

"Have you thought about the fact that you may finally learn Seth's reasons for what he did?" she asked.

"Or excuses," Wendy pointed out. "I think he will give me excuses, halfhearted regrets, whatever."

She had heard from Grace something resembling sympathy for Seth earlier, and she was annoyed by it.

"Why are you standing up for him?" Wendy asked, more than a little perturbed, because Grace seemed the least likely person to do that, knowing as she did all that Seth had put her through.

"I am hardly defending someone who seems to have run out on his wife. You can't really believe otherwise."

"But that's what it sounds like."

"I just want you to know the truth."

"The truth as it exists? Or more likely, as Seth has been twisting it to suit his own purposes?"

It was Grace's turn to be irritated. "Truth is what it is," she declared. "Aren't you able to tell the difference?"

"I don't know anymore. Seth was always a convincing liar. Otherwise I would never have believed him in the first place."

"You think he lied to you from the beginning?"

"What else am I to believe? If he had been serious about our relationship, he would never have deserted me."

Grace placed her hand on top of Wendy's.

"Honestly..." she spoke, "is that why the police were so unresponsive? Were they somehow tricked as well? And what could he have told them anyway?"

"I have no idea, Grace."

"Let me put it another way. Would just another lying, cheating scoundrel of a husband make them act as they did?"

Wendy did not respond right away.

I've thought about Seth like that, she admitted to herself. *They would have been totally cooperative if that was all there was to it.*

"Grace?" she spoke.

"Yes, Wendy?"

"Can you tell me anything? Can you do *anything* to prepare me for what he might say when we do meet?"

Grace dodged an answer. "I think Seth should do the talking," she said.

"You didn't answer my question."

"That's all I can tell you."

Grace's manner bordered on the mysterious. And Wendy did not like it at all.

But she decided not to pick any argument with someone who had been aiding her survival almost from the beginning, only a few months after she had awakened to an unexpectedly empty bed that disastrous morning.

Darien and Stedfast were, as usual, overhearing everything.

"Should I assume human form and be with Wendy?" he posed. "I could be a nurse, an intern, a doctor?"

Darien pondered that briefly.

"It may not be a bad idea," he replied. "Go ahead."

"I thought you would agree."

"Have you decided what your form would be? You just mentioned some possible candidates."

Stedfast had already changed his mind.

"I think I know!" he exclaimed.

"Go with God."

"Is it ever otherwise for you, for me?"

Stedfast left his comrade, and, in an instant, was changed.

Chapter Forty-Four

Wendy's brand-new, state-of-the-art motorized wheelchair allowed her some relative freedom of movement, once she was *out* of bed. But getting *into* it was another story, an experience steeped in pure agony.

Two nurses helped her that particular afternoon.

"Bless you," Wendy said hoarsely once she was sitting down, all the controls at her fingertips.

"As you know, there is an infrared alarm right next to your left thumb," one of the two women, the youngest, told her.

"I won't forget."

"And there's another on the leather belt around your waist, just in case the chair were to tip over."

"I understand."

"We keep reminding patients for the longest while. People *can* forget or become disoriented. It has nothing to do with someone's intelligence."

Wendy thanked them both.

She remained in her room for a short while, wondering where she might go. She was familiar with some of the building's layout.

Seth. She thought about trying to find out exactly where he was. But Wendy would be watched quite closely, or so she assumed, and it was apparent that those in charge of her care would not allow her that confrontation until they were convinced that she was ready.

Brushing Seth out of her mind for the moment, she thought of someone else. Bob Friedl. Wendy hoped that he would come and spend some time with her. It had been several days since his last visit, though he had been calling her daily in the meantime.

During that last phone call, Wendy sensed something was going on. He seemed curiously subdued during their last conversation.

"Bob, is anything wrong?" she felt compelled to ask, her old insecurities surfacing in a new atmosphere that seemed conducive to breeding nothing but apprehension about what was ahead for her.

"Just the normal course of things in political life," he replied, though she felt that he was not very convincing.

"You mean all that's going on in Washington?"

"You're right, Wendy. That stinking mess is a large part of it. Nearly three thousand miles away, a president's immoral behavior and its aftermath trickles down to all of us unfortunate enough to be in political office. If I could do so, I would fly back to D.C. and ring his lousy neck."

Wendy knew of his feelings about corruption in high places, knew that he was not merely spouting some "line," but she also sensed that there was more to what she had detected in his voice.

"Nothing else?"

He hesitated, and did not reply right away.

"Bob?"

"Yes?"

"Is there something else?"

"Why would you think that?"

"Because of the way you're acting. You sound as though all the wind has been knocked out of your sails."

"Sorry, Wendy," he said abruptly. "I've got to go. I'm sure we'll talk tomorrow. God bless."

She held the receiver against her ear for a few seconds after he hung up, then put it back on its cradle.

What's wrong? she asked herself. *He seems to be pulling away from me. Have I said or done anything?*

And then, suddenly, that which might be the truth hit her, hit her so hard that she felt the beginning of a headache, hit her so totally that all of her body seemed numb instead of just the lower part.

Seth again. After the passage of a decade, during which she thought he was gone permanently, Seth was beginning to interfere anew with her life.

When Grace visited later that day, Wendy told her about what had happened.

"So you think he's worried about Seth?" her friend asked.

"It's possible, you know. But that's silly. Why should he be concerned about Seth? Does he think I will have some sort of breakdown? Or that I might become violent, as violent as my present condition allows?"

But Grace could not agree. "It's something else."

"What could it be?" Wendy asked, a begging quality to her voice. "Do you have some suspicions?"

"More than mere suspicion, my dear."

"More than—?" Wendy looked at the other woman, someone she had known for a third of her life thus far, with an abrupt clarity that was nearly overwhelming. "Are you saying that Bob is worried that I might fall in love with Seth all over again?" she blurted out.

Grace actually blushed. "I suppose I should never be surprised by you," she said with some admiration.

The fact was that Wendy had surprised herself with that burst of insight.

"It's ridiculous," she countered. "It's ridiculous for Bob to worry about anything like that. It'll never happen."

"Are you sure?"

"More than I have ever been before in my life."

"So, hatred won't suddenly turn into love?"

"At the beginning, maybe, there was a chance of that, but not after so long, Grace. It will be a big accomplishment for me to face Seth at all, let alone somehow fall in love with him all over again."

Grace stayed a short while longer, then she had to return to her office for some cases that could not be delayed or ignored.

Wendy felt very alone after she left, a slight shiver gripping her. She glanced at the now familiar walls of that room, the earth-tone color, the window looking out at some peaks of the Santa Monica Mountains. She could see three deer passing by in the distance.

So free, she thought, *so—*

That is, until somebody shot them down. She had always loathed hunting, finding no excuse for killing the animals. She had had a running debate with her father, who had been a hunter most of his life.

That awful, awful Christmas, Wendy remembered. *I could have disowned him, I was so upset!*

As usual, her father had typed up a kind of family newsletter that he sent out to relatives and friends. That year, he included a snapshot of a slain deer that he had put in the back of his truck.

"How could you?" she demanded when she saw it.

"What's wrong?" he asked, though she suspected that he knew quite well what her answer would be.

"A creature you've slaughtered!"

"Here we go again!"

"I know what you think, and you and I have called a truce—yes, I know all that, Daddy. But to do this at Christmas?"

He saw how upset she was, and felt sorry for what he realized then to be an insensitive misjudgment.

"You're right," her father acknowledged. "It's not the sort of thing that fits the Christmas spirit. I see that now."

He asked her to forgive him, and, of course, she did without hesitation. Then he took out all the photos from envelopes as yet unmailed, and cut these into pieces and threw them down the garbage disposal. Finally, he took the negatives and destroyed all of them, since most were of similar deer shots.

Now my father is gone, she thought.

How much she wished she could have had him for one more day. How much she wished she could have had her mother back with her at the same time. They were her link to stability and unconditional love and a great deal else.

Chapter Forty-Five

Wendy left her room a few minutes later and went outside, but this short journey took longer than she thought it might.

People stopped her. Nurse after nurse spoke openly of how much, individually and collectively, they admired Wendy, both for her present conduct and what they knew of her work with poor people, troubled teenagers and others—stories of her success straightening out many lives having spread farther than she expected.

A number of doctors came to her and expressed their own appreciation of her strength of will. And a young janitor impulsively but affectionately kissed Wendy on the cheek and rushed off. Others, most of them absolute strangers, shook her hand, patted her on the shoulder, spoke words of comfort and then were on their way.

How many were angels, she wondered, *sent by God to briefly touch my life and, after that, touch someone else's as they continued their travels through the centuries, doing the bidding of their Creator?*

And when Wendy was finally outside, much the same thing happened. She was courteous to these individuals, and, yes, their displays of genuine emotion touched her, but there was something else she felt. Wonder. She wondered why she was getting so much attention.

Some of the comments these individuals made undoubtedly were related to her work but perhaps not a great percentage. The rest were spoken because of how she had acted while at the rehab center.

After two weeks, Wendy had been through a rigorous schedule that would not end anytime soon, that in fact seemed destined to get worse before those in charge of her rehabilitation pronounced her able to reenter the world. But Wendy did what she was supposed to do, did it exceptionally well, and seldom complained, keeping her pain and despair pretty much to herself. And she managed to display enough of her natural faithfulness that others paid considerable attention to her, attention that made her uncomfortable but which she endured with grace.

Every so often she would ask for a rest period apart from what already had been planned, and she would sit in her chair not feeling sorry for herself but praying. This had to be noticed, this had to be admired. And it was, simple moments of quiet prayer. That Wendy would do this and fight the self-pity that sometimes threatened to overwhelm impressed quite a few of those who approached her that day.

"Depending on God has been a part of my life for a long time," she would say to one or the other.

"Even after what happened?" someone would question.

"More so now than ever. I *need* Him more than ever. Faith is harder in good times. That's when we tend to take God for granted."

At last alone, she sat quietly next to the tallest, widest weeping willow tree she had ever seen. A slight breeze touched her cheeks.

Oh, Lord, she thought, *somehow I feel almost happy. It's as though walking doesn't matter. Here I am, on a beautiful day, under a clear sky, smelling air scented with the fragrance of nearby flowers.*

A single tear formed in Wendy's right eye, and trickled slowly down her cheek, but it was not a tear of regret or sorrow or despair this time, for this tear was shed for quite another reason.

I feel almost happy.

An earlier bout with depression was gone, and she could smile, could think of the future without a sense of terror, at least for the moment.

It was odd, she knew, to feel as she did while still in the infancy of being crippled.

"When I could walk," she whispered out loud, "I had happiness, yes, but, somehow, now, it—"

She had been overheard.

Another patient in a wheelchair had pulled up beside her.

"Forgive me," the young man told her, apparently quite awkward about intruding on her privacy.

"Forgive you for what?" Wendy asked.

"For overhearing. I wasn't eavesdropping actually. But I do have acute hearing and, well, I'm really messing this up, aren't I?"

Wendy was amused by this stranger, and she was attracted to him as well.

"That's all right." she spoke, attempting to make him feel more at ease. "I was thinking about something rather strange, under my present circumstances, that is."

"I know what you mean."

Wendy tried to avoid looking at this stranger too intently because he was precisely the type of man she had found invariably enticing over the years: broad shoulders, a muscular neck thicker than average, blond haired, eyes an almost glimmering turquoise, dimpled chin, and a voice, ah, that voice, a voice that struck her as very seductive. In fact, he had features that made him seem a bit like Seth.

Already her palms were becoming sweaty as she glanced at him for a few seconds, then looked away.

"Sorry to make you uncomfortable," he remarked perceptively. "That wasn't my intention, of course."

"No problem," she replied, stretching the truth a bit.

"What you were saying..."

"About when I could walk?"

"Yes, that. It's been the same way with me. I have felt exactly, man, I mean, exactly the same way."

Apparently what she had been undergoing in terms of her feelings was not all that strange after all.

"I can't explain it," she said.

"I couldn't at first," the young man acknowledged, then snapped his fingers and shook his head.

"What's wrong?"

"How impolite!" he exclaimed. "I haven't introduced myself. And yet here I am intruding on your personal time."

"Nor have I," Wendy said, blushing, in part because this young man was so appealing to her.

"My name is Randy...Randy Sutton," he added. "Now I don't feel like so much of a klutz."

"And I'm Wendy MacPherson," she told him. "You know, I do feel better now as well...Randy."

His reaction to her name took Wendy by surprise, for it was hardly the casual one she could have anticipated under the circumstances.

"You are—" he tried to say but became tongue-tied while doing so, his mouth dropping open.

"What in the world—?" Wendy exclaimed, trying to understand what was happening with him.

"I've heard so much about you," Randy finally managed to tell her, his voice trembling just enough to make his vulnerability rather charming.

"Me?"

"You bet!"

Randy's unabashed gee-whiz manner was not forced. She could detect this right away, and that made him all the more appealing.

"What *have* people been saying?" she asked.

"That you're dedicated to helping others. But, for you, it's a personal cause, not just a job or anything like that."

"I could help people *before* my accident. Now, well, who knows? I'm the one needing *their* help!"

He reached out and tapped the back of her hand as he said, "From what I hear, nothing'll stop you." Randy's tone was obviously an admiring one. "We started to talk about how happy you feel right now...." he reminded her. "Remember we were going to do that?"

"But why should it be that way?" she spoke. "What, really, do I have to be happy about these days?"

"Life," he said simply.

"But so different a life, Randy. I...I used to ride horses. Some folks once thought I might be headed for the Olympics as a runner."

She flashed back to the adrenaline rush that she had felt again and again after doing her best on the track field. "Oh, those were the moments...." Wendy said out loud. "I could do so much. I could run...."

No more. What she was saying to herself was obvious. But, then, saying it also reinforced the fact that there was no hope she would ever walk again.

"I've never felt...I've never been totally, absolutely hopeless before," she said, visibly wincing.

"You still can do some of what meant so much to you!"

She looked sharply at him as though he was in some fantasy world and should be ashamed of himself.

"But you *can!*" Randy insisted.

"Please, don't—"

She appreciated what he was trying to do but knew that she could never survive if she kidded herself about the hopelessness of her situation.

"Horseback riding, for example."

"No...stop...you must—"

But Randy persisted. "There's a special brace," he told her. "Believe me, Wendy, I know. I've used it...and it works great."

Wendy was beginning to suspect something about Randy Sutton, and decided to come right out with her suspicions.

"Are you an—?" she began, oddly a little uneasy.

"Am I what?"

Wendy spoke but the words came so slowly that she seemed to be forcing them out of her mouth. "An angel?" she asked.

He began to laugh so hard that his face became bloodred. "Am I an angel?" he repeated, trying to control himself. "Not the way I used to live, that's for sure!"

Wendy was embarrassed, and thought that this might be a good time to say goodbye, and leave.

"Can't we talk just a little longer?" he asked, sensing her feelings. "I wanted to tell you why I feel so happy now. Maybe that'll help you understand your own emotions, if that doesn't sound too presumptuous."

She relented, and listened to him with growing appreciation.

"I've come back from the edge," Randy told her honestly. "After my accident, I kept telling myself that there was nothing to live for, *nothing*. I would require a wheelchair for the rest of my life.

"Think of that! I was a race car driver, Wendy. From hitting two hundred miles an hour to creeping around in a motorized chair, I mean, how could I face *that*? How could I *endure* a future that made me a prisoner of this thing?"

Randy was trembling, tragic old memories regaining his attention once again.

"But *being* this way changed me," he continued. "Before the accident, I was so arrogant, so selfish that I didn't care about anybody else. I had to have my own way every minute of every day. But that time is past, you know, buried by God's forgiveness. It took a while for me to forgive myself but that happened, too!"

Wendy had to suppress a gasp. He seemed radiant all of a sudden, making her wonder if he had told her the truth about not being an angel, but knowing well enough that unfallen angels were not capable of lying since they were extensions of God Who was Truth Itself. So, she had no choice but to accept him for what he was.

"But then...then I nearly died, Wendy," Randy went on. "My car...the car I loved was in flames."

The words rolled out so fast that he had to stop and catch his breath, before he continued to recall that nightmare.

"And it was rolling over and over, Wendy. You've gotta believe that I was prepared for oblivion. And I thought it was coming when I blacked out. It was days later, they tell me, before I regained consciousness."

His expression reflected how he had felt then. "I was alive but...but I was paralyzed from the waist down! And that would *never* change for me. I had to learn to depend on others, to do what *they* wanted, simply because they knew better."

Randy went on to describe the months of pain-filled recuperation he had to endure before rehabilitation could be attempted, injuries throughout his body that were more extensive than her own.

"I had a punctured lung," he continued, "as well as a severe concussion. My heart stopped twice, its activity coming to a complete halt. And, to top it all off, there was massive internal bleeding." Randy was sobbing. "I faced death so many times, so many—" he spoke, "but, always, God brought me back from the brink."

It was Wendy's turn to touch him, and this she did as she brought her wheelchair right alongside his own, gently touched his shoulder, and Randy rested the side of his head against her hand.

"I didn't want to go on," he said a moment later. "If I couldn't race, I couldn't live. Racing was life itself."

"I know...." Wendy said softly. "And then everything we are, everything we need is taken from us!"

"I...I should be encouraging *you*," Randy acknowledged as he raised his head wearily.

"No macho bull here," she said half-jokingly. "You're helping me, you know...another human being facing what I am going through."

"And God is with us every step of the way!" Randy exclaimed joyously. "We must *never* forget that, *never!*"

"You believe?" she asked.

"Oh, yes, I believe, how *deeply* I believe."

"Some have their faith destroyed because of tragedy."

"Not me, Wendy!" Randy seemed to get a sudden new wind, strength returning as he responded to what she had said to him. "My faith has been *strengthened.* I know that only with the Lord in my life can I get through what tomorrow and the next day and the next week and all the rest of whatever is left of my life holds for me."

"I...I would like to see you again," she said tentatively.

"That can't be," Randy told her. "I'm leaving tomorrow. I have a wife, three sons waiting for me.

Wendy was ashamed. "Forgive me...." she said. "I didn't know."

"You and I are here now for a reason," he assured her. "If that's it, if God wanted this to happen, can we even begin to question His plan for our lives, whether we live another day, week, month, year, how much longer?"

"No..."

"I've been blessed."

"You have?"

"So much, Wendy. But, you know, we still haven't decided why we felt so happy a few minutes ago."

Randy waited for her to say something first but when she did not, he took the liberty of speaking up again.

"Life, Wendy," he said. "When we were too busy, wrapped up in our careers, possessed by our professions, we could be standing outside on a day such as this and never notice its beauty, beauty that God has given us." He sniffed the air, enjoying the odors, enjoying the slightly cold edge to it, the invigorating feel as it caressed his face. "Clear today, not too warm," he went on. "And I smell roses. Don't you? Like perfume carried on a breeze."

He nodded toward a man in another wheelchair a few feet away. "I've met that poor soul," Randy spoke almost in a whisper. "You know, his mind...oh, Wendy...is gone, it really is. He is crippled like you and I are, no worse, but we still have our minds, Wendy." Randy's empathy was readily apparent. "He doesn't. I don't know how long he's been through this, not exactly, but it didn't happen yesterday. It's been a while, Wendy, and what a waste! What awful torture is he going through now?

Compared to him, you and I are free, free to laugh and cry and...smell the roses."

A young woman and three handsome boys had just entered the court-yard at the opposite end.

"My family..." he said. "I have to go now."

He asked her to lean forward, which she did, and he kissed her on the forehead.

"Continue being a blessing," he said. "That need not end, you know. And in blessing others, you will be blessed yourself."

She shook his hand and said goodbye, her voice husky, and watched him steer his wheelchair toward his loved ones, feeling sorry in the center of her soul to see Randy Sutton leave.

Continue being a blessing. Wendy MacPherson took those words with her throughout the day and into the night as she fell asleep with them.

Chapter Forty-Six

Wendy was apprehensive.

"Does it have to be today?" she asked, hoping that a deliberate pitiable tone would weaken Grace's determination.

"No, it doesn't," agreed her friend. "Why, yes, Wendy, it surely could be tomorrow. Or the day after that. It could even be next week, you know." She narrowed her eyes as she added, "But, dear, dear Wendy, would that change anything?"

"No, I suppose not," Wendy admitted.

"Then why wait? Today is as good as any."

"Or as bad."

Wendy bit her lower lip as she searched for some reason to tell Grace why it should not be happening at all. "Why do this now or later? Why do it at all?"

"Denial."

"I don't deny anything."

"Yes, you do. You deny that there is any other explanation than the one you've been clinging to for more than a decade."

"I don't want to rehash—"

"You don't want me or anyone else to do it. But *you* have been rehashing it in your mind innumerable times."

"I don't want to go down this road again. I thought I would never have to again. I *prayed* that I wouldn't."

"You mean, that Seth was gone, and good riddance?"

"Yes! Of course."

"Suppose, Wendy. Humor me just this once, okay?"

"Suppose what?"

Grace hesitated for a moment, knowing how fragile her friend's emotions were especially then.

"Suppose that what Seth has to say were to—"

Wendy was able to anticipate the rest of what Grace had intended to say.

"—explain everything," she added, "make me see his side of the story? Have I got that right, Grace?"

"You have. Did you consider that possibility?"

"No, I haven't."

"Why not?"

"Because *nothing* could justify what he did. I can't think of the wildest story ever concocted that would *allow* him to make a nightmare out of what once had been a beautiful dream for the two of us."

"I know some things, Wendy. Please believe that I, that all of us, want what is best for you."

"You seem to know a lot. But shouldn't I be the one with all these mysterious details rather than you?"

Grace ignored that and went on to say, "You may have to face the greatest shock of your life."

"I did *that* ten years ago."

"Yes, you did. But there may be another coming."

"Nothing could be as bad."

"Did I say bad?"

That comment took Wendy aback, and she was about to question it when Grace, smiling, left the room.

What's going on here? she thought desperately. *Why in the world is this being pushed upon me?*

Perhaps the only person who could provide at least a partial answer, acceptable to her or not, was Seth. Wendy closed her eyes.

Lord, Lord, take me from here before he—

Too late. A voice told her, in the very next moment, that it was already too late, and no amount of wishful thinking would change this new stage in her evolving reality.

"Wendy..." the voice spoke, still with the power to make her palms sweaty the instant she heard it. Whether that had to do with attraction or the anxiety of the moment, who could tell?

She opened her eyes slowly, not wanting to confront that which she could no longer forestall.

Seth. He was standing on crutches in the doorway to her room. Thinner, a bit more pale than she had remembered. But still he had some semblance of the old "look."

"No..." she said. "Please, no, this mustn't happen. It can't be *allowed* to happen. I'm not ready. You must understand that I'm just not ready."

He hobbled over to the side of her bed, and as he came closer, she found that her heart was beating faster.

"You hate me, I know," he spoke. "Grace told me."

Grace had told him! But how much? And why? Why had her best friend done this?

"Are you surprised to hear that?" Wendy asked.

"No..."

"Am I supposed somehow to *pretend* that you didn't almost destroy me?" she demanded of him.

Seth sat down on a chair and rested the crutches against the side of the bed.

"Aren't you curious?" he asked.

"Curious? About you?" she repeated as though what he had spoken was little more than gibberish. "About how you've been spending your life?"

"More than that, Wendy, much more."

"Why would I be curious?"

"About my leaving you."

"No, I'm not curious. You tired of me. You found somebody else who was better in bed, and you started sleeping with her instead of me, who-ever she is."

"Do you really believe what you're saying?"

"What *else* am I to believe, Seth?"

"The truth."

"And that isn't the truth? That's what you want me to believe? That you *didn't* have a mistress?"

"It never happened."

Wendy laughed harshly. "Liar!" she yelled at him. "Get out of here!"

"I've been celibate all these years."

He said those words so calmly that she blinked several times before otherwise reacting to them. "Celibate?" she repeated. "You with all that passion inside you? I know how much sex meant to you. I know—"

"I wanted to remain faithful to you, no matter what...." Seth inter-rupted awkwardly, knowing what sort of reaction he would be facing.

Wendy reached for the alarm and summoned a nurse.

"Get away from me!" she demanded.

He was already standing, adjusting the crutches. And crying. "Think it over, my love," he begged her as he bent over slowly.

She spat in his face. "Get the hell out of here!" Wendy screamed, one of the rare moments in her life when she cursed.

A nurse came quickly, and stood just outside in the corridor.

"You'd better leave...for now," she said.

Seth nodded sadly, turned and left.

"For now?" Wendy cried. *"Forever!"*

The nurse waited until Seth was gone before speaking, "You should listen to everything later, when you're ready."

"What is going on here?" Wendy asked. "Everyone seems more interested in pleasing the man who deserted his wife than the one he ran out on.''

The nurse tapped her once on the back of her hand. "Soon..." she said. "Soon, dear."

"Never!" Wendy declared. "I demand that he be kept away from me! I have no reason to show any interest in what he has to say. And how can Seth expect any mercy or forgiveness or anything of the sort from me?"

The nurse left without saying anything else.

Chapter Forty-Seven

So close to death...

An attempt on his life was nearly successful. Somehow his whereabouts had been discovered, and he was shot several times before two deputies in a passing squad car saw what was happening, and intervened, killing his attacker.

And then the battle for life followed.

Seth Darfield had arrived at the rehab center just two weeks before Wendy did. His recuperation in some respects went more slowly than hers.

One bullet had just missed his heart. Another entered his intestines. A third nearly blinded him in one eye.

How could they have found me? he had asked himself over and over. *All these years and I was safe.*

That was what seemed the case, for a time, anyway, before his new world was twice ripped apart.

Maybe that is, in the end, the sum total of their purpose, Seth mused, his nerves taut. *Maybe that is a central part of my punishment, to be lulled into some sense of security only to have it ripped away from me.*

Ten years. As he sat in his room, he recalled moments during that time, the ache he felt all the more severe because of how Wendy had just reacted to him.

He'd been on the run. Seth would live in one town awhile, then be discovered and have to leave to go on to another.

No peace. No joy. Only God helped me to survive without going mad, he thought, wincing as the images took over, images of terror, sleepless nights, food not being digested properly because his stomach was unsettled from a persistent case of nerves.

"I thought you were supposed to protect me!" he would exclaim, shouting at those in whose hands his life rested.

"The process is imperfect," seemed to be the stock answer of the police.

"Which means that my life always will be in danger, isn't that what you're saying?" Seth would retort.

More well-rehearsed answers.

Finally someone told him, "Each new day that you *are* alive is a gift from God. Live your life in that manner, and you'll manage to stumble through somehow."

"Until *they* find me!" he invariably exclaimed.

In ten years *they* had found him twice.

But even when Seth seemed safe, he did not *feel* that way. Every stranger was a potential enemy. An ordinary handshake might be followed by the barrel of a revolver pressed into his side or his stomach.

But that was something that could be seen and felt immediately. What if he were poisoned. Perhaps in a steaming cup of coffee, a glass of iced tea...in anything that he ate or drank. He would not know until the pain hit him, until he was dying, for surely *they* would choose the quickest-acting poison available, lessening the chance that there was time for an antidote.

If not poison, another means of punishment might be chosen.

Perhaps acid sprayed in his face by a passerby. Disfigurement. Yes, that might be enough to satisfy those who hated him. If they could not actually guarantee his *death,* turning that remarkably handsome face into a mass of scars and blotches and otherwise ruined skin might be an acceptable alternative.

Seth had put his crutches aside briefly, feeling stronger, and walked around his room without them.

The two attempts that had been made did not involve poison or acid. In the one case, a bomb proved to be the devastating means; in the second, a semiautomatic rifle was the instrument. In both instances, he was injured; in both, *others* died, innocent people, including a young woman who was pushing a baby carriage with her daughter seemingly secure and peaceful inside it.

After the bomb exploded, mother and daughter died, blown apart so completely that identification of the remains was difficult.

That was the attempt Seth thought most about. That was the attempt that instilled the most fear thereafter in him. That was the attempt he dreaded would be made again and again, until it was successful, dreaded it not only for the uncertainty of his own survival but for the possibility that many innocent lives would be claimed along with his.

When I go, I could take many with me, strangers who were unfortunate enough to be anywhere near me, Seth reasoned to himself. *I always thought hitting women and children were forbidden by these guys. What-*

ever happened to their so-called code of honor? When it comes to me, is that forgotten?

Code of honor. Seth laughed with learned cynicism, thinking of the hypocrisy of men who could talk honor and respect and dignity on the one hand, and practice murder, bribery, intimidation, deceit on the other.

"What will *they* have to face on Judgment Day?" he muttered.

He rubbed the side of his hand across his lips.

So much, Seth thought forlornly of his own situation, *so much fear, so much loneliness, and along with that, so little real joy, so little of everything that constitutes a happy life for most men.*

There had been no women.

And yet once he had the most wonderful lover he could ever have wanted, been married to her, someone so devoted to him that it was almost eerie, unconditionally loving him every second of every minute of every hour of every day they spent together, and thinking of nothing but satisfying him.

Then all of it, this idyllic relationship, the joy it brought them both, evaporated during a single morning.

I entered the valley of the shadow of death immediately thereafter, Seth told himself, *and I thought I would never get out.*

But now... Wendy MacPherson Darfield was back in his life, not far away from where he was standing, and another meeting with her was being urged by those responsible for his rehabilitation as well as her own.

No! his mind screamed. *It would be too hard on Wendy, on me. Some things aren't meant to be, and this has got to be one of them.*

Seth broke into a sobbing fit, and had to sit down, his arms suddenly devoid of strength.

He could not avoid seeing Wendy again, though one part of him wanted, to do precisely that, to avoid any more confrontations like the one that had occurred, old wounds made fresh.

Ten years had gone by. Both Wendy and he had faced the trauma of what had happened, and it had affected them both in various ways.

"How is all that pushed aside so that we can face one another?" he asked of no one. "I have seen how much she loathes me. Surely if she had a gun or a bomb or a knife, she would be tempted to use one or the other. Surely—"

A now familiar voice interrupted him.

"Seth?" that voice spoke.

"Yes..." he replied, knowing by recent experience how the next few minutes would be spent.

"You must."

"But for whose benefit? Can you tell me that? Can you?"

"Both of yours."

Seth snorted with more contempt than he wanted to show but was unable to rein in his feelings.

"The truth must be served, right?"

"Right, Seth, the truth *must* be served. Without truth, there can be only darkness, and darkness has its price."

Seth knew the reality of it. He had been fleeing darkness for many years. Twice it threatened to overwhelm him.

"Wendy will continue hating me," he protested. "Hasn't she already shown that, just minutes ago? You seem to be living in a dreamworld. This is not heaven now. I think it is more like an outpost of hell."

But the voice would not relent. "Do you still love her?" it asked determinedly.

And there was no hesitation in Seth's response as he said, "I do...with mind, body and soul."

"Never forget that. Let your heart guide you. Sometimes the heart can be fallible. But not this time."

"But why now? I am still supposedly incognito. Isn't this all too public for my own safety? Don't I risk my life by being seen with Wendy? And hers at the same time. These people have no conscience."

"I cannot read the mind of my Creator."

"Have you any clues?"

"Not one."

Seth's shoulders slumped, from disappointment as much as from the soreness that he continued to feel because of what the bullets had done to him.

"I might be dead soon," he said almost with relief, death a welcome state after the kind of life he had been enduring.

"Dead soon?" the voice repeated. "Yes, indeed you might but, my dear Seth, dead to this life only."

His heart rate quickened. "Heaven?"

"Your destination now, a week from now, a decade, whatever the Heavenly Father has decided."

"I'm scared."

Seth had had to admit that to himself innumerable times since his nightmare had begun a decade earlier.

And the voice replied with much sympathy, "Understandable, Seth, completely understandable."

Seth cleared his throat as he added, "The way I've been living doesn't breed a sense of security, you know."

"I know so well what you are saying."

And that was as true as the fact that the sun would rise and set day after day. Seth had never been as alone as he assumed. Though he was occasionally aware of an angelic presence with him, he had no idea that such a presence was at his side twenty-four hours a day, seven days a week. Yet it was. A guardian...a guardian making sure that God's plan was being carried out, an instrument of His will.

"I must go now, Seth," the voice said. "You can understand that she, too, needs me right now."

"I want this to work," he responded. "I just don't know if that will ever be possible, now or later."

"It will, Seth, it will."

He turned, smiled just as the being of light and iridescent beauty had become instead a tall, thin, regal-looking black woman who turned, and said, "Be at peace, Seth Darfield. We serve Almighty God. Does anything else matter?"

And then she was gone, to be with the woman he had never stopped loving.

The two angels, Darien and Stedfast, were getting ready to do what the Master had asked of them.

But neither was joyous.

"At last?" Stedfast spoke a bit tentatively, anxious but nervous and awkward at the same time.

"Yes..." his comrade replied.

"After all this time."

For the angels, time had no meaning, and therein was the problem, since they were constantly juggling a course of action in its infinite framework as well as its finite time reference, and could have become confused if they had not been careful.

"There is a reason, you must not forget that," Darien reminded the angel with whom he had spent most of eternity thus far.

"I know, I know," Stedfast replied, "but it does seem that we have done so very little to help."

Darien disagreed.

"That is not true. She has survived for a decade because of us and others of our kind, and, of course, the friend she calls Grace."

"That one is wonderful!" Stedfast exclaimed.

"She is, she is indeed," Darien agreed, "an angel to be proud of."

They waited a bit until they could do so no longer.

"I am ready," declared Stedfast, his reluctance nearly palpable.

Darien's manner was not much different. "As I am, dear comrade,"
he said.

And so the two angels went to do what they must.

Chapter Forty-Eight

There was a garden at the rear of the main rehab building. It was quite small, this secluded spot, but had proven a much sought after location, and, as a result, appointments had to be set in advance, because the very *feel* of it, the isolation, was calming, evoking a peacefulness that was much needed by many of those in treatment, perhaps all of them at some point in the rehabilitation process, their mental condition an integral part of their physical recovery.

Seth arrived there first, closing his eyes briefly as he sat down uncertainly on a rather rickety wicker bench that really should have been replaced. And Wendy followed nearly six minutes later.

He had just started reading a Bible when she appeared in the open from among a profusion of rose bushes.

He broke into a grateful smile. "Sorry for earlier," Seth said, closing the Bible and resting it beside him on the bench.

Wendy looked at him. "You've changed so little," she observed, feeling a measure once again of the old attraction.

"I can't say the same for you," he remarked. "You're lovelier than ever. Age has been kind to you."

She wished she could have avoided blushing but she did not, her cheeks reddening in an instant.

"Wendy…"

"Yes?"

"May I tell you what happened? Finally, after all this time? Will you listen? Will you please do that?"

"Isn't that the main reason we're both here, Seth, whether either of us really want to be or not?"

"So you'll sit and hear what I have to say then?"

"Yes. You're supposed to confess everything, and all the pain I've faced is going to melt away magically. Have I missed anything?"

"I've known a lot of pain, too."

"But *you* ran out on me. *I* didn't desert you!"

Wendy was already immensely sorry that she had ever agreed to such a ludicrous meeting.

"Go ahead," she told him, "roll out the well-rehearsed excuses and lame protestations like, 'She never really meant anything to me, Wendy.' Isn't that one of the things you're about to tell me?"

"No." He smiled patiently. "Wendy, there was never anyone else."

"No? There must be something else you're going to say, of course, something equally stupid that you're going to spout off about."

"There isn't."

"You have nothing else to say to me?"

"Nothing stupid."

"I've gone over a mental list of all your possible reasons, if I can call them that—I don't think I've missed any—and *none* of them are satisfactory, so maybe you shouldn't say anything at all, and we should try to sit here as quietly as we can, doing our duty for those in charge of our care, and then go on about our separate lives, as though none of this right now had ever happened."

"It's too late for that."

"For you, perhaps, but *not* me, Seth!"

"I left..." he started to say.

"Go ahead. I'm ready to laugh until my sides are sore, at least the parts that aren't paralyzed."

"I left because I wanted to protect you."

Wendy did not react with sarcastic laughter but, rather, anger as she said, completely incredulous, "Protect me? From what? I've got to admit that that wasn't one of the excuses on my list."

His eyes darted from side to side, and he was hugging himself.

"From the people who would have taken you down along with me, after using you as bait," he told her. "And they wouldn't have hesitated to do exactly that."

"From the people who—who—" She stuttered, then stopped speaking altogether.

"Fortunately I never told them that I was married," Seth added. "There was never any reason to do that."

"Them?" Wendy repeated. "What are you saying?"

He forced the words out. "The Mafia sent out a contract," he went on. "I was marked for death, Wendy. I was advised by the FBI to leave you behind. They could protect me, they said, but the best way to protect you was to pretend that you didn't exist."

It was as though Wendy's paralysis had spread up the rest of her body, for abruptly she had difficulty breathing.

"You're serious about all this, aren't you?" she said rather lamely.

"As serious as the threat of death that hung over me."

"What a crock!" she spat out the words. "I almost believed you there for a few deluded seconds."

"Wendy...listen!" he pleaded. "There are six undercover federal agents nearby at this center at all times. A couple of them are disguised as doctors, with gowns and stethoscopes and whatever else. Another is posing as a nurse. Two are supposed to look like interns. The sixth is a so-called patient."

As soon as Wendy started to open her mouth, she stuttered again.

"I know that shocks you," he told her, "but how do you think it has been for me all this time? The Feds didn't start doing this kind of intensive surveillance until the first attempt on my life. The Mafia doesn't forgive anyone who betrays them. And that was exactly what I did. I saw that they were beginning to think seriously about getting into the drug business after decades of staying away. I went to the FBI, and they told me what to do. I was an eyewitness to many drug deals. I used spy cameras and recorders again and again.

"Not all the boys, as they were called, were happy about the new drug trade. But they found themselves constantly undermined by the young hotshots who had come into positions of power."

Seth sighed wearily.

"I provided the Feds with plenty of evidence. Doing so changed things more than you may ever know. Not that I have had bodyguards with me all the time since then. I haven't. They let up after a while, figuring that the Mafia has finally given up. Besides, since I'd already told them what I knew, it was fortunate that they bothered with me at all."

He walked haltingly over to her as she faced him.

"Dear Wendy...my love," Seth said tenderly, as he sat on the grass in front of her. "I had to leave you, dearest, to keep you from being drawn into this nightmare that has smothered me for ten years."

His face was contorted by the emotions that were playing across it.

"I worked, in my innocence, for someone who turned out to be a Mafia underboss, the most powerful mobster just below the don himself," Seth told her. "I was more or less just taking care of deliveries but everybody seemed to like me, and I was invited out to lunches and dinners with the guys."

Wendy did not want to believe him. She *expected* to feel strongly enough about this still overpoweringly handsome man to call him a liar but as Seth kept talking, she knew she no longer had any choice but to accept as truth the nightmarish tale that he was spinning with such obvious anxiety. What Seth was telling her was too involved, too complete, too real to be fake, to be even a carefully rehearsed charade. Now she knew why Grace Schaeffer was so certain that she *needed* to talk to Seth.

Grace had known the truth.

"My friend Grace..." Wendy spoke slowly, a bit breathlessly. "She knew before I did, didn't she?"

"A tall, thin black lady...is that Grace?" asked Seth.

"It is. She's wonderful."

"You're right, Wendy," he spoke slowly, "but that's not all. I have more to tell you about this wonderful person."

"What do you mean?" replied Wendy. "Grace and I have been friends for many years. What could you possibly tell me?"

He smiled conspiratorially, then asked, "You are inclined to believe in the existence of angels, aren't you?"

"Of course I am. And it's not a matter of inclination. I *do* believe in them. Why are you asking?" Her face went very pale because it was as though she had peeked into his mind and could glimpse what he was going to tell her.

"Grace is an angel, Wendy," Seth spoke.

"I know...." she said, his remark confirming what she had briefly suspected but had brushed aside as an impossibility.

"How did you find out? Did she change in front of you?"

"She became something so beautiful that I thought I was going mad. *Nothing* is as spectacular as that. I thought what I saw was a dream."

"No dream."

"I wonder—"

"What do you wonder?"

"If she's gone now, her mission satisfied."

"I think she feels very deeply about you. It's more than an assignment from God, this time she has spent with you. It's been more than a mission. I can sense that in my gut, Wendy, I truly can."

"Ten years, Seth."

Thinking back over all that time made her feel depleted, so weak that she could hardly hold her head up.

"Do you believe me, Wendy?" Seth asked. "Do you finally believe me? I could do nothing. I lost you but at least losing you kept you alive. You will never know how much I ached to be with you, to kiss you again—"

He was sitting on the grass in front of Wendy.

"So kiss me now," she said.

Seth stood with some pain, then leaned over her, their lips touching tentatively at first, then—

Nearby a sound like a car backfiring.

Seth jerked his head. "Not again!" he muttered. "Not now!"

Someone who must have been an FBI agent came running in their direction.

"Security breach!" he shouted, an edge of panic in his voice. "We've got to get you out of here!"

"I want to stop running!" Seth shouted back. "I *have* to stop running. And that has to be here, now."

"If you don't come, you'll—"

"All right, all right. Will you take my...wife back inside?"

The agent was about to respond when his shoulders jerked abruptly and blood spurted out of a hole in his chest, a bullet ripping through him. He fell forward, knocking Wendy out of her wheelchair.

"I thought you guys were—" Seth yelled.

A man with pockmarks covering his face stood before them, his pistol aimed at Seth as he said, "No one betrays us and gets away with it."

"*No!*" Wendy screamed as she frantically dragged herself forward, wrapped her arms around Seth's legs and tripped him just as the stranger fired.

A single shot in her chest.

Strangely the assassin did not fire again, his eyes widening, perspiration covering his body in an instant. He seemed terrified, and turned to run.

A second shot. This one was not from the assassin's gun but an FBI agent's pistol. He tried to return the fire but toppled forward, hitting the ground with a pronounced thud.

Angel Stedfast was deeply disturbed.

"*I hope it does not end here,*" *he said,* "*I wonder if I could intercede, and persuade our Creator to—*"

Darien rarely interrupted but this time he felt quite compelled to do so, and said, "*You worry too often. Where is your joy?*"

"*Joy?*" *the other angel responded.* "*How can I be joyous right now? Or ever? Seeing what I see?*"

"*Is our God in control?*"

"*You know that He is.*"

"*Then do you doubt Him?*"

"*Doubt Him? Why would I ever do that?*"

"*Your worry, your melancholy seem to suggest that very state of mind.*"

Stedfast wanted to contest his fellow angel's conclusion but the truth of it abruptly took hold of him.

"*I am...ashamed,*" *he acknowledged.*

"*Do not feel shame. Feel cleansed. For God forgives even angels who have momentary lapses.*"

"*So whatever happens to Wendy, to Seth, they are in His care!*" *Stedfast declared with renewed joy.*

"*That is what 'hallelujah' is all about,*" *Darien replied.* "*No finer word exists than that one, dear comrade.*"

And so the two angels awaited the next chapter in the lives of two human beings of whom they had grown exceedingly fond.

Chapter Forty-Nine

Wendy recovered quickly since no vital organs were damaged, although the bullet had just missed her heart. The attempt on Seth's life had an aftereffect that no one could have expected. It happened one afternoon as Wendy and Seth were in her hospital room, both of them sitting in upright chairs, side by side, holding hands and kissing one another.

Posted outside were two uniformed police officers, demanded by the FBI and readily supplied by Robert Friedl, who met no opposition from the city's chief of police. Even other officials very much part of a bureaucracy-laden city government were exceptionally available to help Wendy.

All visitors had to be authorized in advance, any clearances routed through Mayor Friedl as well as Wendy and Seth themselves. The expenses of recuperation, rehabilitation and protection were covered by a combination of insurance and discretionary funds as well as partially underwritten by the hospital administration.

Wendy's and Seth's job situations could have been murkier but even that fell into place, with offers from a variety of companies, and, where needed, special training to make sure they were qualified.

It seemed for the two of them that their new life together could not have gotten better but they were wrong.

A tall thin man, his face grossly bearing a deep scar, his eyes instinctively darting from side to side, entered the rehab center.

Dressed in a black business suit, and carrying an attaché case, he seemed just the sort of individual against whom Wendy and Seth needed protection.

Unsmiling, he approached the policemen. They jumped to their feet. He quickly handed each of them two letters, one signed by the mayor and the other from the acting director of the FBI. After a few seconds, both stepped aside and allowed him to knock on the door.

"Come in," Wendy said.

The man entered, then shut the door behind him.

"My name is Rocco Mastroianni," he said.

Seth shot to his feet. "Why did they let you in here?" he demanded angrily as well as apprehensively. "Did you bribe those cops or what?"

At first Mastroianni chose not to speak but seemed to be studying Seth as well as Wendy.

"Nothing of the sort," he spoke finally.

"Then why are you here? Why were you *allowed* to be here?"

The other man smiled slightly.

"I have come to tell you that the contract has been canceled."

"The contract has been—" Seth started to say, then lapsed into silence. He sat down again, reaching out for Wendy's hand.

"A woman was shot," the stranger continued. "We abhor any injuries to women and children."

"But it seems you don't mind leaving them without husbands and fathers!" Seth blurted out.

Mastroianni continued as though he had heard nothing. "But even more critical is that the evidence you gave to the Feds has broken the backs of those in the organization who forced the drug business on the rest of us. Any who remain are being taken care of right now."

Seth was stunned. "You really mean that antidrug stuff?" he asked, incredulous, skeptical that this was not just window dressing for something sinister.

"More than ever."

"Why now?"

"My son."

"Frankie?"

"He died of an overdose last month."

Seth's shoulders slumped. "A wonderful kid…" he whispered.

"I know," Mastroianni said. "My son, blood of my blood, was going to be a concert pianist."

"I suspected as much."

"You see, even men like me have feelings."

"I can see that men like you are responsible for whatever morality is left among the families."

"There is more, Seth."

"You've saved the bad news until last?"

"No."

He opened the attaché case and took out some papers.

"The mortgage on your wife's house has been paid off," he said. "The two of you can live there for as long as you want. And if you ever need something bigger, you can sell this one, and have a large down payment."

Wendy spoke up. "We can't accept this," she told him. "I won't allow dirty money to—"

"Forgive me for interrupting," Mastroianni remarked, "not all Mafia money is from crime, you know. We do have legitimate businesses."

"Which are financed by dirty money."

"May I say something else?" he asked.

She told him that he could.

"You have done some nice things for us, you know," he reminded her.

"I suppose I have."

"How many of the children you have helped have been *our* children?"

"I always tried not to let their family backgrounds interfere with whatever I tried to accomplish."

"More and more of our young ones are turning to crime."

"Does that surprise you? Your whole life, for generations, has been built on a foundation of crime."

"To defend our loved ones, nothing more."

"That might have been the case two hundred years ago."

"It is still that way today. We must guard our families, our businesses from the Yakuza, the Russians, the Columbians, others. The battle is *worse* than it was back in Sicily. And now the drugs!"

He focused again on Wendy. "You have helped our sons, our daughters," Mastroianni went on. "Isn't it possible that you might allow us to do some good for you at last? Do you not believe that we should do unto others as we would have others do unto us?"

Ordinarily, Wendy would have gagged hearing such words come from a mobster but there was something about the way he said them that stopped her.

"You want to say something else, don't you?" she probed gently.

"Yes..." he replied.

"Go ahead. You can trust us."

"I am retiring. I have no one. My wife died just a week ago, the loss of our son causing her to have a stroke."

"Will the boys let you just leave?" Seth asked.

"They have already agreed to do so."

"Where will you go?"

"To a monastery in Switzerland."

Seth was taken aback. "To be a monk?"

"Perhaps, or just to separate myself for a time. There is blood on my hands. I want to see if it will ever wash off."

"Forgiveness, sir," Wendy assured him. "It's a central part of the faith that Seth and I share."

"That is what I seek."

He shook Wendy's hand, then Seth's.

"I must ask for one favor," he told them.

"What is that?" Wendy inquired.

"Please...pray for me. I know that sounds strange considering this life of mine. But I mean it sincerely. And I know that you will do what you say, for that is the nature of both of you."

"We will," Wendy said. "We will."

He turned and left, and they did not see him ever again.

"I never seem to learn," Stedfast moaned. "After all these centuries!"

"It is in our nature to be as you say, for we, too, know the essence of free will," Darien reminded him. "That was why Lucifer rebelled. He had the same nature but allowed his darker side to triumph.

"You and I and ten thousand upon ten thousand of our comrades have given the divine side the leadership of who and what we are. Where Lucifer knew jealousy, we felt awe. Where he wanted to be the master, we were then and now content to remain servants of the Most High. Where Lucifer rent heaven from end to end, you and I and others remained to repair what had been damaged. Where our former friend brings, even now, disease and pain and death, we continue to sow strength and joy and eternal life."

Darien sighed as he saw Wendy and Seth embrace one another.

"They will never be apart now," he spoke, "in this life or the next. They will live together, and many years from now, they will die together, ascending finally to the welcome of a heavenly chorus."

"And the mayor? I wonder what will happen to him. He grew to love Wendy so very much."

"Stedfast? Listen to yourself, please. Is that worry I detect asserting itself again? You are incorrigible!"

"Me?"

"Yes, you!"

"How could you think that?"

"I know you all too well, dear friend."

"There is still time for me to learn, you know."

"And after there are no more clocks to tell the minute and the hour, all of that passed away at last, foolishness that it is, eternity will take over. I think, yes, I am quite certain that you will surely need eternity, Stedfast."

The two laughed good-naturedly and went elsewhere, to yet another couple, in yet another place, at yet another point in the chain of service they had been performing since God created all things.

* * * * *